Time Traitors
The Time Traitors Series
Eli Donovan

EDW Books

Table of Contents

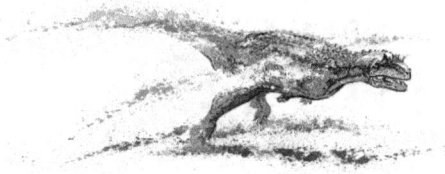

To Larry Wilson, my wonderful teacher and friend, who first believed in Grace.

And to my mom, who helped carry me over the finish line on this one.

Chapter One

GRACE

I've got a one-way ticket out of this geological era burning a hole in my pocket, but, of course, there's a problem on the subway. I should've sprung for an auto cab. The Time Guard finally reinstated my research clearance, and I'm going to screw it all up if I can't get my ass to the city in time.

My train finally lurches forward, but anxiety still crackles along my nerve endings as the city of Berkeley rolls by. Please, oh please. This is my big second chance, and some people don't even get one when it comes to time travel. Only certain research is given time travel clearance—projects that can't be accomplished by more traditional methods.

Like studying dinosaurs in their natural habitat.

Of course, we've all seen the movies. We all know humans and dinosaurs don't mix without lots of chomping and screaming. And what kind of crazy lady would dream of spending years trapped in 73 million BC studying giant murderbirds that want to eat her?

Well. *Me.*

Turns out it's really hard to alter the past in any meaningful way, so the Time Guard allows research projects like mine to proceed—if we're careful. If we don't make too much trouble and follow all their rules.

The train finally pulls into my stop, so I leave the subway and start running. I swallow a growl of frustration as a couple takes up the whole staircase walking arm in arm, giggling together. "Excuse me," I grit out and shove between them.

My breath is coming fast and aching out of my lungs, and I don't know if it's from the run or if I'm about to hyperventilate, but Time Guard HQ is in sight. The Time Guard base is a squat gray building, utilitarian, with no signs anywhere to let the casual passerby know what it is.

Sweat pooling along my hairline, I press a button on the wall and look into a small camera-like contraption at eye level. The techs tell everyone you can't feel a retinal scan, but my eyeballs itch anyway.

A loud buzz sounds, and a lock clicks on the door. I shiver as I step inside, my mouth dry. Doubts bombard me like my insides have turned into a hostile pinball machine. Maybe the university made a mistake reinstating me. Maybe I made a mistake fighting so hard for this?

I try to shake those thoughts away and focus on finding my terminal. The Time Guard's security check is a bit like airport security crossed with getting booked for a crime. It's an embarrassingly thorough process, but the agents move fast. Once I've cleared security, I bustle into the departures area, but stop short when I see my boss, Dr. Paul Trifoso, is waiting for me. "What are you doing here, Paul?"

He's a big man, fit, with deeply tanned skin, a bald spot, and a thicket of curling white hair growing like a tonsure. He smiles, but his eyes are tense. "I'm catching the same boat, Grace."

"You're babysitting me?" The words slip out before I can stop myself. Frustration and hurt's boiling inside me, a twist like food going bad in my gut. "I don't know why you pushed my clearance through if you didn't trust me to get the job done." Never mind I'm not sure *I* trust me to get the job done.

He narrows his eyes. "Grace, after what happened with your husband, you can't blame the university for being cautious."

"Ex-husband. And *I* turned him in." I clench my fingers together to stop them shaking. All my accomplishments, all the work I've done, the advances I've made in my field—none of that matters anymore because my ex-husband was an asshole. My gut jitters again, like there's an earthquake along my nerve endings. Balls, I do not want an anxiety attack right now. I grit my teeth, but I'm too angry to look at Trifoso. "Our dinosaur research is the most important department the university has. Also one of the most dangerous postings. You need someone who knows what they're doing back there."

"Why do you think I've been working to convince the university to give you a second chance, Grace?" His voice is mild. "I know what's at stake. But we can't risk another scandal."

Scandal. Pretty mild word for my ex-husband poaching dinosaurs on the side and selling the bits for profit. And then, *as a bonus*, nearly getting himself and a grad student eaten by a large carnivore. But then Trifoso's always been good at obfuscation and spin. You have to be if you're going to write grant proposals.

He scans the departure area, clearly wanting to change the subject. "We're taking the new Time Guard officer along with us. He's running late."

"All right." I choke down a bitter laugh. One of the unwritten rules of the Time Guard is they'll hold a trip for a time agent but never for one of us civilian researchers. I killed myself getting here on time. This agent probably stopped on the way to get coffee and a bagel.

"Are you hungry?" Trifoso asks. "Do you want coffee?"

"No, take me to the gate." I glance around to see what's changed as we walk. The departure terminal is bigger than it used to be. They must have at least six machines running continuously, zapping people through time and space. There used to be half that many machines. Some of the travelers are researchers like me. Some are time agent "monitors" sent to make sure a historical hot spot doesn't see any action. A time agent friend of mine let slip once they have a standing team of agents stationed at places like the Kennedy assassination and more obscure historical pivot points like Genghis Khan's court.

The strike teams sent to mop up problems—like someone trying to kill Hitler or save Julius Caesar or, or, or—deploy from a different floor.

My face is still clammy from my sprint, and the stale air in here isn't helping. I swab at my brow with my sleeve when Trifoso isn't looking. "How long are you planning to stay in the past with us?"

"Just until you're settled," he murmurs.

I swallow a grumpy noise. That could mean anything from a day or so to several months. Hopefully, he's requisitioned enough rations for himself.

A Hispanic cowboy jostles my elbow then gives me a hat tip by way of apology. I regain my balance in time before I crash into someone in a Victorian gown. The whole terminal is like that: agents and civilians mill about, many in historical dress: a whole crowd of cowboys, a lady in a Jane Austen gown, a truly startling man half-naked with a giant Aztec feather headdress. I recoil as two tall men pass by in Third Reich uniforms.

Apart from the array of dress, the place is like a tiny airport. White-tiled, fairly sterile looking, big walkways, and uncomfortable metal chairs in the corners. There's a cafeteria not too far away with truly awful food. One of those places you try once then, afterwards, you always remember to eat *before* heading to the Time Guard building.

Even though I've been here before, seen it all before, today the bustle of the terminal makes me uneasy. I'm not someone who thinks you should close the buffet just because I've gotten my plateful, but this feels like too many researchers to be working in the past. How can the Time Guard be safely monitoring this many civilian time travelers?

The arrival gate next to us opens and two people stagger out, carrying a third. They're dripping wet, wearing old-fashioned clothes and life jackets. The infamous Titanic detail, I'm guessing. The woman sags under the weight of an injured man. "Medic!"

Trifoso and I flatten ourselves against the wall to make way for the paramedics—another thing the Time Guard has in abundance.

I lean hard on the wall, a sour taste in my throat. There isn't even any blood—it's probably a hypothermia case, but I can't help but remember.

Teeth marks. And blood. The smell of sweat and piss. The poor girl crying while I put the tourniquet on, my hands sticky and red. My husband, Adam, swearing and pacing, holding his own mangled hand. Everything in my life collapsing in one moment.

Fingers brush my shoulder, and I jump away like I've been Tasered.

"Sorry." Trifoso looks at me with concerned eyes, like he's been reading my mind, watching the images unspool. "Are you all right?"

"Just fine." My voice doesn't even tremble.

The medics clear out, taking the injured man and his companions.

I sweep my hand around as the usual hubbub resumes. "Are there more agents around than there used to be?"

"I believe so."

"More time crime going on these days?"

He snorts and lowers his voice. "The Time Guard won't admit it but, yes, I suspect so."

Watching the crowd, it gets so you can tell who's who, even when everyone's in historical dress. The agents all have a studied aura of boredom to them and a certain braced way of carrying themselves. The historians and the scientists like me are usually bouncing with nerves, gawking at everything, curious, excited.

Things are usually low-key in this area of the building. Everyone on this level is here for the research expeditions. The time agents have other terminals a few levels down they use when they need to deploy a strike team. Whether that's to catch time criminals or when they need to stage a large-scale rescue op.

As thorough and paranoid as the screenings on this level are, the research wing of the Time Guard is very much its public face. Everything below this level is a mystery except to Time Guard agents. Even experienced time researchers like me don't know all the Time Guard's secrets.

Trifoso clears his throat. "We'll, ah, have a few more agents stationed with us than we used to have, by the way. Things are a bit different."

"Fine by me. I don't want anything else to go wrong. I want to get on with my work and forget all of the—forget the incident ever happened." Hell, I'd like to forget my whole damn *marriage* if I could.

"Well, no one else is setting up shop in our backyard, I promise. Ah, here's Mx. Vega."

I'd met our new grad student Jax Vega before when Trifoso and I interviewed them several times for the research assistant job. Vega's a grad student from New York with a strong field research background studying hyenas. Dinosaurs aren't their specialty, but I tend to hire folks who have field research experience with *live* animals versus fellow paleontologists who have only been on excavations. Studying dinosaurs on their home turf was *not* the place for someone new to the dangers of fieldwork with live animals.

Vega is stout, but solid with it, and tall. Their shoulders are broad, and they've got well-defined arms that could probably lift our entire supply pallet one-handed. At the interview, Vega had seemed intelligent, friendly, and eager for the opportunity. Now, they look nauseous, and their hand is trembling when we shake. Not a great sign, but I'm hoping it's just travel jitters. "Hello, Dr. Carson," Vega murmurs. "Dr. Trifoso."

I nod 'hello' and Trifoso makes chitchat with Vega: 'how was it getting through security?' 'how was your flight?'

I should be doing the same, trying to build a rapport, but my nerves are swamping me. I'm never a social butterfly at the best of times, but suddenly my brain's decided I've done enough human interacting. The proverbial switch has been flipped, and every move I make feels awkward and distant. Like an inept puppeteer is jerking me around.

I breathe out deep through my nose and gaze over the stacks of crates and heavy-duty cases piled next to my new research assistant. Food. New cameras. Fuel. Batteries. We don't get much in the way of personal items. Clothes. Maybe a handful of books or music to pass our downtime. We each get a box of personal food we can choose to share or not share with each other. I'm pleased to see a box for Trifoso.

Looks like someone packed fresh fruit, and I grimace. "Who brought the peaches?"

Vega frowns and steps toward me. "I did. They had some great ones at a market down the—"

"Dump them."

"What? We're allowed to have—"

I shake my head. "Dried fruit without seeds. I don't know how you got them past the security search, but I'm not going to risk carrying those back in time."

A muscle ticks in Vega's jaw. "Just us *being* there is contamination of the past. What do a few peaches matter? I'll be careful with the pits."

I fold my arms over my chest. "My gig. My rules. Stay here if you don't like it." I didn't use to be such a hard-ass about these things, but I can't afford to break *any* rules this time. I got this clearance by the skin of my teeth. I'm not losing it over *peaches*. "Eat them here or dump them in the trash."

Clearly irritated, Vega huffs a breath out. "Dump them. Fine. I don't care."

Trifoso sidles up to me. "Maybe we should let our new Time Guard agent decide. They're the final authority anyway."

I snort and dig the peaches out of the crate. "Maybe if our Time Guard agent had been *on time* they would've caught this themselves."

Trifoso shakes his head and excuses himself for a restroom break.

I open the produce bag and take a peach for myself. It's perfectly ripe. Soft but not squishy. The skin is velvety against my hand, and the bright, tangy scent blooms in my nostrils, making my mouth water immediately. These *are* good peaches. Shame. I turn toward the general lounge area where folks are sitting in clumps to wait for their own departures. "Who wants a peach?" I yell.

"I'll take one." A man's voice right behind me.

I turn, peach cupped in my hand, and nearly drop it when I see the Time Guard agent standing in front of me. My cheeks go blazing hot, and a shiver starts in my belly as I look at the stranger. He's got skin of a warm fawn brown, great cheekbones, and deep-set dark eyes. The name tag on his shirt reads "Nakamura," and his uniform is tight across his broad chest and shoulders. "Um. Here. Free peaches."

His mouth quirks in a lopsided smile. "Thanks for this. I was worried I'd have to get one of those gluey prewrapped muffins for my Last Meal."

I chuckle. "Truly, a fate worse than death."

Something warm flutters in my stomach, but before I can worry about that, Vega storms over to us. "Do I get one of my own peaches, Dr. Carson?"

"Sorry. Of course." I hand one to Vega but, when they try to storm off, I catch their wrist. "Jax, I'll reimburse you for the peaches."

Their mouth purses, and they look away, their shoulders scrunching in what looks like embarrassment. "I'm sorry, Dr. Carson. Thank you. I—I should have read the packing guidelines more closely."

"It's all right."

"Dr. *Carson*?" This from the sexy time agent.

"That's me." I brace myself but offer my free hand anyway. "I'm the head of the Campanian era time displacement study."

"Agent Nakamura." His mouth twists, and his eyes have gone cold. He shakes my hand but perfunctorily. "I know who you are, Dr. Carson."

Of course he does. I clench my teeth, my whole body tense. "Is this going to be one of those interactions? 'Come on, Dr. Carson, you knew exactly what your husband was up to' and such?"

He cocks his head to the side, one eyebrow raised. "Did you?"

"*No.*" I wheel away from him and start fussing with my luggage. "Enjoy your peach." I've still got a half dozen in the produce bag to get rid of, but this interaction has made me leery of strangers. I do not need any more Time Guard bullshit today.

Trifoso returns to us after his trip to the restroom. He holds his hand out as he approaches Agent Nakamura. "Hullo. Are you the new agent assigned to our location?"

This is when my brain finally processes the time agent's uniform. Agents on assignment don't usually wear uniforms. Usually they're wearing historical dress to blend in. There are only a few very specialized assignments before human history where a field uniform is appropriate. And this agent is wearing standard-issue field kit. Looks a bit like a sheriff's outfit: khaki pants, khaki shirt, but in place of the sheriff's silver star, he wears the silver Time Guard infinity badge.

I swallow. "You're the new agent assigned to the Campanian outpost?"

Nakamura nods slowly, eyes narrowed. "That's me. So nice to meet you, Dr. Trifoso. Dr. Carson. And Mx. Vega, I presume?"

I'm still staring at him in horror when our new time agent jerks his head toward a far corner of the terminal. "Our gate's this way."

Vega and Trifoso fall in line behind him, rolling our luggage pallet down the pathway between terminals.

I puff a deep breath out and make myself take one step and another after Agent Nakamura. It doesn't really matter our time agent already hates me. Probably *every* time agent hates me. Clearly, the company line is I'm guilty as hell and somehow I wriggled out of it. Well, nothing I can do about that. I managed to convince the right people I'm innocent, and now I get to go back to my work. That's what matters.

My palms don't start sweating until our terminal comes into view. I thought I was jumpy before—now my heart is trying to punch its way out of my chest. I'm so close. No time for second guessing, Grace. But the bad memories in my head are always ready to rise to the front. Sticky blood and pulped flesh under my hands. Rustles from the forest, roars in the distance—

I pinch my eyes closed, taking a deep breath in. This is what I want. This is what I've worked for.

Everything will be all right.

If only I could make myself believe that.

The time terminal itself is simple, a plain gray arch with a green light and a red light up top and sliding doors to admit you into the room with the time machine. Green means *this room is cleared to enter or exit.* Red means *shit your pants; you're going back in time.* A jaded-looking technician and her assistant supervise the board, telling us when to go, when to wait. The group ahead of us is dressed like flappers. One man in a tailed coat and two women in slinky dresses with beaded fringe. The doors slide open and they file into the time machine.

My breath sounds harsh even to my own ears as I watch *The Great Gatsby* group disappear behind the doors. Almost there. I don't know whether it's a promise or a threat. My brain is being unbelievably stupid today.

"How are you doing, Doc?" Nakamura's quiet baritone is a low vibration I feel more than hear, like a prickle against the back of my neck.

"I'm fine." I'm not fine, but I'm not telling *him*. The Time Guard is not on my side. Two years of investigations and audits have sunk *that* truth deep into my bones.

He gives me a 'fair enough' sort of shrug. "You should eat your peach. We've only got a few minutes left." Suiting words to action, he takes a bite of his own.

Oh, why the hell not? I dig my own peach out of my bag and take a bite. I close my eyes so I can focus on the tender fruit in my mouth. The tang against my tongue. No fresh produce for a while. I better enjoy this one. I finish my peach in a few quick bites and toss the pit in the trash right next to the terminal. Unsurprisingly, it's full of similar detritus from this time period. Chip bags and soda containers, candy wrappers, a million Last Meals for people leaving the modern era for the past. I'm aching to get to my own favorite time period, but I *will* miss the food here.

No one but Nakamura seems to have perceived my nerves, which seems odd until I notice how Trifoso's sweated through the armpits of his denim shirt in five minutes. Vega looks okay, although they're swallowing, swallowing—ah, nope. They race to the trashcan nearby and start hurling. It's a common enough reaction for first timers. As much as the Time Guard tries to make this place resemble an airport, it's not. And this is about the point where the illusion of normalcy, of safety, starts to fail for people.

Above us, the light clicks from red to green with a force that hits me in my gut. A low hum starts inside the chamber. The door slides open with a loud *snick*. Trifoso startles, knocking sideways into me.

I squeeze his arm. He covers my hand with his own and swallows loud enough I can hear him. Nakamura saunters into the chamber with a visible calm I'd kill for. But I suppose as a time agent this is just another day at the office. Trifoso follows, shuffling into the room, mumbling encouragement to himself under his breath. The terminal technician passes Vega a tissue for their mouth as they walk past.

There's a low mechanical whine starting—the time machine powering up. The vibrations shiver through my feet, against my sternum, in the little bones in my ears. I thought my nerves would get worse now, but hearing the time machine start washes all of that out of me like the tide sweeping the shore clean. I'm ready.

I step into the time machine, and the door slides shut.

The two work lamps are dim in here, but there's enough light to make out the complicated lattice of machinery lining the walls: circuit boards and heat shielding, wires in colorful bunches, and two time tubes glowing like cheap fluorescent bulbs in the middle of the room. Without those two long cylinders none of this works. I've heard reports the Time Guard could easily simplify the design of their time machines, but they don't *want* to. If they made time machines that were light, easily transportable, it would be easier to steal time tubes, and harder to police time travel.

As the door closes with a loud click, the tubes burst to life, humming and buzzing like a beehive at work. A rippling wave like the shimmer on a soap bubble springs up between the two poles. The time field. Nakamura hustles us into a rough line and helps Trifoso push our pallet of supplies through first. As soon as the farthest edge of the pallet touches the time field, the whole thing gets sucked through. *Slurp.* Trifoso jolts. Vega blinks, still sallow around the mouth. My own heart hammers in my chest.

Nakamura grins at the rest of us. "Last chance for second thoughts." He catches each of us by eye, waiting for acknowledgement. Trifoso gives a ragged swallow, but he's the first to step through. His hand brushes the field, and he gets yanked forward. A half-strangled cry breaks from his throat before he's swallowed by the time field.

Vega's next in line, but they hug their hands to their belly and shuffle forward slowly.

I brace myself as the temperature steadily rises. The vibrations deepen, making my jaw ache and my tits bounce so hard I have to hug them or it feels like they might tear off. "Go!" I bark at Vega. The techs can only keep the field open for so long.

I start forward. I'm not missing my chance because Vega's lost their nerve, but before I can pass, the grad student draws their shoulders back and sprints into the portal. It swallows Vega whole.

Nakamura and I are alone in the chamber. Sweat pours down my face, and the room vibrates like a malevolent force that wants to knock me down.

"Let's do it together, Doc." He has to yell at me just so I can hear him.

It's not a bad idea, but still I hesitate. He offers me his hand, but I can't make myself reach for it. Too intimate somehow.

He laughs. "Come on, Doc. Everything's better when you have someone to share it with."

I shake my head but reach for his hand at last.

The room rattles around us and I stumble. Instead of taking my hand, Nakamura wraps his fingers around my arm to help me keep my balance. "Let's go!"

We jump forward, and I actually laugh for the sheer joy of it. *Yes. This.* Nakamura laughs too. We hit the time field together, but as soon as the mechanism of time travel grabs me it's like everything stops. I'm suspended, frozen in amber. I can't move, can't breathe, can't go back or forward. There's just this endless moment, a held breath in the middle of time itself. It lasts forever and only a heartbeat.

I blink and breathe again, and I'm tumbling, tripping, landing hard on the dirt nose first.

Nakamura lands with a loud *"oof"* right beside me.

As I catch my breath, I turn my cheek in the dirt to look at him. It's not a bad view. Even with his muddy cheek smushed into the ground.

He shakes his head to clear it. "Time travel. Not a very dignified way to get where you're going."

"No." I bite my cheek to keep back a smile and sit on my heels to gaze around. We're inside a dome of protective metal fencing, and our research station lies behind me, a small building with our dorms and lab, but I don't care about any of that right now.

For one second, the Cretaceous sun beats down on my skin, and it's like being submerged in a warm bath. But then the light turns bright and hard, and I roll to my feet before my face can erupt in a fresh sheen of sweat. There's a fence between me and the rest of this prehistoric paradise, but I rush forward to wrap my fingers around the chain-link so I can stare out. Lush, overlarge trees are everywhere, surrounding the clearing they made for the research station. This place is a truly green world of conifers and ferns and flowering plants.

A flutter starts in my chest at the familiar hum around me. The forest is alive. The buzz of insects, the wind ruffling through the leaves, and the animals calling softly to each other in lyrical chirps and hoots and squawks.

It starts a longing inside me like thirst in the desert. The forest is teeming with life on the other side of this barrier. Home. Close enough to touch if not for the damn fence. I want to dig my fingers into the lush dark soil and take a deep breath of the turned-up earth. I want to run barefoot through the forest, laughing like a mad woman for joy.

Come on, I silently chant. It isn't *real* until I see one, until I can know for certain this wasn't all some cruel trick. "Come on."

As if summoned by my desperation, something breaks above the tree line, a dark shape in the air. I screen my face with my hand, staring until my eyes hurt, trying to make an identification.

A pterosaur. I can't see the coloring, so the species is uncertain, but the beast pumps its long, graceful wings, scooping speed out of the air.

My cheeks are wet, my throat thick. I use the neck of my shirt to wipe my face. That'll do. Quite the greeting to welcome me home. Although I'm so starved for dinosaurs, a giant dragonfly might've been enough to make me tear up.

"Holy shit," Nakamura murmurs. The cords in his neck stand out as he cranes his head to keep the pterosaur in sight. He's trying to hold onto his Time Guard poker face, but the light in his eyes, the giddy awe I see there, betrays him.

He shakes his head, but he can't shake the hint of a grin off his face. "Well. That's a hell of a thing. We're surely not in Kansas anymore, Doc."

"Nakamura, Kansas doesn't even exist yet." I laugh and crank my head to stare at the sky. I'm home.

Chapter Two
A few miles away...

JULIA

I want to go home. The thought's like a wall in my head. Firm, hard, impossible to get around. Doesn't matter, though, because I've already gone through the time field, and already committed myself to several more weeks of criminality and danger. Besides, I don't have much of a home left anymore.

"*Oy*, Julia!" Daw's voice lands on me like a physical blow, and I'm annoyed when I jump in response. The man's a good-looking thirtysomething, about my son's age, with brown-sugar hair he keeps immaculately combed even in this humidity. Daw's high in the pecking order of our criminal gang—but not as high as he'd like. He's short and looks undersized, almost skinny, until he rolls his sleeves up and you realize he's nothing but wiry muscle. "You planning to earn your keep, Julia, or swan around doing sketches like last time?" He bares his teeth at me in a sneer as he heaves open a supply crate with a crowbar.

I grimace and wander to the other side of camp to find something I can help with. Far away from him.

Our advance team cleared a patch for us in the middle of the dense forest, and the rest of the poaching crew are unloading all our supplies: cages of varying sizes, stun guns, traps, rope for snares. Our three hover-SUVs form a ring around the camp, their landing gear deployed, looking large and solid, intimidating. The bulky vehicles and guns are probably a comforting sight to the newbies on our crew who don't know this forest the way I do.

The sight of the vehicles and heavy equipment camping out in a prehistoric forest still makes my skin crawl, but I shrug it off. *Time is resilient*, I remind myself. The odds of any of this human detritus being left behind to ruin the fossil record is low. Anyway, I'm not supposed to—can't even afford to care about that. If our bosses cared about safeguarding the past, they never would've sent a team of poachers back to steal dinosaurs.

I locate the crate with my drone packed inside and set about unloading my gear and checking it over to make sure everything works. The day is baking hot, but I've found some cover under the perimeter of trees. It's peaceful working in the shade. The babble of voices fades into white noise, and I admire the rustle of leaves above me. Stars of sunlight hit the ground where the leaves don't quite touch, and a bracing breeze fans over my cheeks.

I'm not trying to hide, but a stack of three crates screen me from view unless you're at the exact right angle.

"Why is she here *again*?" That's Daw's voice.

I go still and lean farther into the shade, hoping he doesn't notice me.

"She knows where the dinosaurs are." That's our boss, Xia Wong. She's got a smoky, femme fatale sort of voice with a light Chinese accent. Right now her lovely voice sounds flat, with a thread of tension beneath.

"Bullshit. We were doing fine on our runs before you started bringing your rogue Jane Goodall along."

Oh. Right. I straighten as heat stains my cheeks. *Me.* They must be talking about me. Is this the point where I reveal myself? Spare everyone any future embarrassment?

I scoot my butt farther away so I'm deeper in the shadows.

Xia huffs out a long sigh. "What's your problem with her, Daw?"

He lowers his voice so I have to hold my breath and lean over to hear. "What's to stop Julia from having a change of heart and turning us all in? The scientists in their bunker aren't more than a day's walk. Grace Carson is here—"

Adrenaline spikes through me at the name, leaving my mouth filled with a bitter taste.

"—and your precious Julia already quit on us last time," Daw continues. "Why is Julia back? What's in it for her?"

"Don't worry about it," Xia murmurs, voice bland. "All that matters is: she's here and *I* trust her. You do your job, and I'll handle Julia."

Daw—I'm guessing it's Daw, but I'm still huddled behind a crate so I can't be sure—utters a growl of frustration, then I hear the brush thrashing as he leaves.

I strain my ears, waiting to see when Xia will move off. I have to pee, and my hip is cramping from the way I'm sitting.

Xia pops her head around the side of my crate.

"Gah!" I startle so hard I damn near topple over.

She keeps her face straight, but has to blink hard to do it. "So," she draws the word out. "I don't want you to worry about Daw. I'll handle him."

"Ah. Okay. Thank you." I suck in a deep enough breath to roll my shoulders and force my next words out, "Grace Carson is back?"

Xia flinches but does me the courtesy of nodding slowly. She's a criminal, but she's not a liar. "She is."

"How do you know?"

She gives a little headshake. Not for me to know. Above my paygrade.

But it's easy enough to deduce: Xia has a spy on the other side. Someone passing information, at least. Maybe helping to cover our tracks at the worst. My stomach roils at the thought, but I push that emotion away. I am in no position to judge. And I should try to be grateful Xia's savvy enough to flip someone on the other side to helping us. It's good there's a mole among the research squad. Makes my job easier.

I just need to finish this poaching run. Then I can stop. Stop breaking the law. Stop chasing dinosaurs. Stop everything, if I want.

I hunch low, fatigue washing over me like a cold slap of a wave.

"Hey." Xia eases around the side of my crate and sits so close our knees almost but not quite brush. "I want you to know if you ever wanted to return to your old life with some kind of survival horror story... I wouldn't stop you. And I wouldn't blame you." She flashes me an easy smile that makes my stomach flutter. "I don't want you outing the rest of us, of course, or putting the business in danger. But I understand living like a criminal can be tough. Especially if you're not used to it."

"It's too late for that." I wet my lips and force myself to meet Xia's gaze. "Unless your offer is still good even if I bug out?"

She cocks her head to the side. "You know it's not. My bosses care about results, not sentiment. If you want them to break your son out of jail, you need to finish this run."

"*And* land you the big score."

"That was the deal you agreed to." Her slim shoulders lift and lower in a sigh as she says it, and I wonder what our shadowy bosses are paying *her*. It's probably just an ungodly amount of money, but the bosses knew what to offer me to twist the knife. It makes sense they'd do that to the rest of us too if they can.

"Why do we come back at the same time and place as the scientists do?" I ask, trying to keep the frustration out of my voice. "There are millions of years of dinosaurs we could be exploiting without worrying about running into other humans. And time agents."

She takes a long minute just to watch me, and I figure she won't answer at all. Then Xia settles a bit more comfortably and rests one hand against her cheek. "Well, for one thing, all the places the scientists have been we get great data. Where the dinosaurs are, what kinds. That's less work for us. For another, the scientists being here is a nice sort of insurance in case something goes wrong. We run out of food, something happens to our own time tubes..." She makes a gesture with her open palm and lets me infer the rest: if something goes catastrophically wrong on our run, the scientists are always there for the picking over.

I shiver. "Risky."

"Necessary. *If* it ever came to that."

"Hmm."

She starts to stand, but I reach out to catch her wrist. Her eyes widen, but she doesn't recoil, just raises one perfect black eyebrow in question.

I almost balk under the intensity in her brown eyes, the focused calm. But I square my shoulders instead. "You could walk away, too, you know. You always have options."

She snorts. "Always?"

I put my tongue in my cheek and shrug. "They may not be *good* options, but you always have them."

She purses her lips and huffs like I've knocked her wind out. "True enough." Xia easily rises to stand and gazes down at me. "You mind helping with tent setup? Some of the newbies are having trouble."

"Sure. No problem." I grunt to my feet, and Xia offers me a hand. When our skin brushes, a frisson of electricity passes from her skin to mine, and I hope my face doesn't look as red as it feels.

Honestly, I'm pushing sixty, I have a full-grown son, I've embarked on a second career as a criminal flunky—I don't have time for goofy emotions. And nothing, but *nothing* should be able to make me blush like a teenager anymore.

Xia smiles into my eyes for another long heartbeat then someone hollers her name from the other side of camp. "We'll start the great dinosaur search tomorrow, all right? So rest well tonight, Jules."

"All right." I watch her go. Her hair is a long dark coil over one shoulder, glossy, and the end is as thick as my wrist. Great hair.

I shake the thought away and turn to the pile of my drone equipment. *Tomorrow*. I'll need to scare up some dinosaurs for the crew tomorrow. And make sure we avoid the scientists while we do it. If the scientists—and their guardian time agents—ever find out we're here, then it'll be a mess for everyone. Or a slaughter. I swallow and watch Daw swagger around the other end of camp, the crowbar against his shoulder.

Chapter Three

GRACE

Trifoso comes to collect Nakamura and me within short order, and we all work together to get our supplies inside and start the unpacking. Our research station is new since the last time I was here. It's an ugly squat building in the center of the fenced-in clearing. The research station's been painted a dull green camo in a futile attempt to match our forest surroundings. Solar panels cover the whole roof, and three large rain barrels bloom from one side like toadstools on a tree.

We used to have a larger station a few miles away, but that was when we were the crown jewel of time displacement studies. Before the scandal. Before my ex, Adam, put me and my whole program on the Time Guard's naughty list.

Anyway, this new place is paradise to me because of *when* it is. I'd be happy in a tent, sleeping in the dirt, as long as I was sleeping under a familiar prehistoric sky. (I'd probably get eaten in fairly short order, but at least I'd die happy.)

Jax approaches me, standing beside me as I survey the station. "It's bigger than I'd thought it'd be," they say.

"Oh?"

They shake their head and give a self-conscious laugh. "*How* are they letting us get away with this, Dr. Carson?" They fling their arm out toward the building, still smiling, but looking a little loopy too. "I mean, it's—it's a whole damn building and cars and *people* in the middle of the Cretaceous!"

I fold my arms and give a little shrug. "I'm where I want to be. I don't care what justification the Time Guard needs as long as they let me do my work."

Jax clicks their tongue, clearly unhappy with that answer. "Agent Nakamura!" they call.

Nakamura dusts his hands and wanders over to us, a look of pleasant inquiry on his face. Jax repeats their question, "Why does the Time Guard even let us do this? Be back here?"

He gazes skyward a moment then looks at Jax with a friendly smile. "So, as soon as time travel was invented, it was a sure bet people were going to use it. And use it stupidly too."

"Of course."

"Well, the early travelers *did* do stupid stuff, tried to change history, tried to make themselves famous or rich or president. All that. But it didn't work," he says. "Time is resilient. It's hard to change events in any meaningful way. You might be able to change the flight of a butterfly in Central Park, but no one's managed to stop the Titanic sinking. Time does what it wants. Having learned that, the Time Guard eventually decided to give in to all you academic zealots and let you go back to do your research."

"Hmm." Jax still looks dubious to my eyes as their gaze roves over the dome of the fence.

I tap Jax's shoulder, feeling like I have to defend us 'academic zealots'. "The Time Guard has been letting researchers go back—carefully monitored—for decades now, and we haven't managed to break anything yet."

"Then why does the Time Guard even exist? If time itself is so resilient?" Jax beams as they ask it, still smiling at Nakamura.

"Oh, just in case," he murmurs. "I should've said no one's been able to stop the Titanic from sinking *yet*." He winks, and then he jerks his chin toward the stack of items yet to be unloaded. "Come on now, we shouldn't let Dr. Trifoso keep going by himself."

The unpacking is exhausting, dirty work. The ground's muddy and every single, solitary thing we've packed seems to weigh a hundred pounds *and* come in an ungainly carrying case. A case just the wrong size and balance to be easily lifted. Still, we manage to get the lab supplies, the food, our personal effects, and every last bit of luggage inside while there's daylight left.

The building's empty but clearly lived in. There are dishes in the sink, rumpled beds in the dorm rooms I peek into. Nakamura checks the logs in the com room, the special domain of the time agents, and reports our other two time agents and my other research assistant are all out in the field. He settles into the com room to review records and maps.

We three scientists leave him alone, and I wander toward the back of the complex. Our work area is at the rear of the station, behind a closed door off the kitchen. The lab isn't a huge space, but it's mine. Mine all mine. Battered Cherrywood cabinets with glass fronts line the walls and long black countertops. There's only one sink, but at least we don't have to use the one in the kitchen for our work. The research assistants have one desk to share, and another desk sits empty by the room's only window.

Trifoso lets out a low chuckle behind me. "Welcome home, Dr. Carson."

I bite my lip to keep my grin in check and cross to my area. The chair's got duct tape over the seat, and a mysterious brown stain on one armrest. I sit and trace my hands over the pitted top of the desk. My heart swells, aching happily. A desk. A chair. All the specimen tubes and lab gloves I can want.

Vega knits their hands together and glances from Trifoso to me. "Where do we start?"

I open my mouth to reply but snap it shut and look to Trifoso instead. He is my boss, after all.

But he waves his hands in the air. "This is your show, Dr. Carson. I'm just here to ease the transition."

Uh-huh. I raise an eyebrow at him, but he waves blithely at me. Okay. Fine. "Do you mind showing Vega how to analyze some of the fecal samples? I want to see what the status of the camera trap program is."

Trifoso snorts, but he gamely leads Vega over to another corner to start handling our collection of crap. Literal crap.

Me, I stretch my fingers in anticipation and lift my computer out of its bag. Everything runs on solar power here, so we can't use too much juice for any of our machines. But my laptop is still fully charged from the future. We used to keep the SD cards in a small plastic box with slots, and I poke around the other desk looking for something like that.

I find the container, but there aren't any memory cards. I check the tracking sheet on the box and swallow a sigh. The cards are supposed to be collected every few days as they fill with images. If the dates on the box are accurate it's been weeks since anyone has switched the cards out.

As I poke around the rest of the lab, I find all kinds of other issues. Sloppy records. Tools improperly cleaned, improperly stored. Trifoso and Vega themselves discover several of the fecal samples haven't been labeled properly, which makes them basically useless.

A dark cloud is brewing on Trifoso's face the more we explore the lab. It doesn't help that the other research assistant, Sona Grigori, isn't here to explain herself or show us where she's put everything. We're blundering through, true enough, but how can we be here in the past and not want to dive right in?

Vega at least seems like a good worker. Unasked, they snag a dust rag and start cleaning, organizing, helping set the lab to rights. Trifoso and I work together on making sense of the labels on the fecal samples. Those are the most valuable data in the lab, and it'd be a shame if they weren't useable.

Hours later, Nakamura wanders into the room to call us for dinner. The man's a savior. We're all three starving and, without him, we probably would've worked all night and never noticed the snarling from our stomachs.

There's a heck of a thunderstorm going on outside, but I've missed that too while being head down in the lab.

We throw dinner together out of the oldest things in the cabinet, and the end result is some kind of premade gray mush that claims to be pasta. Just add water! I douse it in hot sauce and share my bottle around the table for anyone else who'd like some flavor in their mush. Nakamura's the only one who takes me up on it.

But Trifoso saves the meal from being too depressing by breaking into his personal luggage for a bottle of champagne. This is why my boss has my undying loyalty. He might be a pain in my ass sometimes, but the man does have flair.

"To the past! We're happy to be here and ready to work!" Trifoso proclaims, glass high.

Nakamura wets his lips as we toast, but doesn't drink more than that.

"To the future! So long. Adieu. We wish you well." Vega takes a long gulp of champagne then beams at all of us, eyes sparkling.

I laugh and hold my own glass aloft. "To our research. May our dinosaurs be plentiful and full of shit."

Nakamura and the rest burst out laughing. He clicks his glass against mine, shaking his head. "Do I even want to know, Doc?"

"Oh, probably not."

"I'll toast to that." And he does, taking his first good swallow of champagne and grinning at me over the rim.

We drink our champagne—good champagne it is too—out of cheap plastic cups, and it's like my blood's been switched out for champagne, fizzy and bright and popping with excitement. Whatever else happens at least I'm in this *here*. This *now*.

Vega takes a long drink of champagne then leans forward on the table to catch Nakamura's eye. I think Vega is trying to flirt with our time agent, in fact, which more power to them. Lord knows everyone sleeping with everyone else is a time-honored tradition of fieldwork. I don't plan to partake, but other folks should feel free. Of course, a time agent and a scientist sleeping together could get complicated—

But it's not my business. That's my mantra this trip out. I bury my nose in my champagne glass.

The front door bangs open, letting in the crashing sounds of the storm. Lightning frames a shadowed figure in the doorway. Nakamura is out of his seat before the rest of us have time to do more than gape. But he relaxes after a moment, and so do I once I recognize the Time Guard uniform under the raincoat.

"You must be one of our other time agents." Trifoso pushes away from the table and stalks forward with a fresh champagne glass in one hand and his other held out to shake.

The figure in the doorway wears a heavy forest camo rain slicker and thick boots crusted to the knee in mud. At Trifoso's approach, the newcomer finally glances up with a grunt and peels out of their rain gear.

When I see our new agent's face my first thought is, *Oh shit*.

Agent Meg Zaran.

Our gazes catch, and she actually growls in the back of her throat when she sees me. "Ah, fuck no."

I've known Meg for years. She's been assigned to this outpost since the beginning, even before my time. We'd always been friendly before.

But I guess criminal charges, even ones you're acquitted of, can change a lot of things.

Rest of dinner should be fun.

Trifoso sputters at Meg, but she brushes past him and glares at me as she yanks a chair out. She collects her plate of slop and digs in, ignoring the champagne. Meg's older, fiftyish but still fit. Her hair used to be a dyed black with blue highlights, but she's let it grow out and go gray since the last time I saw her years ago. It's in two long braids over her shoulders.

Meg forks a few mouthfuls of mush into her mouth then swabs her face with a napkin. She tilts her head, and her jaw is gritted with what looks like anger. "Since you newbies are all here, this is a good time to go over protocols." This speech is supposed to be for everyone, but she's glaring at me alone. "All fieldwork," she says, her voice hard, "in fact, *any* excursions outside the fence, you will be accompanied by a time agent. And if there's more than two of you out, then you will need more than one agent to monitor." Now she shares her glower around to the rest of my team.

"Are you kidding?" I whirl toward Trifoso, my heart pounding. "You agreed to this?"

He opens his palms in a shrugging gesture. "I did what I had to in order to save the program, Grace. It's not a big concession."

I bite my tongue on a sharp retort. It's not a big concession unless you're trying to get close to the animals. Time agents aren't trained to move quietly in the field. They don't know how to sit still for hours taking notes on what a dinosaur is eating, how often it shits or pees, where it mates. All of that is going to be deadly dull to them, and the agents are going to fidget, they're going to complain. "This will make it harder to do our jobs. This will hamper our ability to do research."

Meg snorts. "So what? It's not like your research has any kind of practical application. Dinosaur behavior is hardly a valuable field of study."

Anger blazes through me like dry brush catching after a lightning strike. I could argue that studying the past helps us understand the future. I could talk about how studying animals helps us understand humanity better. I could whip out my doctorate and get into the big pissing contest Meg is angling for.

Except I've had two years of practice taming my temper. So, instead of yelling, I grimace out a smile and keep my voice sickly sweet. "The Time Guard lets the World War II buffs go back to watch Pearl Harbor burn. You think they shouldn't let a couple crazy bastards travel to the dawn of time to study dinosaurs?"

Meg shakes her head as she stabs another forkful of food. But she doesn't say anything else.

A win. Of sorts.

Dinner conversation after that is a bit blighted. Somehow I manage to choke down enough of the hot-sauced slop so my stomach doesn't stay empty. We all disperse to our rooms to unpack. Everyone gets their own room except the two grad students who have to share. Hopefully, Vega and the other student, Grigori, can get along.

It's still early in the evening, but the storm outside makes everything dark and gloomy. There's a sort of communal sense we might as well turn in because what else is there to do?

Alone in my room, I debate the merits of swapping with someone. Several towers of boxes occupy one corner of the room, teetering precariously over the bed. With the door closed, the musky smell of mold and rot fills the space.

I make a business unpacking what I have—clothes and books and toiletries—trying to make the space mine. A knock at the door interrupts me. I don't know who I was expecting, but it wasn't Meg. "Agent Zaran?" I say.

She shoulders past me into my room. "I wanted to get something clear with you."

"Oh?"

"You might have been able to sell everyone else your line of bullshit, but *I'm not buying*."

"But it's only three easy payments of $49.95. Cancel anytime." My blood's hammering through me, a lovely mix of pissed off and embarrassed.

Her lip curls. "You think this is funny?"

"I think I'm finally home after two years of hell." I clench my fists at my sides, fighting my irritation. "Look, I'm in charge of this program, and we need to be able to work together. So maybe you shouldn't be threatening me? Save it for next week." I cross to the door and open it. Subtlety is my strong suit.

Meg crosses in front of me toward the door. "I'm watching you, Grace, and the minute you screw up, it will be my personal pleasure to send your ass back to the future. For good."

"Super. Great talk."

"Fuck you." As she walks out of my room, I notice we had an audience for that charming exchange. Nakamura and two newcomers I don't recognize are standing at the end of the hallway, apparently also on their way to knock on my door.

Isn't it nice to be popular?

Meg slams into her own bedroom without saying anything to anyone, although her face goes a deep red.

I turn to the others and force my expression into something a bit more neutral. "Hello. This must be my other grad student and our last time agent?"

"Correct." Nakamura leads them forward, all of us pretending so hard the awkwardness of the past few minutes didn't happen. "Doc, this is your grad student, Sona Grigori."

Grigori's got olive skin, freckled and tanned, and curling brown hair in a braid pinned atop her head. Her clothes are ragged and grubby, fieldwork clothes like mine. She clears her throat and offers me her hand to shake. "A pleasure to meet you, Dr. Carson. I'm excited to be working together. Agent Srinivasan and I just got in. I was trying to do a night survey of some troodons, but we didn't have much luck."

"Fascinating. I look forward to hearing your observations. I wanted to go over the camera trap progress with you tomorrow too."

Grigori bites her lip, and her cheeks go a little pale. "Of—of course."

I turn toward the last newcomer, another woman. She's got rich, dark-brown skin and wears a black hijab pinned around her face. Her Time Guard uniform is rumpled and mud splattered. She must've been babysitting Grigori in the field. "Agent Srinivasan, was it?"

"Hello, Dr. Carson." She shakes my hand, even though her mouth is crimped with consternation. She and Nakamura are the junior field agents here. Probably awkward for them to watch their boss Meg snap at me. Nakamura is studying me, a notch between his brows.

"Well," I say with fake cheerfulness. "I'm pretty tired, and we've got an early start tomorrow." With that, I nip into my own room and close the door. I lean against it and huff my breath out. Soon enough, I hear the others moving down the hallway, doors closing.

I try to read an old Mira Grant paperback to wind down, but I can't concentrate. Several of the storage boxes are next to my head, hitting me with their musky scent and butting against my elbow.

"What the hell are these anyway?" I shift some of the boxes to the floor to create two small hills next to the bed instead of the one precarious mountain.

When I lift the lid off the first box it's like getting an electric shock. It's pages and pages of field notes and journals, but looking at the handwriting on them sends my heart beating fast. My hands shake as I lift the first packet of papers.

'Spotted a pack of troodons night hunting near the streambed. Judging by calls it was four individuals. Maybe a family group. I'd love to track them to the nest.'

Dr. Carson, the *other* Dr. Carson, wrote these. Reading the lines fills my head with the sound of her voice, practically conjures her into the room with me. It's as if my aching nostalgia, my regret, has some magical power over the physical world. The smell of sweat and old paper rises in my memory. The fidgety rustle of her hands as she pats her pockets looking for a pencil or her camera. The *other* Dr. Carson. My old boss. My mother-in-law. My mentor. My friend.

I thread my fingers into my hair and pull as I read. Nothing earth-shattering in the notes. Just some field observations for a day like any other. The date is years in the past. Before the scandal. Before Adam destroyed both our lives.

Driven, frantic, I peer at the rest of the boxes. Dated by year, okay, then organized into folders by month inside. I scan and shift and dig until I find the last box, the one with the date a week or so after I turned Adam in. Her notes are on top like she wanted me to find them, like she left them there for me. Maybe she did.

The last dated notes I can find don't seem like something that would be useful for our field of research anyway:

'Damn Grace. <u>Damn her</u>. If only she'd kept her mouth shut. I begged her, but she's so goddamn supercilious. So scared of breaking the rules. And now she and Adam are in custody. They'll drag me away too, I bet. Maybe I should walk into the forest, leave all this bullshit behind. Let some hungry dinosaur take me. Let the Time Guard clean up <u>that</u> mess. I'm so tired. This debacle has barely begun, and I just want it all to be over.'

Tears sting my throat. The only official word the Time Guard would ever give me on my mother-in-law was she went "missing". But they always made it sound like she disappeared back home in the *future*. It always seemed suspicious to me, and now this reads a bit like a suicide note. Makes sense the Time Guard wouldn't want anyone to know one of the most famous time travelers in the world had committed suicide by dinosaur.

I scrub wetness out of my eyes and gently place the page in the box. Maybe she didn't even mean to die, maybe she just walked into the forest and let it happen. I'd been tempted by that road myself during the long ugly stretch of the trial, when I thought no one would believe me. When I thought I'd never get my life back. Just drift into traffic without looking. Just sink under the water in my bath and forget to breathe.

I shake the dark mood away and firmly close the lid on the box. I'm here. I'm alive. I fought my way home, so I need to make the most of it. For *both* the Dr. Carsons.

And my ex Adam can go fuck himself. He's ruined things enough, for me and his mother. She's gone, but he can't suck any more of my life down the drain.

Voices pass my door, friendly and laughing. From what I can hear, it sounds like Trifoso is cajoling the grad students into a game of cards. I should stick my head out and offer to join them. Team building, after all. Camaraderie. *Friends*?

Maybe later. I can't quite make myself open that door, can't quite force myself to make that reach to my new team. There's plenty of time for pleasantries later.

And that itch has started under my skin again to be out, to be *doing*. My window is small and circular, like a porthole, but it's enough I can see the rain's stopped. The sun hasn't set yet, although the sky is still a gloomy gray edging toward dark. The smell of the old field journals seems to choke the air, clogging my throat with dust and regrets.

I can't force myself to go through all these old notes. That way lies madness. Still, there has to be another chore I can do to get me out of this room but away from people.

The camera traps! Perfect. There are some near enough to the research station. I can go inventory SD cards, stretch my legs, and get away from this haunted room.

If Meg gives me shit for leaving without an escort, well, maybe I better make sure I'm not caught.

I stomp my hiking boots on and tuck the cuffs of my khaki pants into my socks. I shrug on my trusty brown flannel for good measure.

When I poke my head into the hallway, no one else is around, and the common room is clear too. Maybe the others decided against cards or the game broke up early.

The hinges on our front door have been oiled so it opens easy and quiet. Just like that, I'm outside, breathing the crisp, cool air of a prehistoric twilight.

Chapter Four

JULIA

A massive rainstorm swoops in while we're trying to get camp established, but fortunately we've got most of the tents done, and the cars can provide cover too. I hunker in my lonely single tent and listen to the rain pound outside. The LED lantern hanging from the center of my tent sways as the wind whips at the shelter's fabric. It's almost sunset before the storm entirely eases. I emerge, not at all like a butterfly, from my stuffy cocoon.

The forest is gorgeous in the twilight, leaves dusted with droplets that catch the falling light and gild the whole greenwood a shining gold. I've got an old itch in my gut to go exploring, but my better sense triumphs in time. Only an idiot goes out walking in the prehistoric night.

Now that the storm is over and most of the packing has been abandoned, a small party erupts among the crew. Someone breaks out the cheap booze and starts passing it around. There's laughter and quiet music from another person's guitar. I share a fallen log with Xia as we pass a bottle back and forth until my face is hot and my words are slurring. "I should go to bed," I murmur.

"Do you *want* to go to bed?" she asks.

The air here is fresh and chill, blowing gently over my cheeks until they're colder than all the rest of me. The guitar music is mellow and sweet, some old tune I can't quite place. And my whole side is warm where it brushes against Xia. There's a contentment in this moment that settles right down deep, like digging your toes into summer baked beach sand. Viscerally satisfying. "No, I don't want to go." I could fall asleep right here, leaning on Xia's shoulder...

Or missing her shoulder and splatting in the mud. Or she shrugs me off and asks what the hell I'm doing. I straighten my spine. "Yeah, bedtime for me, I think."

Xia borrows the bottle from me and takes a small swallow as she eyes me over the rim. "Do you need someone to tuck you in?"

And I thought my cheeks felt hot *before*. There's heat lower down too, answering and kindling to the throb of her femme fatale voice.

But I'm probably getting my signals crossed. She's probably offering to help just so one of her drunken crew members doesn't wander the wrong way and get eaten. "I'm, uh, I'm probably all right."

"Fair enough."

It's funny, we were all so eager to get *out* of our tents after the rain storm, but now I notice more and more folks are disappearing *into* their tents. Although not alone this time.

Xia's been watching me stand there, hesitating and eyeing the amorous couples, and she opens her mouth to say something.

But, just as she does, a human scream splits the air from the forest.

Everyone's on their feet, and a few folks stagger out of their tents half-dressed to see what the commotion is. Gunshots follow after several more heartbeats.

"*Hell*." Xia's up and running toward the sound immediately. I follow after her, less sure on my feet. As my stomach gives a sickened slosh, I regret the last few sips out of our shared bottle.

I arrive after most of the commotion has already settled and find just what I expected—and least wanted—to see. A dead body. One of the new hires, young guy, couldn't be more than twenty-five, and he's been ripped open from neck to navel. The smell of shit and blood hits me, and I press my fist against my mouth to keep from vomiting. He's not far from camp. Far enough the searchers needed flashlights to find him. Close enough he might have made it to safety if he'd been faster.

The dinosaur that killed him, a midsized theropod, is dead in the dirt with a shower of bullet holes in its neck and gut.

"It just—just came out of the forest." Another one of the newbies is standing close at hand, her voice high-pitched and threatening tears. There's blood on her shirt, but I'm not sure if it's hers or not. Daw has one arm around the girl. Xia stands apart, just listening, her arms crossed.

"I ran," the girl continues, "but he tripped behind me. I—I should've stopped, should've helped."

"You did the right thing," I murmur. "If you'd stopped, we'd have two bodies instead of one." That's just the sad fact. In the dark, in the forest, unarmed, a human isn't likely to win a fight against a dinosaur.

The girl's gaze cuts to me, and she gives a sad nod, sort of curling in toward Daw. Daw finally coaxes the girl into camp. Xia's third in command, Iris, grimly takes charge of dealing with the body. I have a macabre urge to ask her what she's going to do, if they even care about the fossil record or if they'll bury him somewhere, but it's not my business. And it's not my job to care.

Xia stands there and watches until the body is gone, her mouth pinched and white. I want to put an arm around her shoulders, but I'm worried I'd be too clumsy to do it.

"First blood," she says.

"What?"

She shakes her head. "We've already got a body count. Goddammit, I wish the moneymen would stop sending us here."

I scuff my feet in the dirt and shove my hands into my pockets. "Too profitable?"

"Yes, and they don't weight the human cost in the balance sheet. Fuck, I'm already tired, and we still have to fulfill the whole order list." She digs her fingers into her thick black hair. "Stupid kids. Why couldn't they go fuck in their tent like any sane person would?"

"Too shy? The allure and romance of the outdoors?"

"Idiot children." She turns and tucks her hand into my arm, giving a small tug of my elbow. "Come on, walk me into camp? We shouldn't linger outside the perimeter, or we'll be the next ones eaten."

"S—sure." I keep my hands shoved deep in my pockets instead of taking her hand like I want to. Everything is too dark, too uncertain for me to trust myself. I give Xia a small bump with my elbow where her hand is resting. "It'll be all right, boss."

She snorts, her eyes shadowed and sad. "No, it won't. But we have to get the job done anyway." She disengages her hand from my arm when we pass the perimeter guards. "You be careful when we start the hunt tomorrow, all right? I don't want to pull *your* body out of the forest."

Because I'm *me* or because I'm part of her crew? My head hurts, and I give her a wan smile. "You too."

Then I squelch off through the mud to my lonely tent and cold sleeping bag. As I settle in for sleep, I hear a couple in the next tent over start having sex. Loudly. Enthusiastically.

Fortunately—or unfortunately—I can't seem to handle my liquor much anymore, so I manage to fall asleep despite my neighbors' exertions. The hunt begins tomorrow and, if I don't want to be one more dead body fouling up the fossil record, I need my rest.

Chapter Five

GRACE

The rain's stopped and it's still light outside, although sunset is coming soon. I walk fast as I can to the fence circling our research station and press my palm against the cool metal. It's a thin mesh, finer knit than the usual chain-link so most smaller animals can't get through. I need to find the gate out, and I have a sneaking suspicion if I run into Meg, she'll order me to my room like a teenager sneaking out to a kegger.

As I stand beside the fence, a pressure starts building in my head like it's slowly being squashed, and I rub my temples trying to release some of the tension.

"It's the high-frequency fence."

Nakamura's voice kicks my heart up to racing a mile a minute. I whirl around with my hand pressed over my heart. Why do we do that? The hand to the chest thing? It doesn't change anything but, oh fuck, he scared me. I manage to find my dignity again, and I straighten my spine. "High-frequency fence?"

He twirls his finger in the air to encompass the perimeter of our clearing. "It was one of the security measures added after the incident. To the dinosaurs, all the area around this station for several meters in every direction is filled with an ungodly noise. Humans can't hear it—the frequency is too high—but the dinosaurs can. It keeps them away. Although if you stand here long enough, you'll get a nosebleed maybe. You'll sure as hell get a headache."

"Already there."

He watches me, head cocked to one side. "Were you planning to go out, Dr. Carson?"

My blood jumps with a guilty start even though I had legitimate business outside the fence. "I wanted to find the nearest camera traps and get their memory cards."

He chuckles. "Old-fashioned tech."

I mimic his earlier gesture and twirl my hand in the air. "No wireless data transfer."

"Right." He folds his arms.

Gradually, I realize this whole sneaking out thing looks incriminating as hell. Our first night and I'm out for a walk in the almost dark, sneaking past my time agent guards? *Nothing* suspicious about that, nope. Not at all.

I wet my lips. "Would you like to come out with me, Agent Nakamura? There's still time before sunset."

He pauses and blinks at me. Maybe he'd prepped himself for some kind of denials or defenses. But I can't fight the raw need inside anymore to get out of this fence, and I'll tolerate his presence if it will get me on the other side.

He leans his hand against the fence, close enough to mine I can feel the heat off his skin even though we don't actually touch. "Is it safe to go outside this late in the day, Doc?"

"A quick trip. Sure."

Nakamura sways on his feet a minute, a posture of deciding, thinking. His hand falls on the firearm at his side in an unconscious fidget. His gun is some futuristic-looking thing with a wide muzzle. If that contraption throws bullets, I hope I'm never standing in front of one. "What the hell," he says at last. "Give me the grand tour, Doc."

—eee—

We pass a few cameras, but they're hard to spot in the dark, and some of them are too high to reach without a ladder anyway. After collecting only two SD cards, my shoulders sag in defeat. "I guess this will have to wait for morning." I recognize a familiar trail marker on one of the trees and do a slow spin to orient myself. "But there's something pretty cool nearby. If you're interested?" If the trails and patterns of the animals haven't changed.

Nakamura shrugs. "Sure. I'm just here to sightsee anyway."

"All right."

It's funny, but I don't realize I've done something dangerous until the research station disappears behind us on the path. Maybe there's an implicit trust because he's a time agent, but it only occurs to me I'm out in the forest alone with a strange man *after* we've already passed out of calling distance of the station.

Of course, he's out walking the trail with someone *he* suspects of being a criminal. So maybe we're both idiots.

This research station is in a different location than our old home base, but the territory is still familiar. I've walked this terrain for miles and miles in every direction for years on end. Sometimes I suspect the lay of the land's been ground into my bones.

But I still use the trail markers and the setting sun to navigate instead of trusting my gut. I might take strange men alone into the forest with me and earn my living by studying giant murderbirds, but I'm not *stupid* stupid.

Nakamura puffs beside me as we clamber through the underbrush, squelching in mud. "You *do* have a destination in mind, Doc? Or are you looking for some-where convenient to dump my body?"

I snort. Great minds, I guess? "Shh. There won't be anything to see if you talk too loud."

I'm hoping I haven't made a big promise for nothing, but slowly I start to hear noises over the sound of our thrashing progress. Low hoots and calls, rumbles of sound. Nakamura tenses beside me and gives me a wide-eyed, uncertain look. But he follows me just the same as I creep forward.

We're on a hill overlooking the local watering hole, and a family of sauropods are taking their turn. "These are Alamosaurus," I murmur.

"Alamo?"

I laugh. "Yup. Their name means 'Old Alamo lizard'. They were originally discovered in Texas." They're huge sauropods, nearly a hundred feet tall as adults, and their backs are covered with a bony plate armor.

"I can't... the size of them..." Nakamura can only shake his head in wonder.

They move with a lazy, easy grace, long necks swaying as they eat and call to each other. Maybe it's because I've been gone so long, but the sight of these stunning creatures hits me hard, and I sniff juicily. It doesn't work to stop the flow, though, and soon enough, tears are tickling over my cheeks, wet and cold. Embarrassment heats my face, and I avoid Nakamura's eyes. "I hope I don't cry every time I see a dinosaur. Makes my job harder."

"It's okay, Doc." He says it slow, gentle. No judgment. No mockery.

"Thank you." My voice creaks but it doesn't break. Small mercies.

"Now stop talking. I came to see some dinosaurs." He settles into a squat on the hill and watches them, his eyes bright, and oh help me, but that makes me like him.

The light shines gold off the water, and the long necks of the sauropods sway like dancers in some intricate choreography, smooth and immense. My cheeks ache because I've been grinning this whole time. But even as I admire their elegance, I'm also watching the social interactions between adults, trying to determine the sex of the animals, looking for their young and how protective they are of them. It's a welcome stream of thoughts, an old muscle flexing to life.

Nakamura's fingers brush my sleeve, and I jump away from him, landing on my butt in the mud with a messy squelch.

His mouth crimps in a not-quite laugh. "Sorry, Doc. But the sun's going down."

"Oh. Right."

He offers a hand to me, and I slide my palm into his. His skin's warm, his fingers work roughened. I let go as soon as I'm on my feet and scrape my muddy fingers against my pants.

When I look up, I'm staring down the barrel of Nakamura's gun. It's pointed right at my head.

Chapter Six

GRACE

Before I can do more than form the word "wha..." Nakamura shoves me to the side. "Down!" he bellows.

The gun goes off above my head, a shattering noise that leaves my ears ringing. Something heavy drops beside me, and warm water splatters over my face and clothes. Except when I look down my hands are splattered red, and there's a citipati, an emu-sized theropod, staring at me out of dead eyes leaking blood. I drag a breath in, so deep my lungs hurt with it. "What the ever loving FUCK?"

Behind me, the Alamosaurs trumpet their alarm and chivvy their young away from the water's edge.

Nakamura grabs my elbow and drags me to my feet. He lets me go and toes the dead dinosaur with his foot then holsters his sidearm. "Are you all right?"

I'm shaking, hard enough my knees don't hold me, and I slide into the mud. A crisp wind ruffles over us, stirring the blood-splattered feathers of the dinosaur. Although actually not much blood. It only seems to be leaking from its mouth and eyes. I tip forward onto my hands and knees, creeping toward the animal.

"What are you doing?" Nakamura hunkers across from me, his hands out like maybe I've gone off the deep end and he's worried he'll have to restrain me.

In deference to his nerves, I rock back on my heels. "What the hell is that thing?" I point at his weapon.

"A gun."

"Bullshit. What the—what the hell did that just do?" I gesture at the dinosaur, so very dead but without any visible wounds to show for it.

"We're not allowed to have bullets here."

"Okay."

"They gave us... all right, so you know how an explosion, if you get caught in the blast wave *that* can kill you? Just the concussive force of the explosion can scramble your insides?"

"Yeah."

"So. *That*. But travel-sized for my convenience. And yours since that dinosaur was about to eat you."

I shake my head. "You didn't have to shoot the poor thing."

"Excuse me?"

"You should have made yourself look larger, raised your hands in the air. Maybe made some loud noises. Or warned me, and *I* would've done it." A simmer of irritation hums through my blood as I study the dead dinosaur.

Nakamura frowns, and his mouth opens and closes, open and closes. Finally, he stands and crosses his arms over his chest in a posture of deep frustration. "You're pissed I saved your life?"

I roll my eyes. "I wish you'd tried something else before you shot an innocent animal. And I'm worried about taking you into the field if you're this nervous."

"*Nervous*?"

The feathers on the animal are still fluttering in the wind, which draws my attention to the carcass. With so little damage we could learn a lot from this specimen. Maybe not the internal structures if Nakamura's gun really did turn them to goo, but the structure of the feathers, muscle density, stomach contents—

I pat my pockets, but of course I didn't bring anything with me. Not my field kit, not my specimen jars. No gloves. The animal's feathers are black and brown, with a cream-colored head and a yellow, beak-like mouth with a curved crest on its head. It's a large animal, bigger than me, but lighter boned, of course. I eye Nakamura speculatively, eye those rather decorative muscles of his. "Think you can carry this to the research station?"

"What?"

I stifle a growl. The sun is setting, and I don't want to be out after dark. "Can you carry the body? Or is it too heavy?"

"I... probably not too heavy. But. *Why?*"

"We're not usually allowed to examine remains because we can't be sure how the animal died. But we *know* how this one died."

"So, you're *not* pissed I killed the dinosaur?"

"Oh, I'm pissed. But if life hands you lemons—"

"This isn't fucking lemonade, Doc."

"Will you carry it for me or not?"

Instead of answering my question, he motions me to silence and curls his fingers around my wrist.

I hear it too. A rustle in the brush. An animal breathing in the darkness. The hair rises on my arms, and my shoulders tense with fear.

"No time, Doc." He jerks his chin at me to go first and keeps his gun drawn as he urges me forward.

The sun's going down, and I probably wouldn't be able to convince him to carry the specimen for me anyway. I hope whatever scavenger is waiting in the brush is happy for the meal. With a sigh, I let Nakamura shuffle me home.

There aren't many lights in our research station, but when we walk through the gate, all of them are on. I swallow and groan and head inside to face my dressing down.

Except when Nakamura and I waltz into the common room, Meg is nowhere to be seen. There's just Grigori raiding the recently restocked pantry with her finger in my tub of peanut butter.

I walk into the kitchen and lean against the counter. The thief is still facing away, licking peanut butter off a spreading knife. "Good evening, Sona."

The pantry thief whirls but doesn't drop my peanut butter on the floor, thank goodness. "Dr. Carson. Oh. Hi. Um." She looks all of sixteen, although I imagine she must be twenty-something. Old enough to know not to steal other people's peanut butter.

Still, she's got a few months left on her contract. Best to play nice. For now. "If you'll excuse me, I left a prime specimen on the hill, and I want to see if there's anything I can do to salvage it." I whirl away.

"You are stubborn, Doc." Nakamura falls in step behind me.

"Is that *blood*?" Grigori asks in a wobbly voice from the kitchen.

Absently, I swab my face with the sleeve of my flannel shirt. It's already a brown shirt. I'll disinfect it later.

I pause in the dorm hallway, trying to remember which room Trifoso claimed. Nakamura clears his throat and points. "If you want to talk to your boss, it's that one." I expect him to linger and maybe put in his side of the argument, but instead he heads to the common room to give me privacy.

Holding my breath, I rap smartly on Trifoso's door. When he opens the door, he looks tired and peaked, his skin sallow, his eyes shadowed.

I reach to touch his arm, my errand forgotten. "Paul, are you all right?"

He scrubs both hands over his face. "I took a sleeping pill, Grace. What's going on?" There's a bite to his voice that tells me my errand is unlikely to prosper.

Still, I launch into my plea to take one of the jeeps out to retrieve the specimen on the hill.

But, almost as soon as I've started talking, he lifts a hand to stop me. "Grace, the Time Guard has the final word on this sort of thing. And the Time Guard said no. Why are you bothering *me*?" Lines of tension bracket his mouth.

"You're the ranking scientist lead on this mission right now. That dinosaur could be so valuable to our research. If you'd push back—"

Trifoso's nostrils flare, and he leans forward, lowering his voice to a growl. "Things are different, Grace. I tried to warn you." He sighs. "You didn't antagonize Nakamura did you?"

"No." Not much.

"Good. *Don't*. And steer clear of Agent Zaran. We've got enough samples to sort through as it is. I didn't bring you to play adventurer, Grace. Do your work, keep your head down, and *don't make trouble*." With that, he closes the door in my face.

I suppose I should be happy he doesn't slam it, but it's hard to be happy about anything at the moment.

After the disappointment with the specimen, I finally drag myself to bed and fall asleep.

A soft knock wakes me early the next morning. "Yes?"

Nakamura pokes his head through the door. He's dressed, but his hair is still wet from the shower, and he hasn't shaved yet. He's very handsome and sleep-rumpled, and for one second my own sleep-fogged mind considers inviting him back to bed with me.

I force myself to sit up instead and finger comb the worst of the tangles out of my hair. "What is it?"

"Dr. Trifoso sent me to fetch you. Some kind of kerfuffle with the grad students."

"Oh, hell. What now?"

He leaves, and I throw clothes on, khakis and a blue tank, then follow the sound of voices rising in a strident crescendo toward the kitchen.

"They ate my pie!" Grigori brandishes an empty wrapper in Vega's face. The wrapper is for one of those syrupy-sweet, but oh-so-delicious, vending-machine-style fruit pies.

Vega's face is scrunched with anger, and Trifoso is between the two research assistants, looking harried and annoyed. He hasn't had his coffee yet, clearly.

My boss waves his hands at both students in a *calm down* gesture. "I'm sure it was an honest mistake—"

"My name is all over the wrapper. And the storage bin. She went in there on purpose. She ate it on purpose. I've been waiting for new food for *months*, and Vega just..." Grigori looks on the verge of tears, lip trembling, and it occurs to me how sick she must be of reconstituted mush. I might raid the kitchen, too, in a similar situation.

Vega snorts and folds their arms. "You ate *my* cookies. Fair's fair."

"I did *not*!" Grigori's voice is shrill and indignant, but I can't help remembering catching her butterfingered last night. The plot thickens.

Hell. I scrub a hand over my face. Man-eating dinosaurs I can handle, but this immature dorm room bullshit? No one's noticed me, though. Maybe I'll just slide back into my room...

"Don't wanna play referee, Doc?" Nakamura's voice near my ear is low, a rumble that gives me goose bumps. He's not even trying to sound alluring. He's just got one of those voices.

"Don't move," I whisper and jerk my chin toward the kitchen. "They might notice us if we move."

He chuckles. "What if I want my coffee?"

Grigori lets out a shriek and tries to shove the wrapper in Vega's mouth.

Nakamura and I wince as Trifoso tangles with the two students, wrestling to keep them apart. "How bad do you want coffee, Nakamura?"

"I should've slept in." He grunts and brushes past me heading toward the kerfuffle. Brave man.

Trifoso's got two hands on Vega's shoulder as the student breathes hard, trying to calm down. Nakamura goes for Grigori, assuming a soothing tone, murmuring reassurance to her I can't hear. Her voice starts to rise again, "How dare they accuse me of—"

I put two fingers in my mouth and voice the loudest, shrillest whistle I can manage. Everyone freezes and looks at me. "*Enough.* There has been exactly enough drama about a vending machine jelly pie." I make my voice crisp, using my Professor Voice, and it gets both their attention as they snap to straight positions. "Jax, if someone eats your personally marked food from home, the proper thing to do is let Dr. Trifoso or me know. It sucks, but this tit-for-tat bullshit will have everyone ready to murder each other if you keep at it. Sona, *you* need to deal with this like an adult and eat some other junk food for breakfast. I'm putting you both in charge of the pantry and, if *anything else* goes missing, it'll be coming out of both your pay. Understood?"

Vega grits their jaw, a line standing out strong under the chin, but then they nod. "Yes, Dr. Carson."

"Yes, Dr. Carson." Grigori's lips purse with anger, going starkly white. "Excuse me. I forgot something in one of the jeeps last night." She whirls on her heel, storms away, slamming the front door as she goes.

Vega lets out a disgruntled "*hah*" and stomps to the coffeepot.

Not a great start, but I've got an aggressive list of tasks I want my team to do today. When Grigori doesn't return to eat, Trifoso volunteers to find her. I rush through my own breakfast and gritty instant coffee. Sooner than I expected, Trifoso returns with Grigori in tow. He slides her chair out for her and takes one himself then gives me an "it's all right" look. Nakamura leans against the counter, crunching a granola bar and nursing his coffee.

Now's as good a time as any to go over plans for the day. "Since it looks like the camera traps haven't been checked in a while, I thought a good start might be to collect the memory cards, then we can go over the data tonight."

Trifoso nods approval to this plan. "We can work in pairs."

"If you're all going out today, Doc, you'll need another time agent besides me to go." Nakamura raises his eyebrows over the top of his mug. "Better check with the other agents."

Rats. I'd forgotten I needed even *one* time agent to accompany us. The idea of begging Meg to tag along does not appeal. Maybe Agent Srinivasan will be excited about the prospect of fieldwork—after being out late in the rain last night with Grigori.

As if he can read my thoughts, Trifoso pushes away from the table. "I'll go talk to Agent Zaran. Agent Srinivasan is still catching up on her missed sleep."

Chitchat at the breakfast table is basically nonexistent as my two grad students try to pretend the other one doesn't exist, and then there's me waiting to see if I actually get to do any fieldwork today.

When I'm sure my lungs are about to burst from holding my breath, hoping, Meg emerges. She's in a crisp field uniform, worn around the edges and patched but still clean and pressed. The sleeves are cuffed to show the Time Guard infinity symbol tattooed on her bicep, and her nails are painted a bright cherry red. Clearly, being stationed in the primordial world hasn't made her forget her standards. "Let's get this show going then."

At this pronouncement, we all clear our breakfasts and work on hurrying out the door. There's a lot of scrambling trying to find field bags, notebooks, goggles, the box with the new cameras, and other assorted items. But finally, after maybe forty minutes of running around, we're all ready to leave.

I grab Nakamura's sleeve to stop him. "Don't shoot any more dinosaurs today."

"What happened to your 'make lemonade' philosophy, Doc?"

"Okay. *If* you shoot a dinosaur, then you have to carry it home so I can dissect it. That's fair, right?"

Before he can answer, Trifoso ducks his head in from outside. "*Grace*. Are we going? Cars are this way."

My chest goes tight as we approach the cars in their shed next to the station. They're the same two outdated old hover-models we were flying years ago, with even more dents and scrapes. They look a bit like enclosed jeeps with the wheels cut off, and painted that same dark camo green as all the buildings here.

Vega falls in step with me and jerks their chin at the cars. "Why hover-jeeps? Why not helicopters or something?" Hover-cars are still trying to gain a toehold in the future. Every time the vehicles get close to being approved for private use, the Federal Aviation Administration has another screaming fit, and everything gets delayed again.

My mouth quirks. "Because all you need to fly a hover-car here is a driver's license." I gesture at the clear blue sky above us. "Helicopters are too hard to maintain and too hard to fly in this time period and climate. And regular cars would be useless. No roads in prehistoric times, just shitty game trails."

"Where'd the cars come from?" Nakamura asks.

"Some Japanese manufacturer donated the jeeps to our expedition a long time ago, looking for good publicity, and we've been using the same two vehicles ever since."

Meg lets out a crack of laughter. "And they're going to die on us any day and drop you right out of the sky. You watch."

I roll my eyes. "On that charming note, let's all pile in."

Each jeep seats four, so we'll need both vehicles. Trifoso looks strained, and Grigori's still pouting, but she lets him hand her into one of the jeeps with great ceremony—like a princess and her footman or something. She crosses her arms and looks away, making it clear she doesn't want to speak to any of the rest of us.

Fine by me.

Meg hops into the driver's seat of the nearest jeep. The one without Grigori. Apparently, Meg prefers *my* company to the grad student. How much of a pain in the ass *is* Grigori?

Meg clucks her tongue impatiently. "Coming, Grace?"

"Right. Yes." I slide into the passenger seat beside her, and Vega hops in back.

Meg starts the jeep, and the car lifts with a small jerk as our hover-jeep zips out of the shed and into the air. The fence is really a dome around the whole outpost. Meg zooms almost straight up then clicks a garage door opener thing, and a gate on top of the dome clatters wide. With a burst of speed, Meg clears the gate and takes us into the sky.

My breath catches as the wind pulls at my hair from the window. I grip the window edge, drinking every sight in as the forest rolls along below me. Ferns slowly spiral out, vying for space with cycads. Conifers climb toward the sky, filling the air with a vaguely pine-like smell.

The air is so fresh here, crisp, clean, scraping all the modern pollution out of my lungs. Back in the future, the atmosphere is only twenty-one percent oxygen; here that rises to around thirty percent. So the air here makes our bodies work more efficiently—basically, we're stronger and with better endurance. Although there's a hell of a crash afterward.

Unfortunately, because of worries about increased cell decay, the Time Guard makes everyone traveling to an oxygen-rich environment get an injection of nanobots. It's one of the requirements a lot of researchers balk at because of the "invasion" of it. Nanos aren't my expertise, so I can't get too technical, but the nanobots basically scramble around in my body helping to rebuild cells damaged by the excess oxidation from the Cretaceous air. Sometimes there's almost a tickle you can feel as the nanos work, but I'm probably imagining that.

The nanos are also there in case I die here, to break my body down to nothing and then self-destruct. Can't allow any human corpses to contaminate the fossil record, after all.

The buzz of life from the forest is louder now we're outside. Meg's taking things nice and slow, zooming above the trees but not much higher. Insects zip through the air, the ancient ancestors of bees busy about their pollination. By this point in time, flowering plants have evolved, and they're just starting to perfect their art.

We pass a clearing bursting with vibrant purple flowers, humming with life. Two *Pachycephalosaurs wyomingensis,* the "Friar Tuck" of dinosaurs, are wrestling with each other at the clearing's edge, trampling some of the blooms. Meg notices the dinosaurs and takes the jeep higher, probably so we won't startle them. Behind me, Vega lets out a yelp of excitement.

"Your first dinosaurs!" I grin at Vega.

"Yeah!"

The two young male dinosaurs are beautiful specimens, slightly over a meter tall at this point and five meters long. They're thickly muscled, bipedal, and with the heavy, dome-shaped heads of their species. The pair still aren't full adults, so the spikes on their heads haven't shortened yet to the nubbins they'll become later.

I fumble for my field camera and snap a few pictures as we pass. One looks at us, tilting his bright-blue head with curiosity. His opponent seizes the chance and knocks him over sideways into the flowers. I grin, a zip in my blood that has nothing to do with cell-repairing nanobots. I'm home. I'm where I'm supposed to be.

"Land here?" Meg asks.

"Yes, but please give the pachycephalosaurs a lot of space."

"Yeah, yeah. I know the drill." Meg circles the jeep to the ground then sets us on the very edge of the clearing with a bump of our landing gear. The juveniles hoot with alarm and flee, leaving us humans alone in the clearing.

I take charge as everyone files out of the car. "All right, so we'll sweep north and follow this map to check our existing camera trap locations."

Grigori folds her arms. "I've done those recently."

I sigh, holding on hard to my patience. "Then where are the SD cards for those? And why didn't you enter that into the log?"

She waves a dismissive hand. "I never used the log—"

"I noticed."

Her nostrils flare. "Because for *months* it was just me, working *alone*, and I always remembered what I'd already done. Why would I need the log?"

"And the SD cards? Those are in the lab?"

"Yeah. Somewhere."

Perhaps he can sense how close I am to losing my patience, because Trifoso moves between Grigori and myself. "Well, if the north side is done then let's move south. Sound good?"

"Fine."

"Whatever." Grigori stomps away.

Trifoso pats my shoulder. "I'll pair with Sona. Would you like to show Jax the ropes?"

"Sure. You take one of the new cameras, and I'll take the other. Hopefully, we won't need to replace any of the existing ones, but best to be prepared." I snag the lightweight camera traps in their boxy containers and pass one to Trifoso. The other I stuff carefully into my own bag. The sickly sweet artificial scent of new plastic lingers on my hands afterwards. Great.

We check the maps and compasses—no GPS units for easy navigation in Dinosaurland, unfortunately—and agree to meet at the jeeps before sundown.

After that's settled, we divide into our teams and walk in opposite directions. Somehow Nakamura gets paired with my group instead of Meg. Vega walks ahead of us, taking in the sights of the forest with wide, gleaming eyes. My own mood mirrors theirs. The honeyed gold of the sunshine burns away my anxiety from last night.

"Anything to be worried about, Doc?" Nakamura asks. "Anything to watch out for?"

"If you see something about our size, raise your arms in the air and make a lot of noise. We're strange, so the dinosaurs should flee if you make yourself scary-big." I tap his shoulder with my finger. "No gun unless it's got your head in its jaws."

"And if it tries to eat anything else of mine, I suppose I should let bygones be bygones?" He snorts. "Wait, the scary-big thing is for animals our size. What about something bigger?"

"If we run into a big dinosaur, we're pretty much screwed. So, pray?"

"That's your advice?"

I shrug. "I mean, you could try shooting it with that disrupter gun of yours, but you might just piss it off. I should mention this could apply to carnivores and herbivores. Triceratops can be mean fuckers. You don't even have to do anything—they'll run you down and trample you to paste for breathing wrong."

We walk in silence for a beat before Nakamura clears his throat. "Tell me again why you like this job?"

I laugh and keep hiking. I do love this job. A sense of rightness fills my whole being until it's like I'm walking on clouds.

"First camera should be ahead, Dr. Carson," Vega calls.

"Great. See anything yet?"

Vega stops and does a slow spin. "It's supposed to be here, right? Or am I reading the map wrong?" They bite their lip, eyes squinted with worry.

First day jitters. I glance at the map myself and frown. "Yeah, it should be here." Hell, more sloppy work from Grigori?

"Doc, is this what you're looking for?" Nakamura is bent near the roots of a large tree. One of our cameras lays crushed on the ground, half-covered with pine needles. When I gaze at the tree trunk, there's a pale scar in the bark where the camera was probably smashed away.

"Damn." I take a picture of the camera in the midst of the debris then dig the pieces out.

"Maybe we got some good shots of whatever destroyed it?" Vega murmurs.

"I might be able to do something with a damaged or broken SD card," Nakamura puts in. "If you like?"

I tilt my head looking at him. "You're a computer whiz as well as a dashing adventurer?"

His eyebrows rise. "I'm *dashing*?"

Vega makes a *snerk* sound behind me and quickly tries to cover it with a cough.

My cheeks are blazing hot, but I roll my eyes. "You fit a certain type that could perhaps be classified as 'dashing.' Taxonomically speaking, of course."

His warm brown eyes are brimming with amusement when they meet mine. "Of course."

"Anyway, yes, it would be nice if you could work some tech magic on the SD card." But when I go through the pieces, the SD card isn't among the wreckage. "The card's not here."

"Oh. Bad luck, Doc."

"Hmm." The damaged camera is making the hair stand on my arms, and I look again at the scarred tree bark. Pretty high. Higher than most dinosaurs can reach. And the ones who could wouldn't have bothered swatting a small camo-colored box off a tree, would they?

"What is it?" Nakamura asks.

"Nothing." Nothing but my paranoia running away with me. Broken cameras happen. One of the constants of fieldwork—no matter the time or place, even millions of years in the past—is that animals will mess with your gear. A colleague of mine in Africa had had a bunch of wires destroyed in her vehicle by an enterprising troop of hyraxes gnawing on them. Another friend was often complaining to me about the lengths she had to go to in Gombe to keep the chimps and baboons out of *everything*.

So, sure it was plausible one of the dinosaurs or the mammals populating the Cretaceous could've messed with our camera. Let's go with that. They were like birds, after all. Maybe some enterprising young dinosaur couple had made off with smashed pieces of camera to decorate their nest. Oy. Just the thought of what *that* could do to the fossil record gives me a headache.

I'm very careful to bundle all the pieces together and make sure I have everything. When I start to stand, Nakamura gives me a hand. I don't meet his eyes as I brush past him. "We'll mount the spare camera here then keep checking the other ones down the line."

The first camera unnerved me, but the second and third smashed cameras have me close to hyperventilating. All of them are missing their SD cards.

I run out of room in my own bag after the second one, so Vega takes custody of the third smashed camera we find. "What could be happening, Dr. Carson?" they murmur as they stuff the pieces into their bag.

I shake my head. I've got a theory, a horrible theory, but I'm not ready to voice it yet.

Vega can't read my mind, though, so of course they just say the horrible thing I'm worrying about. "Could the poaching ring be back?"

I pinch my nose and rub. "It's unlikely. The Time Guard rounded up the ringleader, after all, and they're still in jail." As far as I know, Adam is still in jail, anyway. We, ah, aren't exactly on speaking terms. I take a deep breath. "What's likely happening here is one of the animals might be attracted to the scent or appearance of the cameras. The camera traps do have that sickly sweet plastic smell when they're new, and they have all kinds of shiny things inside if you smash them. Maybe some unidentified species keeps knocking them down trying to get a treat." There. Sounded fairly reasonable, right?

I might even have convinced myself except I look over at Nakamura. He's got his arms folded, one hand tracing thoughtfully over his mouth as he frowns.

"What?" I ask him.

He startles and shrugs. "Nothing. You're the expert, Doc, not me." His voice is bland, almost pointedly so.

Fortunately, the rest of the cameras on our route are all right, and we swap SD cards on them before circling around to the rendezvous point.

Trifoso and the others are already there waiting, and he gives a broad wave as we come in sight. "Grace! Do you still have the extra camera? We need to replace two in this section, unfortunately."

My skin goes cold. "Do you have the damaged cameras?"

He frowns and looks quickly back and forth between all three of us. "Did you find destroyed cameras too?" His voice goes hoarse and quiet on the words, as if he's forcing them out.

"We did." I swallow. "Were yours missing their SD cards?"

He clears his throat. "They were. Yes. How odd."

Silence reigns before Nakamura brushes my arm. "'Scuse me, Doc. I need a word with Agent Zaran."

After Nakamura walks off, Trifoso takes me by the arm with a murmured apology to Vega and Grigori. "Be right back. I wanted to get Dr. Carson's opinion on some tracks over here." He tugs me away from the others until we can barely see them. We certainly can't hear them at all.

My stomach sinks, dread and worry raising their ugly heads inside me. "What is it, Paul?"

He gives me a taut smile, one that doesn't reach his eyes. "How much did the time agent see?"

"What do you mean?"

"Of the destroyed cameras."

"He *found* the first one. He was with us the whole time, so he saw all of them."

"And did you, ah..." He scrubs a hand over his mouth, and fresh sweat pops at his temples. "...speculate?"

"About poachers, you mean?"

He hisses like I've hit him and makes a shushing motion with his hand. "Yes. Exactly like that," he bites out.

"I didn't. Vega did."

"Hell. I'll have to talk to them. I don't want anyone running their mouths in front of the time agents."

I chew my lip. "But we're investigating this, right? We *are* going to try to figure out how five cameras were destroyed in such a short period of time *and* missing their SD cards?"

"Grigori hasn't been keeping up with the survey. These could've been destroyed months apart." He's already shaking his head, waving my words away. "Don't fuss, Grace. We'll get more camera traps in the next supply shipment. In the meantime, let's not concern ourselves with things that aren't our problem. Keep the program running. That's what you're here for."

My stomach roils with unease. "You're telling me to look the other way?" I whisper.

He looks like he wants to shake me, and his mouth curls with frustration and anger. "I'm telling you not to be *paranoid*. I'm telling you not to jump at shadows. You don't know what destroyed the camera traps, so why jump to the worst conclusion?" He holds my gaze. "And I'm telling you not to speculate to the Time Guard. About *anything*."

Questions prickle on my lips, like soda bubbles wanting to pop, but I swallow them and nod instead. He's made his position clear. If I think the poachers might have returned, if I believe I've seen evidence of that, he wants me to keep my mouth shut.

Which was exactly what my mother-in-law had asked me to do all those years ago when I found out Adam was working with the poachers. Although my mother-in-law hadn't given a damn about the research program by then. She'd wanted me to stay quiet and save Adam. Save her son.

Save my husband.

"Grace." Trifoso waits until I look at him, then he holds my gaze. "If the Time Guard believes the poachers have returned, then it will kill our program. Kill it dead."

A shivery, shock-cold panic fills my body. When I'd spoken up before, I had naively believed they'd still keep me on at the research station. *I'd* turned him in, after all. Oh, I thought I might have to testify at the trial, and I'd grimly been prepared. But I hadn't in my wildest dreams thought the Time Guard would return after they took Adam and slap *me* in handcuffs too. Adam hadn't accused me of anything, had flatly denied I was involved, but the Time Guard couldn't believe it. How could he have run a poaching ring right under my nose? I had to be involved. Or else I was the dumbest woman alive.

This was the conclusion I'd come to myself eventually. I was dumb and had stuck my head in the sand. In trying to ignore the problems in my marriage, I'd managed to enable massive criminal activity to proceed unchecked.

Last time it happened by accident. Marriage problems feeding into a larger issue. This time, Trifoso was asking me to willingly play dumb, to look away from anything suspicious and not dig deeper. "Paul—"

Trifoso must have been watching me closely, watching the thoughts chase their way over my face, because he wraps his fingers around my upper arm and squeezes. Not hard enough to hurt, but hard enough so my startled gaze flies to his face. "Grace, I think an *animal* destroyed those camera traps. I can understand why you might be worried about other options, but you're overreacting. We can't simply trust your gut."

His last words hit me like a straight bullseye, knocking the breath out of me. The bitch of it is I've been so jerked around and beaten down and desperate these past few years *I* don't trust myself either. Could my judgment be so clouded I'm jumping at shadows?

But no, Vega made the suggestion first. And what are Nakamura and Meg arguing about in lowered voices if they don't think it's poachers either?

Trifoso lets go my arm and turns his iron grip into a friendly pat instead. "Come on, Dr. Carson. It's our first day in the field. Let's not waste it. Right?"

I'd lost everything when I turned Adam in. I'd spent years fighting my way home.

So why should I risk torpedoing my career a second time? Trifoso is my superior. *He's* technically in charge here. If he doesn't believe anything is wrong, then why should I bother pushing the issue? Maybe my anxiety about the past is making me see things, see evidence that isn't there.

Really, I'm making excuses, and I fucking know it. But Trifoso has me good and scared about talking to the Time Guard now. Exactly as he wanted.

And isn't that interesting? Could Trifoso have some kind of ulterior motive? How deep might the rot of corruption go in my program?

I let out a breath through my teeth, which eases only some of the tightness in my chest. "You're right. None of us should jump to conclusions about how this happened."

He laughs and spreads his hands wide. "Exactly. The Time Guard broke the poaching ring, and we have nothing to worry about. So, let's get to work, huh?"

I fall in step behind him. But there's a sick dread in my gut that I'm making a horrible mistake not telling the Time Guard what I suspect.

Chapter Seven

JULIA

I wake up hungover and miserable, but I choke down enough pills to get me moving. Fortunately, Xia decides to start with one of the easy items on our "to catch" list, and we head for the beach. This spot also has the benefit of being very far away from the research station and its healthy complement of time agents.

I don't have much to do once I guide the crew to the local nesting spot of pterosaurs, so I perch myself atop some sea stones. They're bleached white and sanded smooth, and the waves crash into each other below me.

The water should be a comforting sight, the peaceful sea, the soothing waves, blah, blah. Only problem is the sea is *pink*, a saccharine bubble-gum *pink* that shouldn't occur in nature, but it does. *Pink* bacteria—the prehistoric sea in front of me is full of it. Pink seas. Thunder lizards. "God, I hate this place." I hate the heat. The stink. Hate the wild animals wanting to eat me.

Hate the job?

I push that thought away as counterproductive. Whether I hate the job or not, it has to get done, so my feelings don't matter.

Everyone in camp was buzzing about the newbie we lost last night. Dinosaur attacks have become more and more of a problem the last few runs. The beasts know us, know we're soft and tasty. We have to have more and more guards around the camp to keep from being slaughtered. Probably just another sign our crew should abandon this time period and place but, like Xia said, it's so profitable it's hard to walk away. Nothing pays on the time travel black market as well as dinosaurs do.

I reach into my pocket and pull out the fixings for a smoke. I gave the habit up years ago, but we're having so many problems on this run, and smoking calms my nerves. Our fearless leader Xia disapproves, but they're my lungs dammit.

As if my thoughts have summoned her, I hear her sure, scuffing footfalls behind me. Soft steps but quick strides. "Were you planning to help with this shipment, Julia?"

"I'm supervising." I say it around a mouthful of rolling paper so it comes out, "Ah'm suppahvasin'."

Xia scoffs as she eyes my cigarette fixings. "What's wrong?"

I click my tongue. We've only known each other about two years, but I seem to be incapable of hiding anything from her. "Just getting some stage fright, I suppose." Once we cross the small stuff off, then it's time for me to produce the grand finale. Our big payday. And, if I can't, then I've just wasted my time, and I'll never see my son set free.

She puts her hands on her hips, and her silky black hair shines in the sun. "We've done complicated, dangerous runs before. It'll be fine, Julia. We're pros."

"Your customers want a carnotaurus." I shake my head, trying to look calm, rational, even as my mouth goes dry at the thought. "We've never taken on anything that big before."

"Yes, we have." Xia tilts her head. "Technically speaking."

"*Successfully.*" My gut tenses with the reminder of that failure. "We've never *successfully* transported a carnotaurus. Or any big predator. And trying is what got Adam arrested."

"It'll be all right. We've learned from that mistake."

I clench my jaw. "We better have. Or we're all dead."

With a weary sigh, Xia sits on the rock beside me. I've got about a decade on her, at least, but she's so well-preserved and fit she could pass for thirty even though she's probably closer to forty-five. "Just find me the dinosaur, and let me worry how we'll catch it, Jules."

"Fair enough." I drizzle some of my leaf on the paper then lick the cigarette and roll it closed.

Our people work on the beach below us. Xia invested in protective gear for everyone this time: half helmets, goggles, body armor. The gear isn't cheap, but it's easier to protect the experienced folks we have than it is to recruit more bodies for the crew. All things considered, I'd rather we fork over for the body armor.

Two of the younger guys are horsing around, shoving each other, laughing with that *hur hur* noise young men of every era never seem to evolve past. I stick the finished cigarette in my mouth and fish for a light. I just hope none of these idiots fall in the water. Pink bacteria don't play well with the human immune system. And there are salt water crocs to watch out for too.

"Only a couple more days, Julia," Xia says, her tone soothing, "then we'll pack the shipment and split."

"Right." My stomach still twists thinking of all the ways this latest job can go wrong. I take a puff of my cigarette, and the smoke burns some of the tension out of me. There's a big 'If' hanging over my head like a guillotine and hanging over the heads of all my crew. Some of the crew might be idiots, but they're *my* idiots by God, and I don't want anyone else getting eaten by a dinosaur on this run.

Xia eases onto her elbows, lying out on the rock like a sunbather. "I wish we had time for a beach day. Sun feels good."

I blow a smoke ring that dissipates in the sunshine. This isn't how I thought I'd be spending my sunset years, but it's not the worst place to be. Even if it makes me cranky time to time. And I do like the company. *Or is the company the only thing that makes it bearable?* I take another hasty drag. "Any word from your spy at the research station? Does the Time Guard suspect we're here?"

"Who says I've got a spy at the station?"

I make a rude noise and blow a smoke ring at her.

She laughs and waves the smoke away. "All right, all right." Xia's lips purse with worry, but she lifts a careless shoulder. "The scientists arrived the other day, same as us. And we smashed the cameras that got too close to our camp last time. Nothing for them to find, nothing for us to worry about with the cameras gone."

I wince, telling myself not to consider all the scientific data destroyed at the same time. "How did you manage to get an agent to turn to the dark side anyway?"

Her eyelashes flutter, and she sends me a suspicious look out the corner of her eye.

I hold my hands high in surrender. "Right, not my business. Forget I asked."

Xia's jaw clenches. "Better you not get in too deep anyway, Jules. Better you not know too much."

I can't tell if she's trying to protect herself or me or the mission, but I give a small nod and let the silence lengthen.

A group of pterosaurs with red head-crests flirt on the rocks not far from us. Preening. Eating. Enjoying the sunshine, ruffling their leathery wings like vain butterflies. I can't remember the species, but these ones are small, no bigger than seagulls. I've got a notebook buttoned safe in one of my jacket pockets, but I don't let myself reach for it. No time for drawing the pterosaurs or note taking. That's not what we're here for. And I don't want to catch any more shit from Daw.

The sun warms my skin that the sea breeze has chilled, but I've got a pain in my joints telling me a storm's coming. And my ass can't take much more sitting on this rock. Crime is probably a young woman's game, but I don't have much choice in the matter anymore. My options for a cushy retirement were never very good. Now I'd say they're nonexistent. Something wistful and sharp shivers through me, but I shake it off. I made my choice, and I don't regret it.

All I have to do is live with it.

Xia's been watching me, her brows knit together. I cover her hand with mine. She is definitely one of the things that make this life of crime worth living. If only I could manifest enough courage to *tell* her.

"Storm's coming," I say and lift my hand away to shade my eyes. I'm too old for her anyway. Too old, too bitter. All used up and useless except for this poaching business. I squint at the horizon and sure enough, clouds are rolling in from the sea, lightning flashing in their dark hearts.

Xia eases forward, studying the sky too. "We should finish quick. Get this shipment packed."

"Okay. You want me to—"

She pushes to her feet and pats my shoulder. "I've got it. You just supervise." She winks then crosses to our cars and hauls out a large bazooka-like gun. She grunts as she settles it on her shoulder and, with a quick trigger pull, Xia looses a net with weights on the edges. Like a silky spiderweb, Xia's net pins the pterosaurs to their perches.

The pteros squawk and shriek, and I wish we'd remembered to bring earplugs. I stub my cigarette out on the rock then drop the remainder into my pocket. Old habits. I may be poaching the past, but damned if I'll litter. I laugh at myself and push to my feet. It's only in my imagination all my joints creak and lament at the effort.

Several of our people are gathering the net in, collecting our new captive pterosaurs. One of the pterosaurs fights free, leather wings flailing. A newer kid, Quint the Meathead, tries to wrestle the animal into a cage with his bare hands. The pterosaur yanks off Quint's half helmet with his hind claws. Quint fires his sidearm into the air, missing the beast. The ptero scratches a deep line into Quint's scalp before flying off. Quint whips off his mask and holds his bloody head.

"Why did we hire that idiot?" I mutter.

Xia snorts. "To lift heavy things."

One of our more experienced kids, Yao, hurries over to Quint and tenderly brushes her fingertips across his forehead. He kisses her hand and laughs as he bleeds.

Young love. I grit my teeth, my stomach like lead. Love ruins everything. Especially for two young kids too dumb to know they shouldn't be together. But it's not my business. As long as Quint and Yao do their jobs, I don't care who they're... bunking with.

Our people are finishing with the pteros, untangling them from the net, tucking them in cages, carrying the cages to our vehicles. I mosey toward the hover-cars, watching the loading. One of the pteros chirps at me, its eyes liquid dark. If I were of an imaginative disposition, I might think he's pleading with me.

"What does the buyer want these for?" I ask Xia as she lifts a cage into a truck. "More prehistoric delicacies like the triceratops steaks?" I try to keep my voice light as I say it, unconcerned.

"Nah. These beasties are mostly destined to become high-end pets for rich idiots. A few of them might end their days on a plate." She shrugs and finishes loading.

"Oh." I sigh and shake off any guilt that knowledge might trigger. Guilt is something I very literally can't afford. If dinosaur shish kebab pays the bills, well, fry me up some pterosaur.

Still, as the little one gets lifted into the back, he emits a tiny chirrup, a small crystal-pure note of sadness. I shake my head. They're just animals. I swing into the passenger side of the nearest hover-car.

Xia's driving, and she slants me a smile. "Few more days, we'll check the last item off our shopping list. And then we'll get the hell out of here."

Chapter Eight

GRACE

After my chat with Trifoso, I march with him toward the others, and everyone piles into the cars to head to the research station. When we arrive, Meg takes Nakamura aside, and the two of them together rouse Srinivasan out of her bedroom. The time agents disappear into the com room for a conference. I can hear the bolt on the com room's door slide home in the hallway.

"Guess we're not invited," I murmur.

Trifoso glowers at the closed door, his temples sweaty. "Great." He shakes his head. "Well, this is a Time Guard party. They get to make the rules."

"I'll review the footage on the SD cards we did manage to collect."

"Oh, Dr. Carson, please let me." Grigori is standing behind us, hands clasped, shoulders slumped.

Some unworthy part of me figures this might be an act. Maybe Grigori has finally realized we don't have to keep paying her *or* give her a reference if she continues behaving the way she has been.

"Sona?" Trifoso asks.

"I'm sorry for the way I've been acting." She looks at the both of us then hangs her head. "It's been stressful trying to manage all the fieldwork myself, and I felt defensive when you all arrived. But that's no excuse. If you're willing to give me a chance, I'd like to show you I can do this."

By finally doing the job you were supposed to have been doing all along? I swallow the words and glance at Trifoso.

He makes a genial *go-along-then* gesture. "All right, Sona, work with Jax on the SD cards we gathered."

Grigori shakes her head. "Jax is on dinner duty tonight, Dr. Trifoso. Anyway, I should've been doing better about staying on top of everything. I don't mind the extra work."

Brownnosing and maybe trying to avoid working with Jax? But again, I bite my tongue because Trifoso nods and dismisses Grigori to start working on the SD cards.

He watches her go then leans toward me. "I've either given her enough rope for her to hang herself with or she'll step up and prove she's worth our time. Either way, it'll be good to know."

I chuckle and shake my head. "I was worried you were swallowing her bullshit whole."

Trifoso scoffs and starts to make a reply, but just then the com room door opens.

Meg marches straight over to us, her expression stern. "I'd like a word or two with both of you, Dr. Trifoso. Dr. Carson."

Unsurprisingly, the "word or two" turns into an all-out shouting match between Trifoso and Meg. I mostly sit against the wall, watching them have it out as my gut squirms with discomfort. Meg wants to report the missing SD cards to her higher-ups. Trifoso—of course—hates that plan.

"I don't give a damn about your research," Meg bellows, every word bitten out. "My responsibly is to all the people here. To make sure they're safe."

"Bullshit," Trifoso fires back. "You've been *dying* to shut this station down for years. You said as much the other day. You're biased. You're looking for problems where there are none."

"The missing SD cards are suspicious enough to warrant a report," she fires back.

Trifoso crosses his arms, his nostrils flaring with anger. "I disagree. Damage to equipment is a perfectly normal part of fieldwork. Isn't that right, Dr. Carson?"

Oh, *now* I get to participate? Yay for me. I clear my throat and sit forward, looking at Meg. "It's true. It's within the realm of possibility an animal did this."

Meg narrows her eyes, stabbing a finger in my direction. "You don't even believe that." She flaps a hand at Trifoso, red nails glinting like blood. "He doesn't either. He's just not ready to admit this research posting has been a horrible idea from day one." She looks at me again, her mouth pursed with distaste. "Dr. Carson, do *you* believe an animal caused the damage to your camera traps?"

My lips burn as I press them together. I know what Trifoso wants me to say, I know what I *should* do if I want to save my career, save the research program. But, just like Meg, I have a responsibility to keep everyone safe here to the best of my ability. I clasp my hands together hard enough that my knuckles turn white. "Based on the missing SD cards, it seems highly unlikely to me an animal could be responsible for the damage."

Meg lets out a triumphant bark of laughter and slaps my shoulder. "That's all I need to hear. Wait in the common room. I've got a call to make."

Trifoso glares at her, but he pivots on his heel and holds the door open for me. I walk past him, and he catches my arm as he follows me out of the com room.

"I'm disappointed in you, Grace," he hisses the words out once we reach the common room, his teeth gritted. "I thought you'd be more of a team player."

I thought you'd care more about everyone's safety. I let out a slow breath through my teeth. "I can't lie about something like this, Paul."

He opens his mouth to retort, but just then the lights brown out in the research station. "What was that?" he asks.

"Meg sending her message. She has to use the time tubes to talk to the future, and that takes a lot of juice." The lights flicker once more, the room actually going dark, but then everything comes on again in another minute. "And that was probably the Time Guard replying to her message."

His expression wilts. "Oh no. If their answer was that fast, the program is doomed."

I've got a similar fear myself, but I shake it off. "Not necessarily. Time travel, remember. Her superiors could've argued about what to do for days, run it through a committee, had a dozen people sign off on it, and still send their ruling back right after Meg sent her message."

"Hmm."

Meg makes some strangled noise of outrage in the com room. A few minutes pass, then her door slowly creaks open.

Trifoso taps my hand in parting and crosses to meet Meg as she emerges. "Well, Agent Zaran. What's the word from the future?"

She shoots him a poisonous look and flings the paper at his head. "I need to meet with my team." She storms off.

Trifoso scrapes the crumpled paper off the ground and holds it out so I can read over his shoulder: '*Not enough evidence to warrant suspending dinosaur program. Monitor situation. Report suspicious activity.*'

Trifoso and I blow our breath out together on twin sighs. Our momentary spat is forgotten in the swell of our relief.

"Back to work then, Dr. Trifoso?" I ask.

He grins. "Back to work, Dr. Carson."

For as long as they'll let me.

Chapter Nine

GRACE

Three days pass without incident, and maybe the poachers have left, or maybe they were never here in the first place. It doesn't matter because things finally settle down at the research station so we can get some work done. Get some science done.

We've been reviewing the images off the SD cards, everything closely scrutinized by Meg, who's still hoping she'll find the right evidence to convince her bosses to shut us down. Everyone's a bit on edge and jumpy, and there's not much socializing between the Time Guard and the scientists—not in front of Meg anyway.

Me, I'm mostly riding herd on my grad students as we organize the data Grigori hasn't been able to get through. My sympathy for Grigori starts to grow when I realize the absolute mountain of work we've left her with. It simply isn't a job for one person, and the fact she managed to keep her head above water at all makes me respect her more.

We're mostly working on the SD cards, and it gets monotonous clicking through thousands of pictures to type out all the data we need.

There's an interesting set with a family of troodons—a mated pair and a handful of chicks—passing in front of the camera that I mark for later review. But there's also a set where a triceratops just sat in front of one of the cameras and triggered it until the camera's batteries ran out. One picture of a triceratops butt could potentially be useful—hundreds upon hundreds of pictures of a triceratops posterior all from the same angle? Not so much.

"The triceratops butt has defeated me," I declare, pushing away from my desk. Vega and Grigori are still working on their own SD cards. Trifoso is off somewhere else, writing reports or maybe just relaxing. Ah, the privileges of command.

There's other busywork I could be doing besides the SD card stuff. Going through all those old file boxes in my bedroom for one thing, but I can't quite make myself face the ghost of my mother-in-law.

If I can't work, I should relax in my room with my Mira Grant paperback and her murderous mermaids, but I've got an itch under my skin that won't let me sit quietly. It's been days since I've been out in the field, and my blood is restless.

After an internal debate that probably should've been longer, I leave the lab and step outside, prepared to walk the fence if I must.

Nakamura's already out there, head cocked, admiring the stars. He grins. "Hiya, Doc."

I haven't seen much of Nakamura lately. Not since the SD card hike. Meg's been taking him out with her to run patrols and leaving Srinivasan to babysit us. "Were you waiting for someone?" If Meg is about to come out here, then I'll force myself inside. I'm not in the mood to deal with her.

But he shakes his head slowly. "Just enjoying the night. And the stars. I've never seen stars like this."

He's right about the view. Van Gogh's famous painting has nothing on this night. Swirls and splashes dot the blackness of the sky, a riot of color and light that makes me curse our ancestors who decided artificial light was worth losing the stars for.

I stand next to Nakamura as we study the sky. He seems calm, not like someone about to be deployed to hunt down a poaching ring. So they probably haven't found evidence of criminal activity, despite Meg's frantic searching. "Have you and Meg spotted anything suspicious on your patrols?"

"Not as yet. But she's very, ah, determined." He swallows whatever harsher word he might have been weighing and shrugs. "Anyway, I'm getting a lot of experience in the forest."

"Do you two run patterns together or...?"

He shrugs. "Sometimes. Sometimes she goes one way and I go the other, then we rendezvous and report."

I chuckle. "You're not scared of being by yourself in the forest?"

"I, ah, don't usually go too far from the hover-jeep."

That's safer for him but probably not a very effective search strategy. The poachers would hear a hover-jeep coming and hide, surely. "Y'all haven't thought about sending for reinforcements?" I ask.

The first signs of tension creep into Nakamura's face and posture. "Our bosses were pretty clear they don't have more resources to devote to this unless there's an actual threat. Besides, every message we send drains the time tubes. Meg wants to conserve their power. In case we have a more urgent need of the time tubes once new information is available."

In case they need to evacuate this outpost. In case they need to transport captured poachers. Oh yes, it sounds like Meg is definitely preparing for the worst. I can't say I blame her. I'd probably be doing the same thing if I had her job. "Bet Meg can't wait to dismantle this whole outpost nail by nail and send us back to the future."

Nakamura shoots me an unreadable look. "You think she's biased?"

"You heard what she said at dinner our first night." I snort. "And she was practically rubbing her hands with glee when we found the smashed cameras."

He tilts his head in a so-so gesture. "Yes, but she does understand how precarious this program's position is. She'll wait for solid evidence. Not hunches and fear."

Maybe I'm not being fair to Meg. Just because she personally doesn't like or trust me doesn't mean she's a bad agent. Of course, after what she said about our program being worthless, she needs pretty strong evidence before she can move. Just to cover her own ass. It would be temptingly easy to accuse her of bias if she made any hasty decisions.

Ugh, my head hurts. I'm so tired of suspecting everyone, second-guessing everyone. I didn't used to be this way, but Adam effectively nuked my trust in my own judgment. I whirl toward Nakamura. "Do you want to go for a walk?"

He clucks his tongue. "You have itchy feet again, Doc?"

My shoulders are aching, and I should probably go to my room to rest, but the crisp air of the evening dances over my cheeks, and this might be my last chance to get outside the fence for who knows how long. "Short walk," I tell him. "I just want to be out in the fresh air. Away from people for a bit."

He laughs. "Sorry I have to tag along with you then."

"I meant—" Actually I don't know what I meant, but I didn't mean I wanted to get away from *him*. My cheeks heat. "Let's sit by the river a bit. It's only a few minutes' walk, and if they need you, we'll be close. Sound good?"

"Sure." Without another word, he crosses to the gate and opens it for me. Proper protocol would be to head inside and tell someone where we're going, but neither of us moves toward the research station. But maybe Nakamura doesn't want to be told, 'No, stay here' any more than I do.

We walk together into the forest, slow and companionable, following the rushing sound of water. It's maybe a five-minute hike before we're standing on the shore of the river, staring at the calm glassy surface of it. The inland sea is farther off. Maybe an hour's hike or so. "Don't get too close to the water. There might be crocs."

"Of course there are."

A corner of my mouth curls in a smile, and I bite my lip to try and keep that at bay. "You don't like life in Dinosaurland, Nakamura?"

"I like it just fine." He's watching me when he says it, his voice kind of quiet and rough. But he looks away before I can work up the courage to meet his gaze.

He clears his throat. "Anyway, I'm just having trouble getting used to the idea everything is out to eat me."

"Not everything." I shrug. "Just a lot of things."

He chucks my sleeve and ducks his head, trying to see my face. "And how are you handling everything? Is being back here what you'd hoped it would be?"

I huff my breath out like he's hit my stomach. Oof. What's it been like? Mostly tense, like I'm teetering on the edge of an anxiety attack every minute. The only peace I've found at all has been watching the dinosaurs and talking to... I shake my head and pick my way closer to shore. "We shouldn't talk. It might attract the animals."

"Uh-huh." His tone conveys just how credible he finds that statement. Dammit, the man is on to me.

I wander along the riverbank, grabbing a heavy stick and keeping an eye on the water in case something decides to lunge for me. "What made you want to take this assignment?"

After a beat, Nakamura follows me. "I asked you first, you know."

"Good for you."

"Stubborn. That's a new look for you, Doc."

I bite my tongue on a laugh.

He shoots me an arch look but launches into his story anyway. "I just wanted to get here. To the past. The next great frontier. We conquered the West. The oceans. Space. Time is next, and I wanted to be part of that."

"Manifest destiny." I stop on the path to face him, chuckling.

He folds his arms, his face serious. "Look down. What do you see?"

"Tree roots. Mud."

"Lift your foot."

I do, and I see I've left a crisp, perfect boot print in the dirt.

Nakamura voice goes quiet and reverent. "We're the first humans here. Won't be more people around for what?"

"A little over seventy million years."

"Neil Armstrong can have the moon. I'm one of the people making the greatest leap humanity's ever made. And I'm making it seventy million years before he was born."

I cock my head to the side, watching the shadows move over his cheekbones, his lips. I've missed talking to him. Everything's gone a bit Capulets and Montagues at the research station, so we've been keeping our distance. But now there's a zip in my blood, like electricity sparking between our bodies.

He raises his eyebrows in gentle expectation. "Well?"

"Well, what?"

"I showed you mine."

I open my mouth and close it a few times, unsure what to say, what to share—if anything. The easy intimacy of darkness is deceptive, seductive. I know that too well. And Nakamura is entirely too appealing for my own good.

He's probably doing this to draw me out, find out if I know anything, if I'm plotting anything. Maybe this is Phase Two of Meg's plan to shut the research station down.

I shake myself, breaking the intimate spell of the darkness. Nakamura didn't follow me into the night for a moonlit stroll, after all. He's been *assigned* to follow me, watch me, make sure I'm not a criminal.

And Trifoso will probably believe the worst if he finds out I've been alone with Nakamura for so long.

Makes me tired. Makes me sad. I shake my head, the thoughts rattling and clanking, hurting inside me. "This was a bad idea. We should get back."

"Doc—" he calls after me, but I don't stop.

I cut away from him, taking the path up from the river and toward the research station. My cheeks are hot, my stomach in knots, and I'm almost running so he won't catch me and ask what's wrong.

The dark of the forest closes in, the light of the stars disappearing under the canopy of the trees. I left Nakamura behind at the river although I can faintly hear him calling. I hurry, still trying to stay ahead of him.

Something thrashes ahead of me in the bush, and I freeze, my blood going cold. I grip my stick until my hands hurt and brace my feet.

Vega blunders out of the brush and collides with me. I jolt in surprise but don't scream.

"Dr. Carson!" They half swallow a scream of their own and backpedal on the path.

I blink, my surprise clearing away and something much harder and colder settling in its place. "Where's your escort, Jax?"

Vega wraps their arms around their middle. "I, uh, snuck out." They're still whispering, still trying to keep this a secret between us.

"Why?"

My tone is whipping hard, and Vega straightens indignantly when they hear it. "You think I—" Their nostrils flare, and their crossed arms move from a posture of holding heat in to one of defensiveness. "I've been cooped tight in that damn station same as you. I wanted to get out. Trifoso took his usual sleeping pill. Srinivasan was in her bedroom reading with the door closed. Agent Zaran's passed out drunk in hers. I couldn't find Nakamura. So I snuck out. It's not hard. There's no lock on the front door, and they don't exactly do a bed check once you say you're going to sleep."

I wince. Maybe we should. "Come on. Let's go." *Before anyone catches you*, I think but don't say.

Vega makes a grumbly noise but falls in step with me when I start walking. We hike in silence for several minutes before they clear their throat. "I'm sorry, Dr. Carson. It was stupid to sneak out."

And pretty damn suspicious. But I keep that thought to myself.

"I won't do it again." Their voice threads upward on a hopeful note.

"Hmm."

"*You* snuck out."

"Hmm."

I can literally hear Vega's teeth grinding before they speak again, "The escort rules are stupid. Why should I need someone with me to leave the fence? Like you said, it's screwing with our research having them always tag along."

Not very fond of rules, our Vega. "Why did you sneak out tonight? What were you hoping to do?" *Who were you planning to meet?* I hate that thought, and the ugly rearing of suspicion that comes with it. But why would Vega risk so much—risk their job and reputation—just for some fresh air? The more obvious answer is they snuck out to meet someone. I keep hoping we'll stumble over Grigori or Srinivasan, hell even Meg out here somewhere looking to meet Vega for a romp in the grass. But there's no one else. No one who wants to show themselves anyway.

Vega harrumphs beside me. "I just wanted to go out walking. Like *you*, apparently," they toss out.

Goose bumps prick my arms, and I walk faster, ready for the warmth of the station and my own bed. "Let's get inside."

Vega and I don't talk as we hike, and I escort them into their own room before I head outside again and lean against the front door. Waiting.

He takes longer returning than I was expecting him to, but just when I start to worry Nakamura's been eaten after all, he enters the gate and tilts his head as he sees me standing in the doorway. "Lost you in the forest, Doc."

I want to ask him if he saw Vega, if he listened to our conversation, if he suspects Vega of something. I want to ask why *he* took so long coming in from the forest.

Maybe Nakamura was just as happy to shake me off so he could take care of his own illicit errands?

My head is pounding, and I rub my face hard.

"You okay?" I jump when I realize how close he's standing. "You're not about to faint on me?" His breath is warm on my cheek, and I inhale the wet green smell of the forest coming off his clothes.

I ease back, my heart hammering. "Fine. Just tired. I shouldn't have gone for that walk."

"Fair enough." He slides past me through the door. "But I had a pleasant time."

"Nakamura."

"Yeah, Doc?"

Loyalty to my grad student—who's probably just a silly kid, after all, and not a master criminal—wars with my natural inclination to tell the truth, to report weird behavior. Words choke in my throat like I'm trying to swallow rocks. "Are you—will you—"

Nakamura stops and half turns. He keeps his voice low. "I'll have to report Vega leaving the fence to Agent Zaran, but I doubt your grad student was up to anything. Get some sleep, Dr. Carson."

I close my eyes and nod, but I still wait for the sound of his room door to close before I head inside myself. I don't want to catch him, don't want to speak to him again tonight.

I don't want to test how foolish I might be when it comes to Agent Nakamura.

Chapter Ten

JULIA

We've spent most of the past few days filling our "shopping list" with smaller critters, easy to catch and transport. But the time's finally come to make a try for our big-ticket item. And I'm center stage because I'm the best tracker we have.

The Time Guard's pet scientists are severely limited on what tech they're allowed to use on their observations. No radio collars. No tags. No electronic trackers of any kind. Me? I've got my own drone as a scout. If I can just get the thing working.

I fuss with the controls on my drone. A misty drizzle of rain has started again. Not enough to interfere with the job, just enough to leave me wet through and shivering as I configure the controls for this latest mission.

The viewscreen on my controller flicks to life, and I send my drone hovering in front of my face before it zips off into the air. We already know we're in the carnotaur territory. We just need to run them to ground. They're a bit like lions in that they like to hunt at night so they can get closer to their prey without being seen. We've actually allowed a couple days in the schedule for tracking them down, but luck is with us.

I finally catch sight of our targets drinking at the local watering hole. A full-grown carnotaurus, female judging by the dull brown coloring, and her juvenile child. Mama's thirty feet long, ten feet high, a mass of muscle with a powerful neck and bony "horns" above her head. And don't my fingers just itch to take some notes on her child-rearing habits. But Mama's not the real target.

The juvenile is smaller than her, young enough to still have the yellow-and-brown stripes of a hatchling, horns starting to pop on its head. Baby drinks while Mama watches, paranoid, her head on a swivel. An unwelcome twinge coils in my gut. We're going to reward that paranoia. She's right to be worried for her baby.

They're just animals. I hit a button on my controller and send the coordinates to Xia's crew.

This is it. We get this done and I get to go home. We get this done and my son gets to come home.

I keep the screen on to watch Xia and the rest close in. They're darting black figures moving like assassins at the feet of the mama dino and her baby. Mama takes a dart to the chin and another to the neck. She roars loud enough I can hear it from my vantage point above. The hairs on my arm rise at the primal rage in that cry.

The baby is already down, drugged and quiescent. Mama shakes one of the darts free and lunges, her jaws snapping toward Xia's compact form. Mama's swaying from her own dose of tranqs, but she's still fighting to keep our crew away from the baby. Xia tumbles, scrambling and slipping in the mud, trying to grab her gun. Every one of our people is yelling, retreating, trying to hold the dinosaur off but too far away to reach Xia.

My nerves jolt, and I toggle my switch, swinging my drone in front of the dinosaur's face. Mama chomps one of the propellers on my flyer, and blood from her clipped tongue splatters the screen. As the dying drone dangles from her lips, I can see Xia slide through the mud on her knees between the dino's legs. She rams another tranq hard into the dino's thigh then runs away under the dino's tail. Mama dino crunches my drone once more, reflexively, and my video feed dies.

I choke out a scream and sling the strap for my remote over my shoulder. The others are down a slope. I crash through the forest in their direction, my fear strangling me.

A high keen from the mama sounds throughout the forest. I swallow and put on a burst of speed, hopping a log in my haste and immediately regretting it. As my ankle twangs underneath me, I gulp a breath in, grit my teeth, and hobble on. My body clearly isn't made for a headlong rush anymore. I knew that, but I wasn't quite ready to accept it. Oh well.

I hear the water of the river and thrash through a clump of trees. Mama and baby carnotaurus are both down for the count, our people huddled around them, muddy, bloody in some cases. The rain's moving from a miserable drizzle to active splats of water. One lands hard and icy cold straight on top of my head. Like God tapping me with a brisk "what are you doing?"

I stalk toward Iris, Xia's second-in-command. "Where is she? I was watching on the drone."

"Oh, yeah." Iris winces. "Sorry about your drone."

I wave my hands in the air like I'm throwing her words physically aside. "Where's Xia?"

"I'm here."

I whirl toward the familiar husky voice, my heart throbbing in my chest like it's trying to burrow free. She's sitting on a stump, her cheek muddy, her hair falling to shadow half her face. I rush toward her, feet carrying me impetuously forward even as my head starts to have second thoughts. I've already thrown my arms around her, pulled her against me and buried my face in her hair. "You're nuts, you know. Certifiably insane." I take what might be my first full breath in an hour, and the knot where once my heart and stomach were slowly starts to slip loose.

"Hey." She eases back, but only the length of my arm, only a little bit, and her rough fingertips, calloused and cold, trace over my jaw. Featherlight and sweet.

My cheeks are flaming hot, and I hear some chuckles from the crew around us. I try to shift, but her arms band around me. "Where are you going?"

I can't look away. She's got a scattering of freckles on her cheeks, across her nose, and liquid brown eyes. Dark, lushly lashed. We both smell like mud, I'm shivering cold, and there's a dinosaur five feet away that could shake the tranqs off at any moment.

Somehow, though, all that has ceased to matter as she tucks her hand behind my neck and urges me closer. When her lips brush mine, I make a noise like I've been punched in the gut, a deep sucking shock of air pulled into my lungs. Honestly, as her mouth slides on mine it *feels* like something has hit me. Knocked me down, sent me tumbling. I thread my fingers into the wet silk of her hair and kiss her back.

Later, we're a warm tangle of limbs on the floor of her tent. My sleeping bag beneath us, her insulated, down-stuffed one on top. I have to say, sleeping two to a tent is much nicer than one. I can see why everyone went nuts boinking last night.

The rain patters outside, but I'm tucked against Xia, breathing the smell of rain-washed skin and hair, tracing the constellations of freckles on her spine. Her face is pillowed on her elbows, and she turns to slant a smile at me. "Took you long enough."

"You kissed me."

"Yeah, I kissed you as soon as you gave the slightest possible sign you wanted me to kiss you. I've been waiting years for this, Julia-love." She rolls her eyes heavenward and flops dramatically onto her back. "Years."

I lean down and trace a hand over her cheekbone, something fragile and hopeful unfurling inside me. "I'm sorry. I haven't dated since my divorce. I'm out of practice."

She clucks her tongue and rolls to a sitting position. "Gun-shy." And she shrugs her black sweater on as she says it. The languid lover is gone, and my brisk, businesslike leader is ascendant. "I should check the shipment. Want to come?"

Yes. And no. But yes.

She shakes her head, watching my thoughts play over my face then cups my cheek and kisses me, deep and slow. I groan and try to drag her into the warm cocoon we've made together. She slips out of my hands, digging into the fabric pile for her pants. "Ah no, love. You did your bit earlier, but there are still some logistics for me."

"Sorry about the drone."

"Pfft. We got the carno. That's all that matters. I'll buy you a million drones for the next job."

I snicker. She tips forward again, kissing me deep like she wants to drink the laugh off my lips.

Oh God, I can't get enough. Why didn't I do this sooner? "A million drones?" I murmur sleepily. "Really?"

She narrows her eyes and pretends to think. "Okay. Maybe two."

Next job. My brain catches up to our conversation, and the thought stops me cold. There won't *be* a next job for me. This was it. My big payoff then I get to walk away forever. So where the hell does that leave Xia and me?

"Don't dawdle if you want to see the baby," she says.

Since she has pants and a shirt on and she's starting on her shoes, I dig around for my own hastily discarded apparel too.

She tugs her final boot on. "Hurry and dress."

I shake my worries off as a problem for later. Not the time for a conversation about our relationship anyway.

I'm not as nimble as her, but I do manage to throw my clothes on in good time, and I only bang my head on the tent pole once. I follow her into the rain, infatuation speeding my steps. But as soon as I catch sight of the tarp-covered cage occupying a corner of our camp, I stop.

My gut drops and my mouth goes dry. The juvenile looked so small from the air, and tiny next to his mother, but he's a big animal. Somewhat bigger than a horse and massively muscled. Solid. He's awake, but still doped, huddled in a corner of his cage.

Xia starts talking to Iris, going over logistics, going over the plan. "There was a problem with our generator," Iris says, "so we're using solar to power the time tubes, and they'll need a bit more charge before they're ready to go. We weren't planning to catch this thing so quick, and on the first try too. But hopefully the tubes will be charged enough we can start transport sometime tomorrow."

"Any messages from our mole at the research station?" Xia murmurs.

I prick my ears, still dying to know who it is.

Iris steps closer, and I have to strain to hear. "All's well so far. The Time Guard isn't pursuing an investigation, and nothing's shown on the camera trap photos yet."

"Good, good. And what about—"

The dinosaur makes a small trill-hoot from inside the cage, and we all jump in surprise.

The sound acts on me like a bell announcing church services, calling the faithful home. I walk right past Xia and Iris toward the dinosaur. I've never been this close to one before. Not a big one. Not like this.

There's a complicated ache starting in my chest watching the carno. Rain drips from a corner of the tarp, and he shivers as it splatters against his hide. He's mostly protected from the rain, but not entirely. The tarp is folded over so a pool of water's collecting.

I shouldn't.

But I take the step anyway and yank at the corner of the tarp. I'm close enough I can smell him—a musk of dust and the smell of rotting meat, probably from his teeth. Or maybe the pile of droppings in one corner. I'm right next to the cage, my ribs digging into the bars as I wrestle with the tarp. He's such a beautiful specimen, his hide silky and unmarked, eyes a liquid amber close-set on his face. Fascinating. I hope I can sketch him before we have to deliver him to the future.

"Julia." Xia physically yanks me away, and the tarp comes with me, releasing a flood of water that drenches us both better than the misty drizzle could. Xia's fingers are hard on my arms, digging in, and her eyes are wide. "What are you doing?"

Jules, you idiot. I shake my head. "Just fixing the tarp." And gaping at our latest catch.

"You were about to get your hand snapped off more like." That's from Daw. I hadn't noticed him approach.

"I was trying to protect our investment," I put some steel into my voice. "You didn't lay the tarp right. We don't want the thing to catch pneumonia and die." I might be an underappreciated member of this criminal crew, but I know my own value, and I'm not about to take more of Daw's bullshit.

"Right." Xia keeps her hold on my arm. "Iris, you have the guard schedule mapped out?"

"Yes, Xia." Her mouth quirks, and she darts a glance between the two of us before she coughs and looks away. "You, ah, want me to put you or Julia on the schedule for tonight?"

Ah, hell. Well, it's a small camp, and we did tongue kiss each other in front of everyone. And Xia did basically drag me to her tent by the hair and make love to me all afternoon. And I wasn't exactly quiet about my appreciation and... well, I'm not sure what I expected the attitude of our crew members to be, but I definitely should have expected something like this.

Xia just laughs. Her grip on me has gone from forceful to caressing, and she tucks her arm through mine. "Morning shift, Iris. And don't forget to feed the baby." Xia presses herself against me and starts walking. "Come on. Let's get out of these wet clothes."

I grin to show I'm game. Daw rolls his eyes as we pass. I ignore him but, even as we speed toward our tent, I can't help but look back at the dinosaur, like I'm still on that leash somehow. My attention is riveted to the animal we've taken. A hollow, empty worry starts in my gut. I stole something else's child to save my own. And that baby's mama will be *mad*.

"Hey." Xia freezes and tugs me by the shoulder until we're facing each other. "What's wrong?" Her jaw tics and she looks away. "We don't have to go for round two. I hope you didn't feel pressured or—"

I cover her mouth with one hand, shaking my head. "No. Xia, no." I drop my hand and swallow. There's a jitter in my blood making me twitchy and paranoid. "I'm just worrying, that's all. About her."

"About Iris?"

"No." I close my eyes. "No. *Her*. The mama carnotaurus." I meet Xia's gaze, not even trying to hide the tremor in my voice. "She'll come for her baby. She's done it before. We need to be gone by then, or we need to be ready."

Xia gives a slow nod, still watching me like she's worried I might shatter. She brushes a kiss over my lips, butterfly soft. "We'll be gone. We just need those time tubes to charge, and we'll be gone. Don't worry, Julia."

Chapter Eleven

GRACE

After Vega's unauthorized excursion of the night before, I'm expecting a big blowout over breakfast, but the next morning, Meg declares we're finally allowed to go into the field. Maybe she's finally seeing reason. Or maybe she's just as sick of us all being cooped up together as I am. Trifoso seems subdued, but that could be a hangover from his sleeping pill habit as much as worry over our grad student. Vega looks grumpy and avoids talking to me.

Anyway, it doesn't matter the reason Meg lets us out. As soon as she gives her okay, we all scatter. Trifoso grabs Vega and Srinivasan to explore a promising area based on movement from the camera traps. I rustle Grigori out of bed—she slept through breakfast—and send Nakamura to grab a jeep.

Meg declines to join either research trip. "I'm taking a quiet morning off to enjoy my coffee and read one of the books I brought," she says.

I don't quite believe her. We've all probably noticed the bottles hidden in her room, but it's not my business if she wants a morning to herself. I'm more concerned with getting the hell out of there before she can change her mind.

The only hiccup in my plan is Grigori takes way longer to get ready than I would've liked, but, before I know it, we're in our hover-jeep and on our way.

"What are we hoping to see today, Doc?" Nakamura asks as we drive out to our temporary hide for the day.

"Well, there were quite a lot of oviraptors on the camera traps in this area. They're some of the cleverer dinosaurs of this era. It should be interesting just to observe their behavior."

Grigori clears her throat and leans forward to catch my eye from the back seat. "I read your book, Dr. Carson, and all of your papers I could get my hands on."

"And?"

"Are you still interested in tool use among dinosaurs?"

"Of course. I thought we'd seen evidence of it among troodons all those years ago, but the data was inconclusive."

"Well, I think I saw some potential tool use behavior among the oviraptors a few months ago."

"That so?" I try to keep my voice neutral, but I have to bite my lip hard to keep from grinning, and I press my foot a bit harder on the gas to get us where we're going.

We have established hides built, and this one is at the top of a small hill looking down onto a valley filled with wildflowers. Very picturesque. Probably good eating for some of the herbivore herds too.

It's an uncomfortable fit for three adults—even if two of us are on the petite side, but finally we manage to arrange ourselves so everyone is moderately comfortable.

So far today we've seen glimpses of small dinosaurs hopping in the trees, and one of the giant pterosaurs, Quetzalcoatlus, flying in the distance, but nothing for the last hour.

Nakamura stepped out a few minutes ago for a bathroom break, so it's just me and Grigori in the tent. I was iffy about taking Grigori and Nakamura along, but both have pleasantly surprised me. Grigori set up in our tent with practiced discipline, and Nakamura—once the expectations were explained to him that he needed to be quiet—has been doing admirably well. Although I suspect he's been napping for at least part of the day.

Grigori shifts, making too much noise, and I open my mouth to stay something but close it as the foliage rustles in the clearing ahead of us. My breath catches as a group of oviraptors dart into the space. Oviraptors are built like ostriches but with the heads of parrots. They all have the long, sinuous tail of a dinosaur with a fan of feathers at the end. Of course, the crests and coloring on the males are more impressive. The females' feathers are a mix of blacks and russet brown. The males have green plumage and a red head crest. That was one of my favorite discoveries when we first came here: how beautiful the dinosaurs are, their silky feathers, the bright colors. Some of them look so much like modern birds.

The oviraptors quickly settle down and form into groups or pairs. Watching them, the long grace of their limbs and necks, makes me grin.

I slide my hand over carefully for my notes, and Grigori starts to hand them to me, but something in her pockets rattles loudly together as she moves. The oviraptors freeze, their bead-like black eyes darting around, looking for danger. Grigori and I freeze, too, and wait them out.

After a minute or so, the animals settle and return to their behavior. I grab the notebook, carefully opening it in my lap and positioning one hand so I can take notes without looking. Grigori sits with her hands clasped in her lap, probably feeling guilty she nearly scared them off. I just pray Nakamura takes a while with his "business."

The oviraptors continue grooming each other, oblivious to our presence. They ruffle their feathers, using their beaks like oversized parrots. Two of them get into a snit, one's head snapping forward snakelike as he pecks the other with his short blunt beak. That one bounces away, moving apart from the others. He's holding an egg, pecking at it, trying to crack the shell with his beak. He can't seem to get it. He looks around, and my breath catches.

Grigori starts to turn toward me, mouth open, then stops herself. Good instincts. If she scares them away I *will* kill her.

The oviraptor cradles the egg as he bends toward the ground. He lifts a rock in his clawed hands, the feathers on his arms fluffing awkwardly.

Smash. He bashes the rock against the egg. I'm grinning so hard my cheeks hurt, while my hand scribbles furiously, almost disconnected from my brain.

Tool use. In dinosaurs.

Smash. He repeats the maneuver with his rock, and the shell cracks. He crunches his eggshell open then slurps the yolk like a cat lapping at milk.

Grigori vibrates with excitement beside me, and I bump her shoulder to say, *I know.* Tool use among dinosaurs. I've seen the possibility of it before, but this evidence seems pretty conclusive. If only one of the other oviraptors would do something similar, I might be on my way to getting a paper out of this, maybe even my next book.

One of the other animals creeps closer, probably trying to steal the egg. My tool-user sidles sideways, branches breaking under his feet. Then *crack*, the whole ground opens beneath him. The screen of brush collapses in on itself and dumps him into a hole.

"*No.*" I jump to my feet.

The oviraptors take off, jogging into the forest, voicing trills of alarm. The same trills seem to be going off inside me. I start hauling ass down the small hill toward the hole in the ground.

"What just happened?" Grigori calls behind me. When I look over, she's bouncing on her heels outside the camo-colored hide. "Dr. Carson?"

I shake my head and keep jogging downhill.

"Dr. Carson, we're not supposed to leave the hideouts. It's not safe." Her voice threads upward in a whine. She makes an impatient huff sound, but I lose all interest in her as the oviraptor voices a shrill cry from the pit.

"I need to look at that pit, Grigori."

"You're supposed to stay with me."

"Then start running, kid!"

I finally reach the pit where the oviraptor is still trapped. He's honking and twittering, crying out, maybe injured.

"Dammit. *Dammit, dammit, dammit.*" I spit the words out as I slide to a stop at the pit edge. The pit is almost a perfect circle. I bend to examine a piece of the foliage used to screen the hole. It's been cut with a saw. I toss it away, put my face in my hands and rub hard. "Shit." The thing is man-made. This is a poacher trap.

Grigori stops beside me, looks around, then gasps as she comes to the same conclusion. "But *how*? The Time Guard cleared them out last time. Arrested the leader—" She clips the words off and looks over at me.

I can't look at her. If she suspects me, then I don't want to know. "We have to get this guy out."

"How?"

I cast my eyes around, and there's a deadfall log, maybe long enough, a few feet away. I point. "That."

Grigori starts toward it, but I grab her elbow. She looks at me, startled. "What?"

"Watch your step. There might be more traps."

Together we approach the log. We don't find any more pit traps in the immediate area, but I'm sure there are more. Somewhere.

Dammit.

Thunder rolls above us, ominous and deep, echoing my thoughts.

We wrestle the log over to the pit and lift it carefully in. The dinosaur recoils against the pit wall, his feathers fluffed. We get the log in and braced against the side, then run away. I can hear the scrape as the oviraptor claws at the log. A flutter of feathers finally appears over the pit's edge, and he rolls free. He scrambles to his feet then runs away, long legs clawing at the ground. I wish I could warn *him* to watch out for more traps.

Another roll of thunder sounds, then a flash of lightning. No rain yet, but it's coming soon too. All the more reason to hurry.

I hiss my breath out through my teeth. "Do you have a camera? We should document the pit for the report to Meg—Agent Zaran."

"Yeah. Over there." Grigori points toward the hideout where we've both left all of our gear.

"Great. Mine too."

Lightning flashes again. And thunder. The storm's moving closer.

I sigh. "Okay. You—"

There's another crack of breaking foliage, but this one's accompanied by a very human scream.

Grigori gasps. "Nakamura?"

"Go get the jeep!"

"But—"

"*Go.*" I shove Grigori toward the tree we parked underneath. As she crashes away toward our ride, I turn on my heel in the direction of the scream. Not the smartest thing I've ever done—generally in the forest it's better to run *away* from screaming—but then, sane people don't travel millions of years just to study giant animals that want to eat them.

The thunder rolls and lightning sizzles so close I nearly retreat. The bolt hits a tree ahead of me, and ecstatic flame shoots skyward. One of the perils of an atmosphere with thirty percent oxygen is it's so much easier for things to catch fire. Even wet vegetation can burn and spiral into wildfires.

I hesitate but, over the crackle of the new fire, a low human moan sounds. Hell. I head into the forest. A dinosaur jumps out of the trees. I scream and fall, my heart punching at my ribs.

But it's only an oviraptor running from the fire. No threat.

I press my spine against a tree, breathing hard as the beast runs away.

Feeling my way tree to tree, I use them like anchors. One forward. Another. Again. I just keep myself moving until I can get some momentum, until I can get my breathing under control. Then I'm running again. I crash through a spray of ferns, burrs from the forest floor catching on my socks and legs.

A wall of heat blasts me like a physical blow, but I push on, coughing from the smoke.

As I stumble closer, I see a big opening in the ground, another broken pit trap. The fire is close enough burning needles from the pine are dripping into the pit. I kick dirt on the smoldering branches of the trap, but it's no good. The fire is creeping across the ground toward me, using deadfall and dry branches like a straight path.

I hold my sleeve over my nose and scoot as close to the edge as I dare. Maybe I misheard. Maybe Nakamura isn't down th—

His body's on the ground. He's got a bloody scalp, but he's moving, moaning. Definitely alive. Some of the brush screen for the trap fell on top of him, so he's half-buried in it.

Flame drips off the burning tree above to catch in the branches at the top of the broken trap. The dry branches catch fire with a *whoosh*.

"Well, shit." I throw myself at the other side of the pit, scaling down like a monkey, using roots, embedded rocks, slipping and sliding. I drop to the bottom beside Nakamura and start working at the pile of branches he's tangled in, kicking and yanking.

Like the fuse on a stick of dynamite, a branch above me catches fire, spilling flaming debris on Nakamura as it burns. His pants catch fire.

"Perfect."

I kick dirt on the burning, trapped, unconscious man, and it occurs to me that at least here is one person having a worse day than I am. Finally, I smother the flames on Nakamura's leg and return to smashing the clump of branches he's trapped in. The fire burns above us, like a predator waiting on the edge of the trap. Sweat drips into my eyes, and I'm panting. "After all of this, you better still be alive."

Nakamura moans.

"Thank you." I reach down, seeing if I can finally tug him free. He slides out from under the rest of the debris, but damn he's heavy. I look at the high sides of the trap, at the lack of footholds or anything I can use to climb out. I'm not sure *I* can get free, let alone carry him.

The dry roots on the other side of the pit catch fire behind me with a *whoosh* of noise. I whirl, pressing my shoulders against the wall of the trap. The heat pounds my face, sucking all the moisture out of the air. The smoke is blowing upward, but that's not very helpful if we burn to death.

I'm panting, sick to my stomach, shaking as I dig my fingers into the soft dirt sides of the pit.

"Dr. Carson!"

A rope and rescue harness spool down from the hover-jeep above. Grigori waves frantically, and I wave back. My knees want to collapse with relief.

I shove Nakamura into the climbing harness. He's about as helpful getting himself into it as my dolls were when I was dressing them as a kid. He moans and tries to bat at my hands, which my dolls never did when I tried to dress *them*. I tug the rope to signal Grigori to start lifting him. But I don't wait for her to get him out. The fire's still eating at the roots around me. I dig my toes and fingers into the pit wall and scramble. My arms are burning when I finally fling an arm over the top edge of the pit and haul myself out. I run to the clearing where the oviraptors were so Grigori can land to pick me up.

Our gear is still in the hideout, but there's no time to return for it.

Anyway, I'm not too worried about my next book right now.

After his fall, Nakamura comes to in the car. That probably means he doesn't have serious injuries. Grigori is still driving, and I've got Nakamura half-sprawled on top of me in the back seat.

"Ow," he says rather eloquently. He pokes at the knot on his head.

"Do you remember what happened?" I ask.

"Ow."

"Do you know where you are?"

"Shit." He groans.

"Dr. Carson, is he all right?" Grigori asks, her voice shrill.

"Ow." He tries to roll to a sitting position on the seat, flails, then leans heavily against my leg. "Shit. Ow."

"Nakamura," I keep my voice low, but we do need to know if he's in possession of all his faculties or not.

He sighs deeply, looking very put-upon, and glares my way. His irises look almost black. "I fell in a bloody hole. I'm in goddamn Dinosaurland, circa 73 million BC. My head is killing me, but otherwise I'm all right. Any other questions, or can I have a minute to appreciate the spectacular amount of pain I am in?"

"Sorry." I flinch. "You were injected with the nanos before you left, right?"

"Of course. We all are."

"Well, give it a minute, and they'll start doing their work. Making repairs. Helping with the pain."

He grunts. "Yeah, they can start any time they want."

Lucky he has the nanos. His injuries might have been much more severe if the nanos hadn't set to work right away making things right. They can't—or won't—resuscitate someone, and there are limits to the amount of trauma they can fix, but they do have their uses.

After a few more minutes, Nakamura is able to sit up on his own and look at me clear-eyed and calm. "Do you know what I fell into? Was it a nest or burrow or something?"

I worry at my lip, my teeth sinking in hard enough to hurt. I catch Grigori's gaze in the rearview mirror. She gives me a nod, and I don't know her well enough to be sure, but I believe she's telling me if I lie to Nakamura, she'll back me. As if to verify my guess, she widens her eyes and shakes her head in some attempt at telepathic communication. *Just lie to him about the hole, you idiot,* is the gist. Trifoso would be so proud.

I *should* lie to Nakamura. Oh God, I absolutely should. He doesn't remember it was a poacher trap. I could skate right past this morning's terrors, keep working, stay here in the past where I belong.

I swallow and press my eyes closed. "It wasn't some random hole."

Grigori lets out an exasperated sigh but bites it off halfway.

Nakamura scrubs at his face, gaping at me. "What?"

"It wasn't just a hole. What you fell into." I hunch forward and drop my face into my hands. "It was a poacher trap. We've found the evidence Meg needs. The poachers are here."

Chapter Twelve

JULIA

I don't sleep too well overnight. The rustlings in the camp and the nearby jungle leave my nerves raw.

"We have a sonic fence around camp. Nothing is likely to come close." Xia brushes a kiss over my shoulder. "We have guards, weapons. We're safe."

I know she believes that, and I felt safe enough sleeping the previous few nights. But we didn't have a baby carno in camp last night.

We know these animals will defend their young. Fight for them. Search for them?

I guess I'm too restless because in the deepest dark of the night, Xia gathers her sleeping gear, kisses me hard, and leaves with a whispered, "Sorry, Jules, but I need some rest for tomorrow."

I don't blame her, but I definitely miss her heat, and her smell, and her soft breathing against my collarbone and...

Morning comes eventually. I'm still rattling with nervous energy, but I manage to do my duties well enough: inventorying and verifying the species we've got, evaluating what's left of my chomped drone. Xia takes a group out to see if they can score a few more small specimens.

The day is gloomy, the skies gray and heavy with rain, so the solar panels aren't charging as quickly as we'd like. Our time machine is looking a bit worse for wear too. In my—admittedly limited—experience, the time tubes that get us home are usually cobbled-together things. Bits and bobs stolen or 3D printed from incomplete specs. The setup we're using is built inside a shipping container just large enough for us to get the SUVs through. And one large baby dinosaur. There are solar panels atop and a mess of wires and panels soldered inside all around the pulsing heart of the whole machine—the time tubes. Long glowing rods. Powerful and fragile.

Folks in camp are tense, and everyone is keeping a weather eye on the folks in charge of getting the time tubes operational. I don't know if Daw is officially in charge of that group or not, but he's hovering over them and barking like he is.

A cry of triumph from the area of the time tubes draws all of us still in camp closer. Iris catches my eye and grins, and I follow her as she jogs over to see.

Daw is grinning wide and strutting like he invented time travel himself. He points when he sees Iris approach. "Start loading everything, Harris. Let's get the hell out of here."

I freeze. "What about Xia? Shouldn't we wait for Xia?"

"Did I ask you?" Daw sneers, his nose curling. "Go get the fucking carno, Iris."

Iris crosses her arms, a muscle ticking in her jaw. "Xia said to radio her when the time tubes charged and to *wait*."

"What the fuck *for*?" Daw's face is turning a blotchy red, and he throws his arms out wide. He scans the immediate area and spots one of his favorite cronies, Quint, and another meathead nearby. "You two. With me. Let's get the loading started so we can get home." Daw brushes between Iris and me, shoulder checking both of us so we stumble.

Iris rubs her temple and growls. "I'll radio Xia. You keep an eye on those idiots."

"Right." I start toward the carno cage. Clanking and swearing comes from the area, and apprehension sets all my nerves to vibrating. I break into a run. "Sedate him before you move him," I call.

Daw and his minions are wrestling with the carno cage, trying to hook it to the other SUV to tow it close enough to go through the time tubes. The cage heaves, and the baby carno stomps his feet and trumpets alarm.

"Daw, wait!"

Daw hunches a shoulder and keeps fighting with the muddy trailer hitch. I can tell by his posture he heard me. He just doesn't care what I say.

The cage shudders again, and the baby snaps at the bars, causing Daw's minion to retreat from his work in fear. I slide to a stop myself, my heart hammering.

"Help me, damn you," Daw snaps at his minion, voice strained.

"Daw, just wait!" Impatient jerk.

Either Quint's getting antsy driving the truck or there's some kind of mis-communication because he puts the gas on. The SUV zips forward before the trailer hitch is properly secured. The cage comes down hard on one corner, barely missing Daw. He slips. The carno thuds against the front of his cage, and the combination of his weight and the impact against the ground makes the lock snap.

I freeze as the cage door swings open and the baby carnotaurus stumbles free. Daw sputters and scoots away on his butt, trying to claw for safety. The other minion isn't fast enough, and the baby's head snaps out lightning fast to catch his shoulder. The man wails and wrestles, trying to shove the dinosaur off.

My stomach swoops, and I throw myself against the SUV, clawing open the door. Quint's frozen in the driver's seat, but he recoils with a cry when I climb inside.

"Idiot." I paw through the back, trying not to listen to the screams outside, but my hands are shaking as I finally unearth a tranq gun case. I haul it over the seat with an oath and flip it open. "Quint, are you a good shot?"

The meathead beside me only opens his mouth once or twice, his eyes wide as he stares out the window.

I clench my jaw. "Better not to watch, pal." I ram the dart into the barrel of the gun and lock it. Then I force myself to look.

The first man is dead, torn into gleaming red chunks by the baby carno. Daw's still on the ground, cowering next to some supply bins, probably too scared to move. Baby's still chomping the corpse, but he could go for Daw at any moment.

Or me. My heart's pounding hard enough I can feel it in my palms where I'm gripping the gun. I roll my window down and kick the car door open, using the metal as a shield while I take aim.

The sound of the door opening makes the carno's head jerk so he's looking right at me.

I have no idea what dose is in this tranq. It could be measured for those tiny pterosaurs we were hunting the other day. I have no idea how long it will take to work, *if* it'll work. Baby opens his mouth and takes a step—

But instead of running toward me like I'm expecting, the baby squawks and runs the opposite direction—toward the time tube station.

"*Fuck.*"

Baby shoulder checks the container where we have all the wiring and the time tubes. Metal groans, and something shatters inside. The baby lets out a squeal of pain before he careens off the time tube container and starts toward the tree line.

Face grim, Iris Harris steps in front of the charging dinosaur with one of the net launchers against her shoulder. *Fwoosh.* The net plows into the baby, wrapping him tight and tripping him so he slides into the mud. He kicks and screams, tangling himself in the net.

Daw staggers over with a handheld tranq gun and shoots two right into the prone dinosaur. Baby stops squirming.

Huffing and puffing, stomach roiling, I approach the two of them. Although I keep some distance between myself and the dino in the net.

"Daw, you go deal with the body." Iris's voice is flat, her eyes stone-cold.

"In a minute."

"Daw—"

I start walking past the two of them. "It hit the time tubes."

Iris stirs out of her cloud of rage and jogs ahead of me to reach the time tube container. My joints are protesting too much for that. I haven't quite reached the container when a ripple of dismay flows through the camp. I finally catch Iris, and her breathing is quick, like she's strangling down her own panic.

"One tube's cracked," she murmurs.

Daw emerges from the container, stomping and swabbing away some mud on his face. "It's a hairline crack. Barely anything. We should still try."

Iris snorts. "You go first then."

Daw's nostrils flare, and his gaze cuts to me. "Or you."

I retreat a step and tighten my grip on the gun.

Daw's grin goes wider like he's baring his teeth. "Don't worry, Julia. There are enough dinosaurs to test it on first. We don't need a human guinea pig. Yet." He grunts out a mean laugh.

Xia's SUV arrives finally, and she swings out and heads toward us.

My first instinct is to rush her and fling my arms around her, burying my face in her dark hair. But the hard set to her expression tells me it's not the time.

Daw starts talking first. "Boss—"

"Save it." Xia surveys the scene, taking in the tranqed baby carno, the dent in the time tube container, all of our panicked faces. Her face muscles tremble then tense, but she calmly looks over at Iris and raises an eyebrow.

"The time tubes have been damaged," Iris reports. "We don't know how badly yet."

Xia folds her arms, and a muscle in her jaw bunches. "We need to get out of here. Now."

"We'll have the techs look at them," Daw sputters. "We have time—"

"No. We don't. I just got off the com with our spy at the research station. The Time Guard knows we're here. We need to get some time tubes that work." Her gaze cuts to me then quickly away. "By any means necessary."

The wind goes out of me like she just pounded me in the gut. "You want to attack the research station."

"That's our only option now." She steps close and leans her forehead against mine. "I'm sorry, Julia," she whispers.

Chapter Thirteen

GRACE

Everything's a whirlwind when we return to the research station, and a rainstorm starts behind us that sends us pelting inside as soon as we land.

The others have beaten us home to the station from their various research jaunts, and, at first, our news about the poachers is lost in the gaggle of everyone exclaiming over Nakamura's wounds. He's looking much better actually, but Meg orders me to take a look at him with the good first aid kit in the lab.

Nakamura waves that order away. "I have to report something first." Quickly, he tells her what I'd told him: about the appearance of the trap, the fact there were two so close together.

Trifoso glares at me fiercely enough I should be a melted pile of goo. He tries to cut into the discussion between Meg and Nakamura. "We don't know it was a trap. Those could be from some unknown anim—"

Meg's lips curls with disgust. "*Enough.*" She stabs a finger at Nakamura. "You, get patched up. I'll send the message." She turns on her heel and slams into the communication room. And, lest Trifoso think he can further argue his case, she bolts the door behind her.

I puff my breath out and look around at everyone. Srinivasan sits on the couch, face carefully neutral, but her hands are clenched into fists against her knees. Probably waiting for the other shoe to drop. Or for Meg to emerge and bark her next set of orders. Trifoso won't look at me. Grigori is glaring like I just lit her room on fire, and Vega's got a brittle look on their face, half confusion, half devastation. The ride's over. Our research program is dead, and I'm the one who killed it. I squeeze my eyes shut, fighting a burn of tears. "I'm sorry, everyone. I had to tell them. I had to."

Nakamura nips my sleeve with his fingers. "Help me out, Doc?"

"Yeah." It's not like anyone else is talking to me at the moment. He strips out of his burned and bloodied uniform shirt while I haul the big first aid kit out. "You don't look too bad. Probably just clean some of these deeper scratches, salve for the burns."

I'm digging through the kit, but he catches my hands. I glance at him, startled.

"You did the right thing, Doc. The only thing you could've done. Don't let the others get under your skin."

His hands are warm, and he smells like sweat and a day outdoors. With just a hint of smoke from the fire. His dark hair's tousled out of its usual tamed waves. He's disheveled and dirty, and for just a minute there's an ache in my teeth, a sudden need to see what it would be like to kiss him. I step back, pulling my hands free.

Nakamura clears his throat. "Sorry, Doc, didn't mean to overstep. I—"

"Nakamura." Meg raps on the doorframe to get his attention.

"What is it?"

Her face is grim, lips pinched so the skin is white around her mouth. "Someone's sabotaged the time tubes. We're completely cut off from the future."

Meg's pronouncement doesn't fill me with the proper dread it should. No, my first unworthy thought is: *great, more time for me to work.*

Nakamura slides out of his chair and throws his shirt on, buttoning it in record time. "*Sabotaged?*"

"Come along to the common room." Meg grits her jaw. "I only want to explain it once."

We pile out of the lab and take our spots in the common room. Everyone's already there, the scientists crammed together on the overstuffed couch and Srinivasan looking stern while she leans against one wall. I unthinkingly cross to the couch and perch on the arm next to Vega. Nakamura hesitates then moves a few steps behind Meg. All three of the time agents stand not quite in a row facing us scientists.

Us vs Them. The thought makes me shiver. We should all be on one team, but it doesn't work that way. A deep cloud of suspicion has risen between our groups, almost like a physical wall.

"So." Meg folds her arms over her chest and spreads her feet. "Someone stole a key component of the time tubes so they aren't working. I'm giving whoever that was a chance, now, to confess and return the part so we can get the time machine operational." Meg's gaze roves over all four of us on the couch.

The grad students avoid her gaze and shuffle nervously. I don't believe either of them are guilty. They're probably as uncomfortable as I am.

Trifoso glowers at Meg but says nothing.

Me, I frown at her and shake my head.

Meg raises one eyebrow and tsks her tongue. "All right, well, *that* was the easy way. Time to search your rooms. Srinivasan, with me. Nakamura, keep them here."

"Wait one fucking minute." I pop to my feet and throw a hand out to stop her. "Are you searching the time agents' rooms?" I cock my head to the side. "Are you going to let Trifoso and I search *yours*?"

Meg's mouth twists like she's bitten something sour.

"It's only fair, Agent Zaran," Nakamura puts in, voice low.

But Meg's shaking her head.

Vega mutters, "Maybe they're all in on it." Not quite under their breath.

"Excuse me?" Meg barks.

Vega startles then raises their chin and meets the older woman glare for glare. "Why should we trust anyone on your team? You've been shadowing all of us scientists since we've been here. We aren't allowed anywhere without you. But you three can come and go as you like. If anyone's working for the poachers, it's much more likely to be one of *you*."

"Draw straws." Srinivasan sighs. "One scientist, one time agent, and they search the rooms together. All right with everyone?"

We all trade looks and finally nod ascent. Nakamura cuts the straws and I hold them so everyone can draw. Vega gets a long straw and so does Meg. Vega swallows nervously but follows behind the senior time agent.

I watch their retreating backs then hop to my feet.

Srinivasan grabs me by the arm, yanking me hard enough I stagger. "What do you think you're doing?" she asks.

I jerk free of her hold and rub the sore spot on my arm. "I was getting my laptop so I can work." I let my eyebrows climb to my hairline, and Srinivasan has the grace to look embarrassed. "Permission to enter the lab, Agent?"

"Yeah. Right. Sorry." She hunches her shoulders and moves out of my way.

I work for as long as I can, continuing to update the logs for the camera trap images. As soon as his room is cleared of suspicious items, Trifoso stomps into the bedroom, slamming the door. Off to take another sleeping pill?

Grigori hops to her feet, hollering, "Please do my room next. I want to go to sleep. I want this day to be over."

Which reminds me she helped me rescue Nakamura from the trap. No wonder she's rattled.

Even though Srinivasan's room was supposed to be next, Vega and Meg search Grigori's. And, once it's pronounced clear, Grigori drags herself out of the common room with a murmured good night and softly closes the door.

I keep working even as the images on the screen blur. Even as my fingers start typing nonsense strings of characters.

"Doc." Nakamura's voice is soft, warm.

I blink my eyes open. The common room is empty except the two of us. Everything in me is lazy and warm, heavy. So heavy.

"Doc." He gives me a gentle shake. "They're done with the room search. You can go to bed."

I blink again and scrub hard at my face, trying to shake off my drowsiness. "Done? Did they find anything?"

His mouth sets in a harsh line. "No. We'll search the rest of the research station in the morning. Once everyone's gotten some rest. Srinivasan's on night shift to make sure no one tries anything. She's catching a quick nap while I hustle you off to bed. The rest of us are supposed to sleep."

I close my laptop and set it on the common room table. "Are you my official escort then? To make sure I don't do anything shady?"

He lifts one shoulder in a shrug. Not quite an answer. He does see me to my door, although we don't speak.

How would this interlude have gone if none of the awfulness this morning had happened? If he and I had spent the day in the sun and open air, happily watching dinosaurs, would things be different now? Would I say something? Ask him? Touch him?

The Time Guard doesn't let you use time travel to undo a mistake, to fix something dire. Once it's happened, it has to happen. You can't go back and save your army buddy from getting shot. You can't save your father from a car accident or your sister from drowning. Can't stop some shit politician from ever entering the race. That's why no one's been allowed to kill Hitler, stop the Titanic from sinking. Stop this wretched day from happening.

He's watching me, and he lets out a tired sigh then. He lifts his hand as if he might brush the hair off my cheek, but that invisible wall sprouts between us again. Scientist vs Agent. Us vs Them. And his hand falls instead to slap against his thigh. "Sweet dreams, Doc."

"Good night, Nakamura."

Chapter Fourteen

JULIA

Xia's words about attacking the research station hang in the air between her and me, then another rainstorm sweeps in, pounding us with water.

She wheels away, as if it physically hurts to look at me. "Daw, Iris, with me. Julia, I'll see you later." She sprints toward one of the SUVs, probably for a consult with Daw and Iris.

My dismissal couldn't be clearer if she had physically shoved me away.

I corral some of the beefier members of our crew and get them to drag the poor baby carno into his dented cage. The door still closes, and we have spare locks. Hand shaking, I brush my palm over his scaly side, feeling the breath rise and fall. "Sorry about all of this," I murmur then I close the cage door and lock him in.

There's a knot in my chest, and my head's aching. The windows of the SUV where Xia is having her conference are steamed over with fog. I can hear raised voices even over the storm. Tempers must be running high.

I spit into the rain and turn toward my own tent. "Fuck 'em." Xia shutting me out stings like lemon on a wound. I'm tired of waiting to discover if I'm about to become a murderer as well as a criminal. I go to my tent and try to sleep.

Everything in there is cold without her, and the ground is hard on my bones. I'm chilled deep in my marrow, like I'll never be warm again. Tears sting my eyes, and I swipe them away. "We got the carno, and we have to get him out. Finish the job, and forget everything else." I'm not in this for Xia anyway. And I already made my choice. I chose my son. Over my reputation, my own safety. I've sacrificed so much already, what does a murder really matter? "I made my choice," I grit out, still trying to throttle the thick emotion clogging my throat.

You can always choose again. The thought drops like a stone into my stomach, and I curl up tight, biting back a sob and aching, aching.

"Julia." Her voice is soft, questioning, and I go still, trying to pretend to be asleep. It's the coward's way out but, dear God, I don't have energy for a difficult conversation now.

But Xia's younger than me and more of a stubborn cuss, I guess, because she shakes my shoulder. "Julia."

"What?" I bite out.

"I'm sorry."

"That's it?"

"That's it." But her tone is softer than the words might imply. "We aren't doing anything tonight. We'll give the techs a chance to mess with our time tubes, and we'll run a test with some of the less high-end cargo to see if it goes through."

I prop myself on one elbow to look at her. "So we're not attacking the station?"

"Not yet." She cups my jaw. "But I can't rule it out as a possibility, Jules. I just can't."

I grind my teeth, not even angry, wanting to say a million things at once and nothing at all.

"Boss." It's Iris's voice outside the tent. "You need to get on the radio. Our spy in the research station needs to talk to you. Sounds pretty rattled. Something about a murder."

Chapter Fifteen

GRACE

Later, in the quiet dark of midnight, something startles me awake in my room. I regret I haven't left a flashlight close, something—anything to help me orient myself in the unfamiliar dark. I lie in bed, breathing hard, listening, wondering if I'm dreaming, wondering why my heart is hammering. Everything is quiet around me—the kind of quiet we can't get any more in the future. No ambient noise. No airplanes. No cars.

Everything's fine. I roll over, scolding myself for an overactive imagination.

And then I hear the sound that must have woken me—a long, drawn out scream. Human.

"Ah, shit." I toss my covers off and slap my hand against the wall until I can find the LED tap light mounted next to the door. I pause long enough to get my boots on then run out of my room. Someone else slams out of theirs at the same time as me. I recognize Nakamura's broad shoulders as he pounds down the hallway ahead of me, dressed in sweats and a pair of boots as hastily donned as my own.

He tosses a look at me. "You don't have to come, Doc."

"You might need backup," I puff out, fighting to keep pace with him.

He gives a small nod of acknowledgement, then we hit the front door. He yanks it open and doesn't even wait for me before he runs outside into the dark. I clatter out after him. The screaming's still going on, someone yelling "Help!" over and over.

A human comes running at us in the dark. Nakamura throws a hand out to stop me and puts himself between me and the other person. But, as they step into the light, I recognize Vega. They're wearing a PJ set with cutesy flying pigs all over them.

Vega slams into Nakamura and clings to him, sobbing. "Oh, please. By the fence." Vega is breathing hard, gasping words out with difficulty. "I don't know what she was doing outside. She's dead."

"Who?"

"Agent Zaran. Something ate her." Vega gags, tears leaking out of their eyes. "I wasn't even sure it was her at first, but I recognize the tattoos."

"What are *you* doing outside?" Nakamura's voice is soft, but there's steel in his tone.

"I woke up, and I was having trouble getting back to sleep. I went to the kitchen for a snack. The front door was open and, when I went to close it, I heard these..." Vega swallows convulsively. "Crunching sounds. I thought it was scavengers having a meal close to the fence. It was probably dumb, but I wanted to try and see them. I didn't get to see hardly any dinosaurs today with Trifoso, we came home so early. When I got close I saw..." Vega shivers. "It's—oh *please* just go get the body." Vega stumbles toward the station, legs wobbly, and I step close to tuck my shoulder under their arm to keep them upright.

Somewhere in the midst of all this, Trifoso has appeared. "What's happening?" He's still wearing his day clothes, and I catch a hint of alcohol coming off him. Not champagne this time. Maybe tequila. God, I hope he wasn't mixing his damn sleeping pills and booze.

"Get Jax inside." Nakamura starts toward the fence line.

I catch his arm to hold him. "Don't go by yourself. You don't know what's out there."

"Right." He seems rattled, distracted, and he slings Vega's other arm over his shoulder so we can help them inside. We get Vega to their bedroom, waking Grigori in the process. "What's happening?" she asks.

"Stay with Jax for a minute, please?" I murmur.

Nakamura's already out of the grad students' room and bellowing Srinivasan's name.

I scrub at my own face, trying to make myself focus. Right. Srinivasan was supposed to be on guard duty. So where's Srinivasan?

I head toward the front of the station myself so I can get to our lab, but Trifoso catches my wrist. "Grace, what the hell is going on?"

He's holding me tight enough to hurt, and I twist free. "Something happened to Meg. I need to get some things from the lab."

His eyes are squinty, and he looks very much the worse for wear in the better light of the common room. "What do you mean?"

"She's dead, Paul. And you probably want to make yourself some coffee."

He tries to grab me again, but I dodge him and half sprint into the lab. I grab the first aid kit out of one corner even though I'm pretty sure Meg is past the point of needing it. There's also a tarp on the supply shelf, and I grimly snag that, too, and a shovel.

Srinivasan is conferring with Nakamura in the common room as I emerge from the lab. She's got red creases on her face and watery eyes—like someone who fell asleep on her arms at a desk maybe? So much for guard duty.

Srinivasan runs her gaze up and down my body, probably taking in my terrific PJ-boots combo, but Nakamura looks no better.

"Are we going?" I ask.

She opens her mouth, maybe to tell me to stay put, but Nakamura's already at the door. He's got his sidearm strapped on over his sweats. I hate the thing, but the sight of it does provide some comfort. Srinivasan is armed too. Before I can second-guess grabbing a weapon myself, the two time agents charge out the door, and I have to scramble to keep pace.

Nakamura takes the lead, shining a flashlight on the ground ahead of us. The ground's wet and muddy from the rainstorm earlier, and we all have to place our feet carefully to stay upright. As soon as we get close to the fence, I hear the crunching noises Vega mentioned. My stomach lurches. The light sweeps, shaky in Nakamura's hand, and settles on a pack of three dinosaurs stooped over a kill on the other side of the fence. Their bodies mostly block the carnage, but Meg's hand has been separated from the rest of her body, and her bright-red nails glint with their candy shine in the flashlight beam.

Srinivasan starts retching behind me.

One of the dinosaurs looks up from the kill, snout bloody, and its intelligent eyes fasten on us. It looks like a gobivenator, a scavenger. An opportunist. Normally, they wouldn't go after prey the size of Meg. The size of us. But, with a snout already full of delicious human, it's foolish to believe these animals won't attack us too. Especially if we try to scare them off their kill.

My heart's racing is making me sick, and we're all frozen in some monkey-hind-brain fear response. Another dinosaur raises its head and chirrups at the first.

"Doc," Nakamura's voice is a frightened hiss. "The gate's open."

Srinivasan lets out a low groan beside us.

Although Meg's body is outside the fence, she never managed to close the gate before the animals got her. Or maybe Vega left the gate open after discovering Meg. It doesn't matter. The gate is swinging wide enough for any of these three dinosaurs to walk right on through.

My mouth dry, I set the first aid kit and tarp down and swing the shovel high in a two-handed grip. Cold in my bones, trembling, I cross toward the gate where the dinosaurs are, and I lift the shovel. I swing my shovel at the fence and bang it against the bars as loud as I can. I start yelling, too, I'm not even sure what. I just make as much noise as I can while inside my stomach curdles.

The dinosaurs startle, and one bolts immediately as soon as I begin my racket. The other two recoil and move off a few feet, but they don't run. They watch me and wait.

Suddenly, Nakamura's at the gate beside me, banging the butt of his weapon against the metal, raising his arms above his head and hollering fit to wake the whole world. When he joins me, the dinosaurs both turn tail and run.

The remains of their meal are all over the immediate area, gore and bits of Meg's innards. The blood is shockingly red as Nakamura runs his flashlight beam over the scene. Although there isn't as much blood as I'd expect.

"Fuck." Nakamura scrubs the back of his hand over his mouth and swallows convulsively, going pale.

I take a deep breath and close my eyes to compose myself. "We can't leave her out there, and we can't wait around. Those scavengers might return. Or more like them. We need to move the body." I have to start thinking of it like that, or I'll never move. The body. Not Meg. Meg's gone. The body is business to be taken care of, practical and grim. The loss of Meg is something to process later. Emotions too deep and complicated to easily turn over now in the middle of this crisis.

Briskly, I bend to open the first aid kit and pull out gloves and a face mask. I wish there was an apron, too, but I guess I'll just have to dump these pajamas when this is all over. With a confident step I am far from feeling, I tug open the gate and circle around the fence line to Meg's body. Nakamura grabs his own protective gear and follows on my heels. With a stifled groan, Srinivasan brings up the rear. Together, we load Meg's poor ruined corpse onto the tarp I brought and drag her into the safe perimeter of the gate—much too late to do any good.

Once she's inside the perimeter, with the gate shut behind us, we pause.

I clear my throat. "Before anything else, I would like to examine the body."

Nakamura raises an eyebrow.

I sigh. "I'm not being morbid. I'd like to measure the bite radius, see what kind of wounds they inflicted. See what the killing blow was. I want to figure out how she died, if I can. And why."

Nakamura scratches at his neck, staring at the tarp-wrapped body. "I'd like to figure that out myself."

We get the body inside and into the lab. I put a cap over my hair and an apron over my clothes then I get my tool kit and move to examine the remains. I'm used to performing necropsies, not autopsies, but the basic fundamentals are the same. Blood. Fat. Organs. Bone. I'm not doing a full examination anyway. The Time Guard will want to do that when we send the body forward.

If we *can* send the body forward. No one's mentioned anything about the time machine being fixed.

I shake that thought away and force myself to focus. I'm hoping to get a general idea what the hell happened anyway. Nakamura posts up across the table from me.

When I lift one of Meg's arms—the one that still has a hand—her muscles are loose and don't fight me. I suck in a breath. "Primary flaccidity. No rigor mortis yet. She hasn't been dead long." I swallow, and my gut is hollow. "Less than two hours most likely."

A muscle bunches in Nakamura's jaw, and he punches the table. He's probably thinking what I am—was there something we could have done to prevent this? Moved faster? Listened harder? Slept lighter?

I get my ruler out and start making notes on the bite radius of the wounds.

A convulsive movement from Nakamura startles me. He reaches to close Meg's eyes with his gloved hands. He's shaking. We, neither one of us, are used to this kind of thing. A dead human on the table. A dead colleague. I would've even called her a friend, once upon a time. Before the drama with my ex-husband.

As my eyes fly to her blood-specked face, my own composure cracks. The dinosaurs mostly went for her abdomen, masticating her intestines and organs. Her face is shockingly untouched. I'm slipping, spiraling, caught by the serene expression on her face. A lump forms in my throat.

"Doc." The sharpness of his tone catches me and snaps me back to the task at hand. Nakamura's gaze roves over the rest of her, and he steps away from the table, glowering. "There's not enough blood. Right? Look here at this bite on her leg. It doesn't look like it bled at all, does it?"

I examine the area and have to agree. There's hardly any blood and, that close to the femoral artery, her whole leg should be soaked in red. My chest goes tight, like someone's squeezing my heart in a vise. "She was dead before the dinosaurs got to her."

"We need reinforcements." Nakamura starts to scrub at his hair but stops himself, remembering his bloodstained gloves. He catches my gaze, his own wide and worried. *"Fuck."* Then he yanks his gloves off with a snap and tosses them in the biohazard bin on his way out the door.

After he's gone, I bend my head, trying to breathe shallow so the rank smell of her innards doesn't hit me. I might not be able to find what I'm looking for; the dinosaurs might have destroyed the evidence. But I still meticulously work my way over Meg's corpse. Shifting her clothes out of the way, carefully pressing and pulling on her body. Finally, just below her rib cage, I find what I'm looking for: a thin stab wound, probably one of many, but the evidence of the others has literally been eaten away. Still, this is all I need to see. Meg wasn't careless. She didn't get herself killed by dinosaurs. She was already dead when they started eating her.

Chapter Sixteen

JULIA

"A murder at the research station?" Xia caresses my jaw, a parting reassurance, then takes off after Iris at a jog. I never undressed for bed, so I scramble out of my tent and follow along, limping because my ankle is still not happy with me after all the dramatics today.

When I finally catch them, Xia's already got the portable radio in hand. She shoots me an exasperated look, rolling her eyes at the mole on the other end. "Look. Calm down. Just tell me what happened?"

"I tried to call earlier, but everything was so tense and hectic." Our mole's voice crackles over the radio, breathing hard, tension vibrating in every word. They're using some kind of voice scrambler so they sound robotic. Anonymous. How very paranoid of them. "We found one of your goddamn pit traps today. Fucking Grace Carson practically fell into it. I told you not to get too close to the compound, dammit. I managed to smooth over those smashed cameras and now *this.*"

"What happened?" Xia's voice is level and calm, but I can see she's gritting her teeth, visibly fighting to hold onto her temper.

"They wanted to send a message," the mole says, "call for reinforcements, but I snuck in and stole one of the wires this morning, just in case you lot needed more time with your shipment."

"That was good thinking." Xia keeps her voice light, mild.

"Damn right it was good thinking. I was fucking panicking. Pit traps. I can't believe you idiots. Did you even consider what would happen to me, to my reputation, if I'm caught helping you?"

Did you? But I swallow those words. Unproductive. If our spy has got cold feet, then taunting will not help.

"Agent Zaran started poking around," the mole whispers, voice raspy over the radio, "She searched our rooms tonight. She must have found something in mine. I thought I was so careful. She dragged me outside, to talk she said. She offered me a bargain, turn you all in for reduced jail time."

Xia's breath hisses out of her. My own gut clenches, churning with sudden fear.

"What did you do?" Xia asks, the slightest bit of a snap coming into her voice.

"She's dead."

"*What?*"

"I panicked and I-I killed her. God, you were so careless. You need to come now. Right now."

"Now?" Xia says.

"*Yes.* Don't you see?" The mole's voice is a like a harsh bark, biting the words out over the radio. "Before the Time Guard finds out Meg was murdered. I tried to cover my tracks, but it might not work. Get here before the time agents get the tubes working and send their message to the future. You need to get here before everything falls apart. Shit. I've got to go." The line goes dead.

Xia rubs her head and shoots me a worried look. "What do you think?" she murmurs.

I rake my fingers through my hair, my heart trip-hammering. "We could still wait this out, hide in the forest and wait for everything to blow over."

"*Hide*? Why are we even discussing this?" Daw stalks forward and cuts between Xia and me. "You may want to spend your golden years in this death trap, fine, but I don't. I want to go home."

"We *all* want to go home," Xia snaps. "We just need to be sure we don't make a big mistake trying to get there."

"Look, I know I fucked up with the carno today." Daw thumps his chest. Even apologetic, he's still got to display like a damn gorilla. "But *I'm* not trying to get everyone killed. We've got what we need. We know there's a working pair of time tubes. We can't wait anymore."

Xia calmly stares his down. "Attacking the research station is a point of no return I'm not ready to cross yet. I told you that."

"The Time Guard knows we're here! And there's a dead time agent." He practically slaps the radio out of her hand as he gestures. "If they find that part to the machine your spy stole, then they can report everything and get reinforcements. *What the hell are you waiting for?*" Daw stalks off. A few of his cronies peel away from the group surrounding the radio. Xia shakes her head as she watches him go.

"You're not following him?" Iris asks.

Xia snorts. "Not when he's in a mood like that."

A car engine roars in the darkness, the familiar hum of one of our hover-jeeps. I jump, and Xia's eyes widen.

"That son of a—Iris, go with him!" Xia gives Iris a shove to get the younger woman running then takes off herself.

Iris reaches Daw's car first and swings inside, but either she can't stop him or she secretly wants the raid to happen, too, because the hover-SVU climbs steadily into the sky then zooms out of view.

"Hell." Xia's shoulders slump in defeat before she draws herself tall and turns toward me. "You should go to your tent, Julia. Get some rest." She slaps my arm, distantly, her gaze already far off, planning.

"Xia."

She shakes me off. "No time, Jules. I'm sorry." She gathers the rest of the camp together and starts murmuring orders. Soon the whole place is a flurry of activity, and I lose her in the rush of bodies. But I finally find her by the other vehicles, where she's loading them with personnel and weapons.

"What are you doing?" I ask.

She's stowing a long rifle in one of the hover-SUVs, and she doesn't meet my eyes. "I'm following Daw. He's went off half-cocked, and he doesn't have enough people or supplies to get the job done. If we're doing this, we need it to work."

Heart hammering, I grab her arm. "Xia, please." I don't even know what I'm asking her for. Or maybe I do, but I'm not foolish enough to say it out loud. Not now, when the choices seem so stark.

She looks at me, but only for a heartbeat before she has to look away again. "I'm sorry, Julia. I would've liked to do things your way. Civil. Nice. But I need to salvage this mess. We need those time tubes one way or another, and Daw just shortened the timeline. I need to go. We don't have time to do this gently." Her face softens as she cradles my cheek, pity and affection both shining in her eyes.

My cheeks burn.

She keeps her voice soft. "It doesn't have to be an attack. Maybe the scientists will be reasonable. All we need to do is borrow the time tubes, after all." Xia pauses, and her hands clench and unclench against her thigh. She's cool, not cold. She doesn't like what we're talking about any more than I do.

Xia's shoulders sag but then she straightens, wipes all expression from her face, and slams the door shut on the SUV. She turns toward the rest of the camp and pitches her voice loud, "Saddle up, everyone. We're going to get some time tubes."

Chapter Seventeen

GRACE

With Meg gone, Srinivasan is in charge. And practically the first thing she does is assemble all of us in the common room: scientists on one side, Time Guard on the other. (The *very* first thing she did was let me catch the world's quickest shower to get Meg's blood off. So at least she has some mercy.)

Srinivasan and Nakamura are both in uniform, both wearing their sidearms. It's all very official and intimidating—as it's meant to be, I'm sure.

I'm wearing khakis and a denim shirt, but the rest of my team is still in the clothes they slept in. Trifoso, especially, seems awkward having this discussion in his dirty clothes from yesterday. He's bleary-eyed, but he seems sober, at least.

Srinivasan clears her throat to make sure she has our attention, then she starts, "Based on events tonight, our number one priority is finding that missing part for the time machine. Either the original that's been stolen or a replacement. Grigori, I want you with me in the com room looking. Dr. Trifoso and Mx. Vega, search the kitchen. Nakamura and Dr. Carson, search the lab. We *need* to find that part and get the hell out of here." She's outwardly calm, but there's a vibrato of fear in her voice. "We'll check with each other in thirty minutes and swap partners. Everyone, stay alive until then." She grimaces and waves her hands to dismiss us.

Our lab is the last place I want to be, but still less do I want to subject Vega or Grigori to the sight of Meg's body, basically unzipped, gleaming red with gore on the examining table. I grit my teeth and put my mask on to stifle some of the smell.

"Do you want to search one side and meet in the middle or work together?" I ask.

Nakamura shakes his head. "Together."

Right. In case one of us is up to something. The hair rises on my arms, and I start pawing through the cabinets, taking things out, patting the back of the shelf. Everything is dusty, and the organization could be better, but no one seems to have hidden anything here.

"Really, I'd like to review Meg's movements," Nakamura mutters as he does the next cabinet. "Figure out what she was doing before she was killed."

I flinch. "Whatever Meg figured out got her killed."

He tilts his head. "Was that an observation, Dr. Carson? Or a warning?"

"What? Ah, jeez." I shoot him an irritated look. "A warning in the sense that are you sure you want to be digging your nose in?"

"I can't exactly let this one lie."

"Right." I start searching through the drawers with all the poorly labeled fecal samples. Now I'm sorting literal shit. Lovely. I stack the sample containers neatly on the counter as I empty the space.

Nakamura leans against the counter beside me, a distant look on his face. "So, help me figure this timeline out, Doc."

"I can try."

"Meg's in here working or in her room trying to sleep. The killer finds her and says something to lure her outside."

"Srinivasan didn't see anything?"

He gives a wry smile. "Srinivasan claims she fell asleep at her desk."

"Great alibi."

He raises one finger in the air. "Ah-ah, but all of us have that alibi. So do you."

I wave my hand, conceding the point. "Someone lures Meg off, kills her. Drags her outside the gate so the local scavengers can dispose of the evidence. Wait, she's got the nano inject, right? Shouldn't her body have started to disintegrate immediately?"

He shakes his head. "There's a delay built in to the nanos so you can attempt manual resuscitation." His mouth settles into a grim white line. "Or attempt an autopsy. Those scavengers who ate her probably have a pretty bad bellyache coming on." He scratches at his jawline with one finger, making his stubble rasp. "Using the scavengers was clever. If Vega hadn't been outside at the right time, there probably wouldn't have been much left of Meg by morning. Which..." he lowers his voice. "I'm not sure I buy Vega's story."

I grit my teeth. "You just want to believe it was one of us scientists because then the Time Guard remains infallible."

"Hey—"

I slap the counter. "Srinivasan had the chance too. The best chance of everybody, despite her sleeping excuse. And you had as good a chance to get out. Vega made a valid point: all you agents had much more freedom of movement than we did. And either of *you* would know better how to sabotage the time tubes than we would."

His face goes hard. "All of us agents have been sleeping at night, same as the scientists, and no one was assigned on the night shift as a guard. Any one of you could've been sneaking out to work with the poachers. Hell, Doc, how many times did *I* catch *you* trying to sneak out?"

I straighten, anger firing my blood. "I wasn't trying to sneak out. I was taking the air. And I invited you with me. Maybe I'm the one who stopped *you* sneaking out?"

We glare at each other in silence, the air charged, both of us breathing hard and rattled.

Pop. Pop. Pop. It's a strange tinny sound. Popcorn? We're not allowed to have popcorn because of the smell—

Nakamura tackles me from the side, dragging me to the ground.

My heart's beating fast, hard, and I stiffen my arms, trying to hold him off, clawing for his face. *"What are you—"*

He grips my wrists together, one large hand pinning both of mine. "Those were gunshots, Doc."

Chapter Eighteen

JULIA

It's a quiet ride to the lab. As we approach and the perimeter fence comes into view, my stomach sinks into my shoes. The fence is a dome all around the building—to keep the pterosaurs out—with an automated gate on the top so the hover-jeeps can fly out.

Daw's car has already landed, and his people cut their way through the fence at ground level. Makes sense the research station's defenses would be easy to breach. They're trying to keep out dinosaurs, after all, not people.

We haven't even landed next to the lab ourselves when I hear gunshots and spot muzzle flare coming from below.

"Shit," Xia murmurs.

I fumble for the radio. "Daw, *copy*. Daw, what the *hell* are you doing?"

"I'm getting the time tubes. However I can," he snarls back. "Get off the radio, Julia."

Xia gently takes the radio as she circles for us to land outside the perimeter fence.

Just then, one of the scientists' hover-cars takes off like a rocket from the ground. The hatch on top of perimeter fence barely opens in time, and the hover-jeep jerks as its hood scrapes against the partially open fence.

Xia fumbles for the radio. "Team Two, follow that car." Our other hover-SUV, still airborne, peels away to give chase. "Try to take them *alive*. And don't damage the car. They might have the time tubes."

After that, Xia brings us down for a harder landing than usual. She sucks in a long, deep breath and reaches for the radio. "Iris? Iris, status report."

Iris replies at once. "No casualties so far on either side. We've got one captive and at least two escapees. Quint and Yao are sweeping the inside of the station. Daw and I are manning the perimeter to ensure no one else makes it out."

"Do you need us to come in? Do you need reinforcements?"

"Not yet," Iris says. "Hold your position in the car in case anyone else manages to slip past."

"Sounds good. Be careful. Over and out." Xia reclines against the car headrest, closing her eyes.

I wet my lips, my heart hammering. "Now what?"

"We wait," Xia murmurs. "And we hope Iris can keep Daw in check."

Chapter Nineteen

GRACE

More loud pops. From outside, I think. Muted. They sound like firecrackers. But Nakamura's right; they are gunshots. Someone is attacking the lab.

I twist my arms, and he lets me go. My hands are shaking. Gunshots. I understand what he's saying, but for that first crucial moment, I'm frozen and can't decide what to *do*.

Run, fight, hide. The words burst in my brain, and I snap my head around looking for a weapon. My first year as a grad student instructor, I had to take "active shooter" training. In case someone ever came into the classroom with a gun, I needed to know what to do. But "run, fight, hide" were options for the real world, for the future. I'm in 73 million BC. There's no back up coming to rescue me even if I can run or fight or hide.

"Can you repair the time tubes?" I whisper.

"I'll have to try, won't I?" He cracks the lab door open. Looks out. Hallway's clear, apparently, because he motions me to follow. We slither into the hallway and run in a serpentine pattern down the hall—another legacy of my active shooter training: you're harder to hit if you zigzag.

"Hey!"

Two people with long guns step into the hallway. Nakamura grabs my arm and shoves me ahead of him. I maintain the serpentine zigzag run, and a bullet pings off the wall across from me. Another ricochets off the floor by my feet.

The lights in the building cut out. It's not too dark to see, but apparently it's dark enough to screw the poachers' aim because we make it through the hallway unscathed. Instead, we hear running feet behind us.

I hit the time room door and fumble with it, pushing the door open so hard I jar my arms. Nakamura shoves me inside. He tries to tug the door shut, but a big arm slides between the door and the jamb from the other side, keeping it open. The two of them jostle together, the door wavering. I don't have time to see who wins.

I rush to the time tubes. No time to make repairs or try to boot them up. No time to get safely away. Alas, the dreadful irony of a time traveler with no time.

I hesitate, my hands trembling. If I'm wrong about what the intruders are here for then we're dead. But we're dead anyway, so I might as well gamble with my life before I lose it, right?

I yank the time tubes out of their casings. They're about half the length of my body, thin like a fluorescent light bulb and about that fragile.

"Quint, get back!" A woman's voice. "Shoot through the door!"

Nakamura springs away, eyes wide.

"Stop or I'll smash the time tubes!" I holler it at the top of my lungs, my voice shrill. "I will *smash* the time tubes. *I will smash the time tubes.*" I scream it a few more times, like a kid having a tantrum in the toy aisle. I want to know they hear me. I want to know they understand.

"You wouldn't." The woman's voice again.

"I can survive in that forest until help comes. Can you?"

"Dumb bitch." The man's voice.

I jerk my chin at Nakamura. *Get behind me.* He complies, staring at me with a furrowed brow. I can't tell if he thinks I'm brilliant or crazy. Both?

"I've got the time tubes against my chest and face," I call. "If you try to shoot me, you will destroy them. If you shoot me anywhere else, I'll fall and smash them even if I'm dead. You understand?"

Silence for a breath then, grudgingly, "Yes."

"Good. Guns down. Slide them through the door."

Another long pause. Too much to ask? I'm not used to bargaining with criminals. But then the door creaks open and the guns slide in: one, two, three. Two long ones and a handgun. I hadn't even noticed the handgun. I use my foot and drag them closer until Nakamura can pick them up. He does, slinging one over his shoulder by its strap, tucking the second gun into his pants.

My stomach plummets. If you'd asked me yesterday if I trusted him, I would've said yes, but after everything that's happened... It scares the shit out of me he has the weapons, and I have nothing. But my hands are full.

"We're opening the door and coming out," I yell. "Remember what I said. Anything happens to me and you lose the time tubes."

"Come ahead then." It's the man's voice. Surly, unhappy.

My nerves are jangling like an alarm bell. We step out of the room, and I brace myself.

When I walk into the hallway, I'm facing two people dressed all in black, a petite Asian woman and a huge brute of a blond guy. They're both younger than me, early twenties. Both athletic with hard eyes. They could probably kick my ass ten different ways before I take another step if I wasn't holding their future hostage.

I cradle the time tubes close, one of them cold against my cheekbone. "Get in the room then get on the ground, flat. Hands behind your head."

Nakamura makes some noise behind me. It sounds like approval.

The girl walks past me, chin high, pissed as hell. The man follows her. His burning gaze makes my shoulders itch. I turn as they walk, keeping them in sight and keeping the time tubes between us. I can feel Nakamura's warmth at my back.

Both poachers are inside the room. "On the ground." I use my professor-voice, loud, no nonsense.

The blond guy's nostrils flare, and his hands curl into fists at his sides like he's dreaming about hitting me.

"Do as the good doctor says, please." I think Nakamura does something with the gun because the intruders both sink to their knees, resting their cheeks against the cold tiles of the floor.

I wish we had something to tie them with. *Oh well.*

Nakamura hustles past me into the room and wheels a boxy maintenance cart into the hallway with us. "Wha—"

He yanks the door to the time room closed then he braces the maintenance cart against it. With some pleasure, I notice the door opens out that way. We can't restrain them, but we *have* trapped them inside the room. I smile.

He grins too, and my gut swoops with something close to pleasure. "Head for the cars?"

"Best bet." I jog down the hall, trying to move swiftly while still listening for other people. *Is anyone dead?* My nerves are like a string stretched between two posts, and I'm terrified everything in me will fray and snap. I hate to leave the others behind, my grad students especially, but I don't know how we can go looking for them without getting ourselves killed.

I lead Nakamura out the side door and slink around the main building toward the storage shed for the hover-cars. I push the heavy utility door open to the garage. The sight of the hover-jeep ahead, half-illuminated by sunlight, inspires me to rush forward into the work area. *Almost there—*

Something crashes into me from behind. Bangs into my head hard. I stagger forward as my vision goes black. I'm dizzy. Nauseous. I press a hand to the wall but fall to my knees anyway. The time tubes clatter to the floor.

"You idiot! We need those!"

I don't know who's yelling. My palms are burning, my knees aching. On all fours, I breathe through my teeth, trying to refocus, reorient. Recover.

Someone slams their arms around me, constricting as they jerk me to sit up on my knees. I find myself staring down the barrel of a rifle. Nakamura falls to his knees beside me. Behind the legs of our attackers, I catch sight of Trifoso tied beside the hover-jeep, gagged, blood on his forehead.

A male poacher yanks me by the hair. I can hear his grunt of pleasure as he hurts me. "Hey, Iris, I think this one is the infamous Dr. Carson. What a treat."

"Shut up, Daw." This is the other poacher, a woman's voice. She leans down to meet my eyes. "Hello, Dr. Carson." Is she the poachers' leader? She's tall, muscular, with cool-toned dark skin. Her hair's twisted in longs braids pinned around her head. "Now, Dr. Carson, we need your—"

I am never to find out what the poachers need from me because suddenly the din of pounding feet and squawking obliterates every other sound. Three panicked oviraptors barrel into the woman, Iris, spinning her round and knocking her off her feet.

I whirl and punch the male poacher Daw in the balls. He doubles over, useless for the moment.

One oviraptor steps on Iris as it runs away, its foot sinking into her belly. She lets out a pained "Oof!" noise. The oviraptor runs into the workbench and flails around, banging into things like a bird caught inside a house. How did it get in?

I crawl for Iris's gun and grab it as she claws for the strap. I kick out and catch her under the jaw. Yelling, holding her nose, she releases the gun. I roll to my feet and hit her hard with the butt of the rifle, a sick hollow melon sound coming from Iris's head. She's out.

I pivot to see Daw looming over me, about to grab my neck. But then Daw wobbles and tips forward. I duck out from underneath him as he crashes into the concrete floor. He lands hard, his face cracking against the ground, knocking him out cold. When I look over, Nakamura is on the floor, one hand still gripping Daw's ankle where he must have tripped him.

Nakamura pops onto his elbows. "You okay?"

"Yeah."

The oviraptors, three of them, are bunched in one corner of the room. They hiss at me when I get too close, and their eyes are wide. "We have that acoustic fence around the perimeter, why did they..." I trail off at the same time Nakamura shoots me a dry look. "Right. The lights inside. The poachers must have cut our power." You kill the electricity, you kill the acoustic fence.

"It'll be all right, Doc." Nakamura hops to his feet, not even winded by the recent bout.

Fast, efficient, before they can shake off their daze, Nakamura restrains the two poachers using their own belts. He takes the poacher Iris's extra ammo and knife.

I kneel beside Trifoso and cut his ties with the pocketknife Nakamura passes me. Trifoso rips the gag off then spits. He's breathing heavy, and a sheen of sweat coats his skin.

"Is Vega with you?" They'd been paired together to search the kitchen.

"No," he says. "I was taking a bathroom break. I heard the shots and climbed out the window. I thought I could loop around the outside of the building and try to find the others, but these people grabbed me." Trifoso retrieves the time tubes from the ground. I hope they're all right, but we don't have time to check.

"Any sign of Srinivasan or Sona? Did the poachers say they had more prisoners?"

"No." Trifoso is panting. "They just grabbed me and tied me up. I didn't see anyone else. Although the second jeep is missing."

My palms are sweating on the gun. "We have to get word to the future. Let the Time Guard deal with this."

A line of bullets hits the ground, ricocheting off the concrete or punching through the jeep doors. The bullets come from behind us. Our jeep is immediately shot full of holes. It collapses to the ground with a crash, steam rising from the hood.

I dare a peek around the shed door and just outside the perimeter fence sits a large vehicle painted with forest camo. The poachers' ride, probably. Such a bad idea, but it looks empty, and all the poachers seem to be *inside* the research station.

"There! Come on." I race forward, my heart thumping as I worry I'm leading us into a firing line. But the giant hover-SUV is empty, the area around it clear. Almost as one, the three of us pile into the vehicle. Nakamura and I trip over each other trying to get into the back seat.

Trifoso slithers into the driver's seat. "No keys!"

I hear shouting, and the front door of the research station bangs open. Bullets hit the car like raindrops. Relentless. My mouth is bitter with the taste of adrenaline. A bullet pings off the metal by Nakamura's head. He ducks, his body so close to mine I can feel the slick sweat on his skin.

"Look around," Trifoso calls. "Maybe the keys fell—"

The rear window spiderwebs. I tug Nakamura out of the next bullet's way by a fistful of his T-shirt. We overbalance and end up sprawled in the back seat—me on top.

"Doc, this is so sudden," he says.

Jackass.

As more bullets hit the car, we both duck. Nakamura rolls on top of me so I'm better shielded. Showers of glass trickle over his shoulders. Then, as suddenly as it started, the assault stops.

Trifoso uncurls from the ball he made of his rather large form in the front seat. "Wh—"

From the forest, a primeval roar sounds, and all the blood in my body turns to ice water. We're outside the fence in a car that won't start.

"What was that?" Nakamura asks.

I open my mouth, but I can't make any sound come out.

Trifoso shoots me a worried look from the front. "A carnotaurus. Let me see if I can hot-wire this thing."

But the roaring grows louder, moving closer, followed by a rhythmic *thump thump*. Too much noise for one animal.

A stampede.

Oviraptors and other small dinosaurs curve around the sides of the perimeter fence, like a wave breaking against a lighthouse wall. An entire menagerie of prehistoric life is on the run, hauling ass to get away. Some of them bang against the hover-car, like birds hitting a window.

Mixed in with the fleeing dinosaurs, I notice half a dozen poachers run for their lives. Some screaming. One man falls and gets trampled.

The car jerks with the impact from the animals, and one of the side windows cracks, dotted with the blood of whatever dino rammed into it.

"We need to run, Doc."

I don't want to, but we'll be stomped into jelly at this rate. Throat dry, heart racing, I crawl toward the car door.

Before we can hop out, the cause of all this mayhem races into view: a full grown carnotaurus. She's thirty feet long, ten feet high, a mass of muscle with a powerful neck and bony "horns" above her head. The Lady Carnotaurus bounds through the trees, cracking branches, angrily bulldozing her way toward us.

"Doc?" Nakamura shakes my shoulder, and I jump at the contact. "Doc, you okay?"

"Fine."

"We have to go."

He starts to move, but I grab his arm, holding onto him as I watch Lady C. The dinosaur charges across the clearing, head whipping around on her powerful neck. She sniffs, hesitates.

Iris, the poacher who attacked me, staggers out from around the side of our breached compound, stumbles through the half-standing fence. She must have wriggled free from her ties. Her head is bloody, her nose still bleeding. I want to cry out for her to stop, run away, but it's already too late. Iris stops, stares at the dinosaur, and screams.

Lady C. tilts her head, contemplative, and then—

I look away but can't stop the sound from reaching my ears. The fleshy crunch. Nakamura's arm bands around my shoulders, squeezing hard. I lean against him, taking comfort where I can as the thick metallic smell of blood hits my nose. Behind me, Trifoso exhales loudly. My own stomach roils.

With Lady C. distracted, it's now or never. I climb out of the seat and use the edge of a tarp to clear away some of the glass littering the bed of the SUV. We're in luck. There's a knapsack with supplies, along with a dented first aid kit. I hand the pack off to Nakamura so I can carry the time tubes. "Come on." I take a deep breath then lead us at a jog into the forest.

Behind us, Lady C. just keeps feeding.

Chapter Twenty

JULIA

I'm perched on one of our hover-SUVs, biting my nails to the quick and praying for good news as the sound of gunfire fills the air again. Of course, I'm not even sure what "good news" would be anymore. With all the gunshots, it seems likely there have been casualties.

I chose this. I let this happen.

I slide both hands over my face and press my fingertips against my eyes. Is my life worth this? My son's freedom?

Another gunshot cracks the air, startling me. Xia rubs my back, poised by the radio. We're waiting for contact from Iris or Daw, but all the shots ringing out suggest they have their hands full.

I want a smoke, but my hands are shaking too bad to make one. Xia and I are hiding in the tree cover, with no line of sight on the entrance. The idea is, if we're needed, the time agents won't see us coming from under the trees. Unfortunately, our position makes it much harder to figure out what the hell is going on.

Xia thumps the top of the car. "Where the hell is Iris?"

A roar echoes through the forest, making me jump. I stiffen, recognizing the sound.

Xia tenses, biting her lip as her eyes go wide.

Pulse trip-hammering, I shake Xia's arm so she'll look at me. "Radio our people. Tell them to stay inside. Tell them to shelter in place. Even if that means they have to surrender to the Time Guard."

"*What*?"

"You *know* what happened last time we tried to wrangle with a carno unprepared. Send the damn message." Desperation spikes inside me, and I snatch for her radio to call our people myself.

She holds me off with one arm, glaring. "We need those time tubes. We can't just—"

Before she can finish, the forest ground shakes with a loud sound that rattles my bones: *thud, thud, thud*. Another roar echoes.

"Go!" I shove her toward the driver's side as I whirl to dive for the passenger side myself.

Xia blanches when she feels the vibrations rolling through the ground. She's done arguing. She hurls herself into the SUV and starts the engine. Seeing her haste, the other two members of our cohort throw themselves into the back seat.

The mama carnotaurus enters the clearing. Her head swings around, and I notice her mouth is bloody. Her nostrils quiver while she scents the air, and my skin prickles. She voices another roar as she charges toward me like the bull she was named for.

I slide into the passenger seat as the carnotaurus rams her head against the side of our vehicle. The SUV rocks and bobbles, but Xia's a pro. With nerves of steel, she revs the engine and yanks on the controls, throwing us nearly vertical into the air.

Behind us, the dinosaur vents a great bellow of frustration.

I let out a rattling breath between my teeth. "Well, that could have gone better."

Chapter Twenty-One

GRACE

The three of us keep running for about the first hour after we clear the research station, trying to put as much distance between us and the poachers as we can. As soon as Nakamura decides we might be deep enough in the forest to have lost any pursuit, he calls a halt. By this time, my skin is covered in a layer of sweat, my clothes soaked and sticking to my body.

Nakamura passes me our canteen without me asking. I nod silent thanks but carry it to Trifoso first. He's panting, unable to speak, and only nods before taking a deep swallow. He has enough restraint not to spill any of the water as he gulps it down, though. That's good. We don't have any to waste.

Trifoso is a fit man for his age, but we're setting a hard pace. His skin looks sallow, and he's pale around the mouth. After drinking, he collapses into the hollow of a giant tree's roots, bracing his spine against a large root and closing his eyes.

"Check the time tubes?" I ask Nakamura.

"Yeah." His mouth sets.

We sit together with crossed legs on the ground, guns to one side, tubes on the other, and he lifts the first tube for inspection. He runs his hands over it, checking for cracks. Even the smallest fracture means we're stuck here. The first one seems fine, but as soon as he lifts the second toward the sunlight we both swear. There's a visible crack down half the length of it.

Trifoso must be watching our body language. Once I spot the crack, he kneels beside us. "Is it bad?"

"Not good." Nakamura takes a deep breath through his teeth but otherwise keeps his impassive poker face in place.

My own panic is boiling like a hot pot, but I manage to get a question out without bursting into hysterical tears. "Backups?"

Before Nakamura can answer, Trifoso cuts in, his voice bouncing with hope. "The original lab. The old research station."

"Didn't it get torn down?" I ask.

"No."

"Does it have backup tubes?"

"No." Trifoso's voice wobbles on the end, close to a sob. He clears his throat, and his voice is stronger. "There might be spare parts for them, though. And that's where Agent Srinivasan and the others would probably head for safety."

I turn to Nakamura. "Is there any chance some of the others escaped the poachers? Any chance Srinivasan got through to the future to call for help?"

Nakamura's eyes narrow with some strong emotion, and he shakes his head. "Seems unlikely."

Trifoso grunts, like the words are a punch to the gut. "You don't know that. The other car was missing, after all."

A muscle tics in Nakamura's jaw, and he glares at Trifoso. "If someone had gotten through to the future, the Time Guard would be here. They can't interfere with events that have already happened, they can't *stop* the attack, but they can return to the literal moment after their informant left." He slaps his thigh in frustration. "If only the Time Guard had listened to us about the damn camera traps."

Trifoso draws himself up. "Are you blaming this whole thing on me? There wasn't compelling evidence—"

Nakamura cuts a hand through the air to stop Trifoso. "There's no point hashing all that out. What's done is done."

But Trifoso blusters on. "I don't like your attitude, Agent. And you're the ones who failed to find the poachers when they were squatting in our backyard. Or maybe you didn't *want* to find them." Trifoso's on his feet, fists clenched as he faces Nakamura. Trifoso has about a foot of height on him, but Nakamura is broad, brawny with muscles.

Ah, fuck, I was hoping the pissing match wouldn't start until, well, never.

But Nakamura doesn't rise to Trifoso's bait or the challenge. He just veils his eyes and stays crouched beside me. "My team did the best we could. I'm sorrier than I can say that it wasn't enough."

Before Trifoso can open his mouth again, I cut into the discussion. "So, the old lab sounds like the best option. It'll be a rallying point, and there'll be supplies if nothing else." I push to my feet and barely stagger at all when I stand. Nakamura slaps the canteen into my hand with a stern look, and this time I take a deep gulp.

"Fine, great. Let's just get there," Trifoso says.

Nakamura nods, half laughing under his breath. "If we don't get eaten first."

I pat his shoulder. "That's the spirit."

He snorts.

Trifoso rolls his eyes and shuffles past me. Nakamura catches his arm, yanking the other man back. I start forward, ready to intervene.

Trifoso shrugs Nakamura off, whirling with his fists raised. "Get your hands off m—"

"*Wait*. Look." With one boot, Nakamura toes aside some branches to reveal a giant hole ahead of us on the game trail. "A pit trap."

Trifoso deflates, but his jaw is clenched. "So? How do we get past the trap?"

Nakamura tilts his head, studying the ground, then points. "This way."

The three of us edge around the pit trap, following Nakamura's careful lead. As soon as we're past, Trifoso falls in step with me, grabbing my arm and picking our pace up so we're farther down the path than Nakamura.

"Do you trust him?" Trifoso's breath is harsh against my ear. "How did he see that trap? How could he possibly have known it was here?"

"Paul—"

"He's probably working with them. He's probably leading us to an ambush—"

"I noticed the brush was too heavy on the ground." Nakamura strolls up to us, easy as you please. "In my profession, I'm paid to be detail-oriented. To notice things. This way, Doc?"

I nod, and he gives me a crimped social smile then walks ahead of us, allowing us privacy if we want to keep talking about him.

Trifoso stumbles. We've barely started this trek, and he's already flagging, as if his tirade against Nakamura took the last of his strength. Looking at Trifoso, a familiar tightness starts in my chest. We've lost so many people on this damned, doomed expedition. I don't want to lose Trifoso too. Even if he is being an asshole.

As the three of us trudge through the forest, Nakamura trusts me enough to let me lead our column. Probably because I'm the only one who's actually been to the old research station.

With the heat of the day, moving is like swimming through warm, wet cotton. The hum of insects and the high chirrups of dinosaurs sound in the background, eerily similar to the sounds of a modern forest. I'm tired, aching, and we're all slowing down, but I'm still pushing hard. We can't afford to slow, to stop. A plant whips at my face, and I barely duck in time. Trifoso's shirt gets caught in a prickle bush, and Nakamura has to help me untangle him.

Ahead of us, the distinctive sound of a branch cracking shatters the quiet. I freeze, and the others hunch, hiding in the heavy ferns with me.

Nakamura mouths the word, *Where?*

There. I ease forward with my stolen gun. Nakamura follows, holding the handgun. Trifoso dawdles, pressing against a tree, swabbing his sweaty brow.

Crack. Another branch breaking. *Crack*, another. I exchange a worried look with Nakamura. Are the poachers *trying* to get our attention? Following the sounds, I peel aside a large fern leaf.

A family of troodons, Mama, Papa, and a clutch of five babies, huddle around a large insect hill. The adult troodons stand about waist-high to a human, eight feet long nose to tail, one hundred pounds each or so. The adults look a bit like giant roadrunners: fine-boned but fast, brown-striped feathers, wing-like arms, a menacing, sickle-shaped claw on each foot.

Mama Troodon balances a narrow branch with her feet and uses her snout to peel away the leaves, making a bare stick. The babies hop and wrestle each other, yellow-and-brown puffballs of down and manic energy.

"Do these guys eat people?" Nakamura whispers.

"They're troodons. Omnivores. They've attacked lone humans before and a group of us once when they felt threatened. But generally, no."

Nakamura raises an eyebrow. "And what were you doing to threaten them, Doc?"

"Measuring their eggs, counting their clutch. My moth—a colleague tried to take an egg to study. The parents objected."

Mama Troodon hands the pole to her mate. He sidles closer to the insect mound. The babies hop and chirp with excitement.

Nakamura grips my arm. "Time to go."

He's right, of course he is, but—"*Wait.*"

Papa slides the stick-tool into the hole. He fishes in the mound then draws the implement out. Hundreds of insects crawl along the wood. He holds the twig out so the babies can pluck the squirmy, fluttery bugs off to eat.

Watching this is like fireworks bursting inside me. Dazzling bright and beautiful. "*Tool use.*"

When I look over, Nakamura's staring at me, his pretty brown eyes warm. My cheeks heat—and from more than just the weather.

"What?" I ask.

Nakamura chuckles. "Making lemonade, Doc?"

I roll my eyes and give him a small shove. I try to stop smiling, but I have to bite my lip to do it.

Crack. Another branch breaks nearby, but it wasn't the troodons.

The dinosaur family freezes. Papa drops the pole, and Mama chivvies the babies into the ferns. One baby rushes back, pecking up bugs off the ground. Mama returns, scolding, and herds her little rebel away.

I freeze, holding my breath as Nakamura and I wait to see what's coming behind us.

Trifoso crawls into view, cracking another branch under his elbow as he does. When he sees the two of us, he looks like a harried parent who's finally found his lost child at the mall. "There you two are. Jesus."

I fight a hysterical laugh, swallowing it into a cough. Nakamura flicks a glance my way, his own eyes dancing.

Another branch snaps.

Trifoso flattens to the dirt, and we three crowd together, trying not to move. I close my eyes but force them open again as the sound of human voices reaches me.

Two poachers move through the trees. One of the poachers is Daw, who I remember from the garage, and the other is that beefy twenty-something blond guy who first burst into the research station.

Daw's got a fat lip and a cut on his eyebrow but seems otherwise unharmed.

The young guy steps on the troodons' abandoned fishing pole, snapping it under his boot. Bugs scurry away to avoid being crunched.

Daw glares at his partner. "Will you watch it? You might as well throw a parade."

"What's the plan when we find them?" the big guy asks.

"Boss said take them prisoner until we have the time tubes."

"The *boss* said." When I see the sly wink the big man shoots Daw, my skin prickles.

"Yeah." Daw snorts. "I say, if you get a shot, take it. We don't need them alive to get the tubes."

I shiver. Nakamura's nostrils flare beside me.

The younger poacher grins and follows Daw into the dense brush.

We wait until they're out of sight, moving in the opposite direction, then we return to the game trail and we *run*. We run until the light and our strength fail us.

Chapter Twenty-Two

JULIA

Once we manage to regroup after the carnotaurus attack, we split into groups and start searching the forest. Some on foot, some in cars. We search for hours, combing the woods, trying to find the scientists and the time tubes. No luck. And we have that relentless mama carnotaurus dogging our tracks every step of the way.

When the sun sets, we have to return to camp. I've got an itch under my skin thinking about those missing time tubes. I don't believe the scientists could have used them to go forward. If they had, then the Time Guard would have already descended on us. But if they haven't used the tubes yet, that probably means they were damaged somehow.

In which case we're all screwed, and I better start building my summer home here.

The sounds of camp settling for the night are usually soothing, homey: folks chatting over their nightcaps from a flask, the rustle of blankets, laughter between lovers, soft croons and croaks from the forest.

Tonight it's too quiet, as if the forest is still in shock from the violence it's seen. And, whenever a small sound does penetrate the oppressive silence, the noise scrapes my nerves raw.

I walk the perimeter of camp, staying in the circle of light from our fire, but not close enough to be drawn into a conversation. The farther I go, the fewer people there are. No one likes to go toward the cages—especially after today. No one but me.

Moonlight gleams on the bars of the large cage, mostly hidden in the shadows of the trees. The only other light in this part of camp is the flashlight I brought with me. We still have the sonic fencing, though, so I should be safe enough outside the firelight.

As I approach the cage, the *clink* of chain links reaches my ears, and the sounds of a large animal breathing. The dinosaur puffs and twitters under his breath like a frightened bird.

I shine my flashlight over him, admiring the pattern of short spikes along his sides, the beautiful striping pattern of his scales. I used to dream about being this close to a dinosaur as a girl. Now, here I am, breathing the same air as one. Keeping this magnificent creature in a cage. On a chain.

I pat my pockets, looking for smoke fixings. I'm running low, and we obviously can't make a supply run until we get the time tubes. Maybe I have some in my tent.

"Julia, you *know* you shouldn't be over here. It's dangerous." Xia's voice.

I abandon my search and nod toward our baby boy in the cage. "Not a fan of the breed?"

"I just want to get him delivered to our customers. Although, after today—" She breaks off, looking at me out of the corners of her eyes.

"What?"

"*Maybe we should dump the cargo*," Xia says. In Mandarin. A sure sign she doesn't want most of the others to know what we're saying. The only other person in camp who understands Mandarin is one of the younger women, Yao, Xia's niece. "*We don't have the time tubes to transport it,*" Xia continues, "*and every day we try to hold the animals, it gets more dangerous. We already know his mother is tracking us."*

I cluck my tongue. *"We don't know that was the same female. Could have been a coincidence."* A comforting lie, but Xia's so rattled it has me nervous.

She snorts. *"You've studied these animals—"*

"Not carnotaurus. Not specifically."

She waves her hand. *Details.* "You know dinosaurs. You know how obnoxiously smart they can be. Hell, we had to stop capturing troodons altogether because they would pick the cage locks."

"Troodons are *exceptionally* smart." There was even a theory about tool use—I shake my head and take another long drag. "Any sign of your mole?"

"No sign. So much for the mole waiting with open arms for us." Xia's mouth quirks, but she accepts my subject change. "Meg Zaran *is* dead, though. We found her body in the lab. It looked like scavengers had gotten to her. Just like the mole said."

I shiver. "Your spy seems pretty dangerous." An unsettling thought. If the mole is willing to kill a time agent, they probably won't hesitate to kill one of our people.

Xia folds her arms, like she's steeling herself, and holds my gaze. "Julia, we have to talk. There were some casualties today among our folks."

The night's warm, uncomfortably so, but my skin is chilled now, clammy. "How many?"

"That stampede spread us all pretty far, but everyone who's alive has reported in probably. Three people are missing. Iris is one of them."

"Iris?" My throat goes thick with emotion. Iris Harris is a good kid, smart, reminds me of—*Don't.* "Have we found any remains?"

Xia swallows. "Yes, one body near the entrance to the lab. There wasn't much... It's probably Iris."

My eyes sting with water. "We were too slow. We needed those tubes. Daw was right." I bite the words out.

"No—"

"We should have done the raid sooner. As soon as our tubes broke."

She rubs my shoulders gently.

I want to lean into her, forget, but if I fall apart, I'll never be able to put myself together again. And I still have too much work to do, and the faint, dying hope we can finish this damn run successfully. I shrug her hand off. "How long until sunrise?"

"A few more hours," she murmurs.

"First light, we're going out?"

"That's right. And, Julia, worst case, but we might have to... Well. There are two time agents unaccounted for, and they aren't likely to surrender easy. We're on borrowed time. Are you okay with what we might have to do?"

I flinch, my stomach roiling. "You want my permission? This is your show."

Xia holds my gaze. "I want to know you won't hesitate to do what we need you to do." She circles her hand to take in the camp, the rest of the group that managed to make it. "For your son?"

I hiss my breath out. "Low blow, Xia." But she's right. This is my crew. The people who've been watching my back in the forest for two years. And this is the side that can get my son his freedom.

I slump my shoulders. This isn't what I wanted, but I guess this is what I signed up for when I decided 'yo-ho, yo-ho, a criminal's life for me.' "You can count on me." The words burn coming out of my mouth, like I've eaten something acrid.

Xia cradles my face in her hands. "That's all I need to know. Come sleep in my tent—just sleep. It'll be a long day tomorrow."

Shit, it's been a long *year*, but I fall in step behind her. She's right; I don't want to be alone tonight.

Just to cap our already awful day, another storm starts before we make it to her tent, and we're freezing and dripping when we climb inside.

Xia has the talent for falling asleep fast in all kinds of conditions—including with wet hair, her head pillowed on my shoulder. I'm not so lucky, and I spend I don't know how long staring at the top seam of the tent, my mind whirling with all the ways things could go wrong.

Xia traces a hand against my cheek without opening her eyes. "Sleep, Jules. Worry tomorrow."

She's right. Who knows what tomorrow will hold? Although I'm pretty sure it's going to suck.

Chapter Twenty-Three

GRACE

Right before sunset the storm front that's been threatening all day rolls in like an avenging god. Lightning flashes in the sky. The clouds grumble. It starts slow with a small *tic tic* against the leaves and plops in the dirt. Then, as if someone has turned the tap to full, water pours out of the sky, and all of us are drenched.

The water's as warm as a shower. It feels good against my skin, cleansing away the dirt and sweat. I tilt my head and open my mouth to take the water in. When I glance over, my gaze catches with Nakamura's. There's a laugh line tucked in the corner of his mouth. My skin heats, tingling with physical awareness of him.

I shiver and look away. Not the time or the place. Anyway, I have shit judgment when it comes to men. Best to avoid the breed altogether.

Trifoso's been holding our canteen up to catch the rain. Once he's got it full, he glances between Nakamura and me, his eyes narrowed. With a grunt, Trifoso stomps past me, knocking a big leaf over and splashing rainwater all down his shoulders. He shivers and tries to shake the water off. "Perfect. Marvelous," he mutters.

Nakamura slicks his wet hair out of his face. "We should stop."

"I agree," I say.

Trifoso sags against a tree, looking haggard. I wish we had better medical supplies, proper shelter. And time tubes that work. I snort. Might as well wish for a pony, too, at this rate.

The trees are tall enough, lush enough, when we huddle together under the big ones we don't get too wet. I hate to stay in one place too long. Hate it. But we can't blunder around in the dark, especially when some of the big predators will be out and about at sunset, looking for dinner. The rain should give us a short reprieve, but I don't want to push our luck.

Anyway, Trifoso doesn't have much juice left, I can tell. If we keep pushing, then odds are good I'll only end up getting him killed.

We crouch shoulder to shoulder, passing the canteen and a couple ration bars from the pack I stole from the poachers' car. You always pack at least seven days' worth of supplies when you go into the field. Anything can and does happen, so it's best to be prepared. Good for us that the poachers followed this common sense. Still, these supplies won't last long feeding three people.

I dig one last foil-wrapped item out of the bag and huff at the sight of a candy bar.

"What?" Nakamura asks.

"It's my favorite kind." My mouth starts watering just thinking about the sweet chocolate, the thickness of caramel against my tongue, the crunch of nuts. There's only one bar, though. What kind of monster packs only one candy bar for fieldwork?

I clear my throat and glance at the other two. "Split it?"

Trifoso waves my offer away, still hunched over trying to catch his breath.

Nakamura clucks his tongue. "I'm not big on chocolate. You go ahead, Doc."

I don't care if he's doing it to boost my morale or because he pities me or what—I wolf that candy down in three bites and hum with happiness at the chocolate on my tongue. I should've saved some for tomorrow, but it's been a bitch of a day, and I don't have the self-control for that right now.

Nakamura gives a slow chew of his gluey rat bar as he watches the forest. "Why aren't we seeing more dinosaurs?"

"This area's had a lot of action recently. The gunfight. The stampede. It probably scared the animals out of the immediate area. But they'll return soon. And they'll probably be hungry."

Nakamura scoffs. "Paranoia. Such a charming quality in you, Doc."

I roll my eyes. "Anyway, there *are* some dinosaurs around."

Nakamura freezes, rat bar halfway to his mouth. "Yeah?"

I laugh and point to a tree across from our shelter. In the foliage, a flock of small birdlike dinosaurs, turkey sized, are clustered on a low branch, huddled for warmth like us. About the size of peacocks (but without the fabulous tails), these guys are heavily feathered on their arms and serpentine tails, with black coloring around their faces and cream-and-brown striped feathers on the rest of their bodies.

Nakamura chews and swallows. "Those are dinosaurs?"

"Velociraptors."

"*Those?*"

"Yes."

"*Those* are velociraptors?"

"Yup. Full-grown adults, too, judging by their plumage."

"Huh." Nakamura cocks his head sideways. "Velociraptors. Not as advertised. Do they taste like chicken?"

"You can't eat them, Nakamura. Prehistoric bacteria don't play well with modern human digestion."

He narrows his eyes, still considering. "Dunno. Might be worth it not to have to live on rat bars."

"'Scuse me." Trifoso pushes to his feet, walking toward the forest.

"Paul?"

"I need to piss, Grace. Stop fussing."

I close my mouth with a click of teeth. If I'm coddling him, it's only because he looks like shit. But I don't say that. And I don't stop him going off to pee in private. I notice him holding the canteen up in the rain to refill it again.

Nakamura breaks off part of his granola bar to give to me. "You handled yourself well. Before. You don't panic, do you?"

I tear the wrapper of my own finished ration bar, fidgeting. "Oh, I do. But I've got an anxiety disorder. I'm used to panicking at having to make a phone call. I have very specific triggers, and getting attacked by poachers isn't one of them." I try to laugh, but it comes out more choked than I want, and my face starts burning. My anxiety attacks aren't usually something I tell people about. Especially in a professional setting. But a full day running for our lives has pretty much obliterated whatever professional boundaries I might have had.

Fortunately, Trifoso saves me further embarrassment as he returns. "You two shouldn't talk so much. It'll attract the animals." Trifoso nudges me with his elbow, jerking his chin toward the tree line. "Take a walk, Grace? I thought I saw some interesting remains of a troodon nest over there."

I frown, but the look on his face tells me I shouldn't say no. As we stand to walk away, I notice Trifoso oh-so-carelessly lifting the knapsack with all the supplies up to his own shoulder. Nakamura notices, too, but just shakes his head as my boss leads me by the elbow into the forest.

We go only far enough so Nakamura can't hear us, but Trifoso makes sure to keep the other man in sight through the leaves. He draws me to the ground, perhaps to maintain the illusion we're looking at a nest. "We need to get away from this guy, Grace. You know he could be the one who killed Meg."

I rear back, startled. "*What?*"

"It *had* to be one of the time agents. Nothing else makes sense."

My head is aching. "Nakamura hasn't done anything to make us distrust him." *Yet*.

The brush crunches, and Nakamura pushes a leaf away to look at the two of us. "You two, on the other hand," he drawls, "are making *me* downright paranoid.

How do I know you two aren't working with the poachers, planning to turn me in?"

The men square up to each other again. And they're both idiots as far as I'm concerned. I push to my feet. "We have more important things to worry about than this infectious suspicion. Nakamura, no one is planning to kill you in your sleep. Paul, we need all the help we can get in the forest, and you know it. We can sort out the rest later."

Trifoso grunts, but I can tell by the way he's clenching his jaw he knows I'm right. Nakamura's smile is all teeth as he glares at Trifoso. I jab the agent in the gut to get his attention. "What are we doing about predators tonight?"

Nakamura's tension immediately ratchets down. He shrugs. "Trees are the safest bet tonight. Doc?"

"Yeah."

Trifoso swallows loud enough I can hear him. "Trees?"

Before I can stop myself, I look to Nakamura. He nods, letting me know that he'll help me with Trifoso if necessary.

Seeing this, Trifoso squares his shoulders and walks briskly toward the nearest tree, muttering, "*Trees,*" darkly under his breath.

It's not graceful but we all manage to get up in the tree. I take first watch, cradling a gun. We rig a sling sort of thing for the time tubes, and Trifoso has charge of those because he's not great with a weapon. We figure it's better for Nakamura to have quick draw capabilities, and he's willing to trust us enough with the time tubes to let Trifoso keep them. All of us tie ourselves to the tree so we don't fall off while we sleep.

I've got caffeine pills in my knapsack, and I pop several with no compunction. The poachers won't be looking for us in the dark—it's too dangerous—but the night-hunters of the forest will be.

The rain keeps animals away at first, but then, a few hours into my watch, the rain slows to a drizzle. Branches rustle all around me, the wind through leaves. High-pitched, chilling animal calls sound in the night.

When my watch is over, I lean toward the lower branches, trying to keep my voice low. "Paul!" No good. I can hear snoring from the lower branches, and I'm pretty sure it's Trifoso. "Paul, it's your watch. Paul!"

"He's out cold, Doc." Nakamura's voice floats up to me in the darkness, a warm baritone drawl. "And he needs the rest."

Branches rustle and Nakamura climbs to perch on the thick branch beside me. I can only see bits of him in the darkness, moonlight sliding over his arms and face. "I can take the extra watch, Doc. I've slept, and, uh, I think I'll handle missing sleep tomorrow better than you."

Such a gentleman. He means he's younger and in better shape than me, and the annoying thing is it's absolutely true. Every muscle I have has been twinging and aching all night, and my eyelids are so heavy I'm scared I'll nod off midword. But I've got Trifoso's voice echoing in my head, too, that Nakamura might not be entirely trustworthy. Someone had to have been working for the poachers, or why was Meg dead? The fact I desperately didn't *want* it to be Nakamura didn't mean he was safe.

"Did you fall asleep on me, Doc?"

I laugh under my breath. "Just contemplating things."

"Ah." The branches creak as he shifts his weight. "Can I make the argument you might as well trust me as not?"

"But why?"

"If I wanted either or both of you dead, you'd be dead. And if I'd killed Meg, no one would've found her body." His voice is dead level as he speaks, and the hair rises on my arms.

For perhaps the first time, it sinks in for me how dangerous Nakamura is, how easily he could probably dispatch me and Trifoso and tell any story he likes. I shiver. "Your argument is I should trust you because you haven't killed us yet? Oh, and I should have more faith in your hypothetical murdering skills?"

He claps a hand over his mouth to stifle a laugh. "Shit, Doc, when you put it like that..."

The animal calls of the forest stop, and I freeze, listening, straining with every muscle.

Nakamura babbles on, oblivious to the stillness, "Okay, try it this way: I need you and your Dr. Trifoso alive. If dinosaurs start chasing me, and you two aren't around, who am I going to trip?"

"*Shh!*"

"I was joking."

"Shut up."

Nakamura finally notices it too. The waiting anticipation of the darkness.

Heavy feet pound through the brush. A monumental shadow moves in the blackness and stops beneath our tree.

I can smell her now. Old blood and rotting meat and the stink of wild animal: a bit like a wet dog magnified times a thousand. I hold my breath as Nakamura gags beside me. The giant carnotaur, my infamous "Lady C." has found our tree. I can hear her moving beneath me, brush crunching under her feet, her scaled skin brushing against the leaves. If I close my eyes, I know I'll flash back to hiding with Adam, waiting for her to leave, waiting to stumble home to our lab so I could destroy my own life. Turn my husband in.

You know your life is shit when washing all the blood off isn't even the worst part of your day.

I shake my head, pushing the memories down. Why is Lady C. here? Has she found us, or are we just unlucky enough to be stuck in her territory?

Her head lies just below Trifoso's branch. I can still hear him snoring.

Lady C. shifts, freezing. She breathes in deeply, a rumble of sound, then *sniff, sniff*.

My hands are slick against the gun, and my chest feels tight.

I jump as Nakamura's palm slides over my forearm. His fingertips follow my bones up to my hand, leaving a trail of goose bumps behind. As if he's reading my frightened thoughts, he squeezes my closed fist. Gently. Carefully. *It's okay, Doc.* I hear the words as clearly as if he's said them aloud.

I steal a quiet breath and take one hand off the gun to press his fingers. *Thank you.* Without hesitation, I pass him the gun, then I pluck a football-sized pinecone off the tree by my head. Winding back my arm, I throw and release the pinecone in a perfect spiral. It sails over the trees to crash through the foliage sixty yards away. Lady C.'s head whips around, following the movement. She runs off to chase the pinecone-football.

"Touchdown," Nakamura whispers. "Nice arm, slick."

"Thanks."

Nakamura catches my hand to press it again. I can't even see his expression but just imagining warmth there, admiration, even half the things I'm feeling for him—my face heats in a blush I am *so grateful* he can't see.

In the branches beneath us, Trifoso lets out a loud snore.

What am I doing? I jerk my hand free from Nakamura's. "Okay. You take next watch," I whisper, letting him keep hold of the gun. I untie my safety straps and climb to a higher branch. Immediately, a chill wind whips us, dancing over my skin, raising gooseflesh along my arms. I curl into myself and try to go to sleep.

I wake once in the night, late. I turn my head, rubbing at my eyes, trying to figure out what woke me. A grunt or something? Branches and leaves rustling? Is that what my pre-waking brain remembers?

Maybe it was just an extra loud snore from Trifoso? The night is quiet, and my brain is sodden with weariness. I close my eyes and fall asleep again.

"Grace." Someone's shaking me. I try to roll away, digging my face into the skin of my arms. "*Grace.*" Trifoso's voice, low urgent.

"No." I come up hard against my safety straps, and Trifoso's fingers dig into my arm as he stops me from falling out of our tree.

Adrenaline buzzes through me as I roll back, trying not to look at the twenty-foot drop to the forest floor.

"Grace." Trifoso's face is grave.

"What?" I scrub my hands over my eyes. Thirsty, groggy, and I have to pee, I start unbuckling my safety straps, ready to be out of this goddamn tree.

"Grace." Trifoso stops me and puts a hand under my chin to make me meet his eyes. "Nakamura's gone."

"*What?*"

Chapter Twenty-Four

GRACE

"Nakamura is gone," Trifoso says. "He took the spare gun and part of the food sometime in the night. He's gone." We're at the bottom of the tree, going through what supplies are left to us.

I shake my head, staring at the rations, at the gun we still have, at the time tubes. "This doesn't make any sense." A rumble sounds in the distance, echoing my inner tumult. Thunder? Or a thunder lizard? The morning sky is gray and miserable. I can taste the coming rain on the air, and my clothes are still damp in places from yesterday's storm.

"It makes perfect sense, Grace. I warned you. I can't believe you trusted him to take a watch."

I glare at Trifoso. "You don't get to judge me for sharing the load. You know you're not in top condition. If I'm supposed to get you out of this, I need to lean on Nakamura."

Trifoso looks away, his face twisting. "I can handle myself fine. I'm much better today."

I'd already noticed how stiffly he was moving when we climbed down the tree, and he still hasn't managed to catch his breath. I rake my fingers through my hair and stare again at the supplies assembled on our blankets. Something's poking at my brain, a wrongness I can't pinpoint— "The tubes."

"What?"

"Why wouldn't he take the tubes? They're his only way home."

"They're broken."

"Broken tubes are better than nothing. He's Time Guard. He must know the fatality stats on travelers who get separated from their time tubes. He wouldn't walk away from a set willingly." I hate where this train of thought is pointing, hate to even say the words. I've known Paul Trifoso for years and yet...I swallow and quietly ask, "What did you do to him?"

"I can't believe you'd ask that." Trifoso draws himself up and makes a great show of looking indignant. But he holds my gaze too long, and his hands are fidgety. If he'd had nothing to do with Nakamura's disappearance, he'd be angrier. Frustrated. Not awkward like this.

My mouth is dry, my stomach roiling. I've trusted Trifoso implicitly because he was my boss, my mentor, my old friend. Have I made a horrible mistake?

More rumbling starts in the distance. Definitely thunder this time. Dry lightning cracks the sky.

Trifoso glares at me. "We don't need him. And it was only a matter of time before he turned on us."

My stomach swoops in an ugly mix of shock and disgust. "So you turned on him first?" I press a hand over my eyes, too tired, hungry, and worn down for this. "Did you kill him?" I whisper.

"No!"

The anger on his face makes me believe he's telling the truth. At last. He's still sputtering. "I can't believe you would even—"

"Where is he, Paul?"

Trifoso flexes his jaw then spits out, "I had some of my sleeping pills left, so I dosed the canteen and gave it to him."

Sleeping pills. Srinivasan had fallen asleep on watch too. I retreat another step from Trifoso.

Oblivious, he continues talking, "After Nakamura passed out from the pills, I hauled him away from here and lashed him to a tree with his belt. I left him a gun and some rat bars. I don't want him dead, Grace. I just don't want him with *us*."

"You drugged and tied up an innocent man, alone, in this forest. A shot to the head would have been more humane, and you know it!" I start repacking the supplies, my heart hammering. "Do you remember where you left him?"

"Why?"

"So I can cut him loose, you asshole. If he's still alive." Tears burn in my eyes, which just makes me angrier. My hands tremble as I pack our supplies together. Another ugly thought has taken hold, so ugly I can't even look at him. "Did you do it, Paul? Did you murder Meg?"

"*What?*"

"Those damned pills of yours! Did you slip one to Srinivasan so you could off Meg?"

His mouth works, open and closed, like a fish flopping on dry land. "I—I don't count my pills, Grace. Anyone could've taken one. And I only had them on me during the station attack because I didn't want anyone finding them during the room search. It's—it's nobody's business."

He means it's not *Time Guard* business. "Paul, I don't—"

The brush rustles. We freeze, but then one of the troodon babies shoots out of the trees, lashing its tail and scolding in indignation before disappearing again.

Trifoso puffs out a relieved laugh, but I'm frowning. I bend to grab the gun.

Six black-clad poachers burst out of the trees, two moving on me and the rest heading for Trifoso.

The gun's too far, so I grab for a tree branch and swing it at the nearest poacher, the petite Asian girl from the lab yesterday. I connect and her head snaps back. Blood pours from her nose.

Someone rams into me from behind, knocking me forward. Huge arms band around my chest, constricting my air. "That was my girlfriend, you bitch." He squeezes harder, pushing all the air out of me.

The other poachers have already subdued Trifoso. He's on the ground between them with a bloody nose.

The man from yesterday, Daw, comes sauntering out of the tree line. "Let the lady breathe, Quint."

With a grunt of annoyance, the younger man, Quint, loosens his grip on me. I gulp in air and cough, but my vision clears.

Trifoso pushes up on his knees. "Who are you people?"

"Unhappy neighbors." Daw gives a hunted, worried look at the forest. "Where's the rest of you? Where's the time agent?"

"He's making a coffee run," I grunt.

"I sure hope he doesn't forget the creamer again," Trifoso puts in.

Daw's mouth twists. "That's fine. We'll get him."

I snort. "And my little dog too?"

"Still the same tasteless sense of humor, I see," a new voice calls out from the brush.

Hearing that voice, every muscle in my body stiffens with shock. Medusa might as well have walked up. All I can do is stare as the other woman walks into the clearing. She's tall, pushing sixty, too skinny, but it's all wiry muscle. Her tanned skin is weathered from a lifetime spent in the sun. Her hair, which she used to wear in a braid down to her butt, is close-cropped in a bob, the color of silvery salt and pepper, with more salt than pepper. Cold brown eyes meet mine, and the muscles in her face twitch with tension—with raw emotion—as she studies me.

My own face is numb. All of me feels numb. "Hello, Julia."

"Dr. Carson?" Trifoso gasps.

"What?" I say and, at the same time, the other woman—my ex-mother-in-law Dr. Julia Carson—says, "Yes?"

Julia and I look at each other. I don't know about her, but I'm remembering all the other times that happened after I married Adam. We used to laugh about it. Oh God. *Julia*.

Trifoso is still sputtering, in shock maybe. "Dr. Carson—*Julia*. Julia, *you're alive?*" He pushes to his feet and starts forward, his face furious. "You let us believe you were dead! We had a memorial. We named a scholarship after you."

Julia's mouth twists. "Thank you?"

Trifoso's guards haul him away. Not gently.

"What are you doing here, Dr. Carson?" I ask, resigned, sad.

Like a dam breaking, Julia's face contorts, seething with rage. She slaps me, and fire erupts along my cheek. I taste blood. She slaps me again, and my head snaps the other way. Both sides of my face are throbbing. The man holding my shoulders releases me, and I fall weak-kneed to the ground.

"You dumb bitch." She spits at the ground in front of me. Her hands are shaking. "Why couldn't you stay away?"

I stare at her, and we share another long look—long and painful as having your heart wrung out like a wet dishrag. *Julia*. She's working with the poachers. She's one of the people who's been chasing us through the forest with guns. "What the hell are you doing, Dr. Carson?" I don't ask what happened because I know. She's here because of Adam. I actually mourned this woman. I *missed* her. And now this. *This?*

I grind my teeth, but one feels loose, so I stop. My whole body is trembling. "Adam doesn't deserve this kind of loyalty, Julia."

"Shut your fucking mouth, Grace." She turns away from me, face scrunched, heading toward Daw.

"Julia?" It's the meathead, Quint, who tried to juice my guts out.

"What?" Julia says.

"What are we doing with them now we have the tubes?"

"Wait for Xia."

"Why wait?" Daw levels his gun at Trifoso's head. Trifoso swallows.

A ripple passes over Julia's face. Remorse? Grief? She stares at Trifoso then looks hurriedly away. "No. We'll bring them to camp."

I let my breath out through my teeth. Trifoso looks like he might pass out.

"But—"

"*I said bring them.* You don't want to fuck something else up, do you, Daw?" Julia snaps. "And we keep looking for the others—"

Gunfire erupts from the tree line, kicking up dirt right in front of Julia. She stumbles, and the other poachers scatter.

I roll to my feet, sweeping the tree branch up with me. I swing it hard and connect with the head of one of the guys holding Trifoso. The man goes down. Trifoso tackles his female guard at the knees then slithers forward and gathers the time tubes in his arms. I haul him to his feet as more gunshots sound and we run hard for the trees.

Chapter Twenty-Five

JULIA

Daw takes careful aim at Trifoso. Gut clenching, I knock his arm upward just as he fires. He wheels on me, his face furious.

"*Alive*, Daw. We want them alive." At his incredulous look, I wet my lips. "At least until we know what's wrong with their time tubes. We might need hostages to bargain with."

A bullet zooms between us, dead center in the tree trunk. We drop to the ground and crawl under cover. My heart is trying to punch its way out of my ribs. The bullet missed me by inches, and Daw too. "This guy's a lousy shot," I murmur.

"Or a very good one."

"Get those prisoners!" I yell to the rest of the crew. "Alive! And be careful with the time tubes!"

———

GRACE

I'm running as hard as I can, my muscles on fire, my throat burning.

Trifoso puffs behind, holding his ribs, flailing. I keep checking to make sure he's not too far behind me. "Where... are we... going?" he asks.

"Away!" I round a bend on the game trail.

My throat connects with something. I sputter, choking, and fall, hitting the ground. The big poacher, Quint, steps out from behind a tree. He actually cracks his knuckles as he glares at me.

Trifoso throws himself on Quint, trying to get him in a choke hold. Trifoso is the same height as the poacher, but the younger man has about a hundred pounds on him. Quint's built like a tank.

I roll over, pushing onto my hands and knees, trying to catch my breath, too dizzy to stand.

Quint elbows Trifoso's ribs. Once. Twice. Trifoso falls, crying out, holding his side.

Still on the ground, I swing my branch at Quint's boots and knock his legs out from under him as he starts toward me. Quint rolls fast, though, and pins me. I wriggle under his weight, gasping.

Quint lurches off me. I crane upward to see Trifoso grab Quint's leg, trying to yank the man off. Quint lashes out, and Trifoso's head snaps back as a foot connects with his mouth.

Without hesitating, I rake my nails over Quint's cheek, and the skin opens under my hand, drawing blood. Quint howls in pain and swings his arm toward me. My head snaps sideways from his backhanded blow. My skull knocks against the ground. The world goes fuzzy. My face throbs in time to my heartbeat.

Quint pins my hands with one of his and hauls me to stand. The poacher kicks Trifoso again—a casual blow, an afterthought. "A little help here!" Quint calls out. "Julia! Daw, where are—"

Clunk. A sound like tapping a watermelon. Quint's eyes roll into his head. He drops to the ground—

And there's Nakamura, grinning in triumph after wielding the rifle butt on Quint's hard head. "Hiya, Doc."

I cradle my face and spit blood. Two of my teeth feel loose now. "Paul, are you all right?" I crawl past Nakamura toward Trifoso, helping him sit up. "Paul?"

"I'm all right. It just hurts." Trifoso winces as he sits up.

Nakamura, meanwhile, has tied Quint up with his own belt and shoelaces. He's also stripped the poacher of his knife, gun, and extra ammo. He stands apart from Trifoso and me, watchful and waiting.

I clear my throat. "Glad to see you're okay."

Nakamura's gaze flicks to Trifoso, who's still wheezing on the ground. "Did you know what he was planning, Dr. Carson?"

"No—"

"She didn't." Trifoso sits on his haunches, one hand pressed to his side. "I didn't tell her. I didn't trust she'd help me."

Nakamura looks at me, giving a small nod to acknowledge this. He's still tense and glowering, though, and truly I don't know what to say. How do you apologize when someone left you for dead in the forest?

"Thank you for coming to help us," I whisper.

Trifoso tugs on my hand. "Grace, we need to run."

As if God was waiting for his cue, a rainstorm starts. Torrential, biblical rain. Bit excessive. Is God having a bad day? Or just pissed at us?

I help Trifoso to stand and let him lean on my shoulder. He can barely walk.

"I'll take him, Doc." Nakamura crosses closer. Pauses. Frowns. He reaches for my cheek then stops himself.

"What?"

"Your face."

"The poacher hit me—although Paul got the worst of it," I murmur. "My moth—the other Dr. Carson took a crack at me too."

Nakamura's eyes go hard, like stone, and he turns on Quint. The poacher stirs as the first of the raindrops hit his face. He opens his eyes, blinking. Groggy. "Wha... what happened?"

Nakamura grins, friendly-like, then punches Quint in the head. Quint goes down like a rock. Goodbye, Quint. Sweet dreams. Fuck you very much.

Nakamura loops Trifoso's arm over his own shoulder, taking the weight off me. "Let's go."

From the forest, a familiar roar sounds: Lady C.

The other bitch is back.

I duck under Trifoso's shoulder opposite Nakamura. "Let's hurry."

JULIA

Grace Carson. Grace bloody Carson. Nothing's gone right in my life since that damn girl came into it. I wish I'd given the order to have her killed when I had the chance. Or rejected her grad school application when I'd had that chance. That might be a smarter wish.

Dr. Trifoso, though. I'd rather not have Paul's blood on my hands. If it comes down to it, I'd rather not have Grace's blood on my hands either, but needs must drive.

Xia and I stand together under a tree. We're still mostly dry, although the forest around us might as well be underwater. Xia presses her radio to her ear to hear over the rain.

"... rain washed the tracks out," one of our people, Yao, yells from the other end of the radio.

"They're tired," Xia says. "They don't know this terrain like we do. Find them."

The carnotaurus roar echoes through the brush, like the pistol shot starting a race.

Xia darts an uneasy look around then signs off, "Command out."

"Yes, ma'am. Wilco. Team Two out."

Xia clips the radio to her belt and turns to me. "What do you want to do, Jules?"

Seeing Trifoso rattled me. It was probably naïve to hope I could go from academic to career criminal to cold-blooded killer without some significant growing pains. "You heard that roar. Mama's home and on the war path."

Xia plants her hands on her hips, her brow furrowed. "We still need their time tubes."

I let out a shuddering breath, my nerves jittering. "People got eaten yesterday playing tag in the forest with those scientists."

"Can you come up with a better way to get out of here?"

"No." Another roar sounds, and a cluster of birdlike dinos shoot out of the trees—*Hesperonychus?*—nearly clipping some of our people's heads before they glide away. "We do need those time tubes."

"Then let's go get them." She cups the back of my neck, and her face softens. "It doesn't have to be you. I mean, you don't have to be there if we—when we..."

I shrug her off. "Let's worry about the tubes. We can decide what to do with the people later."

Chapter Twenty-Six

JULIA

Our crew moves methodically through the downpour, guns out, scanning every nook and crevice of the terrain on the game trail. Xia pushes away a heavy leaf, and the startled velociraptor who was sheltered there flees into the forest. Ahead of me, Xia's boots crunch over a mat of branches. One branch falls through a hole in the mat.

—*ℓℓ*—

GRACE

I'm huddled with the others, holding my breath. All of us are covered head to toe in mud—camouflage. Water pools at my feet and continues to rise with the constant pouring of the rain.

An errant branch falls through the screen over the top of our hole and lands with a muted splash.

Nakamura's hand twitches around his gun, but he doesn't fire.

My body is stiff, cramping from standing so unnaturally still for so long, but we don't dare move. Only my eyes move—looking up.

More footsteps sound above us, and I worry my heart might shatter my rib cage it's pumping so hard.

JULIA

I toe another branch through the hole then squint to watch it fall.

GRACE

The branches creak above us, and I can see the shadow of someone standing on the edge of the pit. I roll my shoulders, readying my gun. My hands are surprisingly steady considering I'm about to shoot someone—

JULIA

I sidestep to avoid falling through a crack. "Watch your step, guys—"

GRACE

"—this is one of our pit traps." It's Julia's voice.

My finger tenses against the trigger.

Trifoso closes his eyes, shaking, mouthing wordless prayers.

I wet my lips.

"Walk around the trap this way," I hear Julia call out. Followed by the unmistakable sounds of the poachers moving away: the crunch of branches and the suck of mud from above as they walk.

I hold my breath and silently wait until all sounds of the poachers' movements fade. After ten minutes, I just about collapse to the ground once I lower my gun. My poor body must be out of adrenaline by now. "I could really do with some lemonade anytime now."

"Well," Nakamura drawls, "I got a fresh batch of lemons here anytime you're ready to start juicing."

"What?" Trifoso frowns.

An actual giggle—probably half hysteria—breaks from my mouth.

Nakamura's dimple flashes.

I shake the fey mood away. "What do we do now?" With a grim laugh, I itch at my muddy face. "I don't suppose you have some Super Secret Time Guard Device hidden up your sleeve that can get us all home?"

"Not at the moment." Nakamura flashes me a grin. "But if you can get me to your old lab, I do have a spare set of time tubes there."

"*What?*"

He has just enough shame in him to look embarrassed. "When they decommissioned your old lab, they left the security intact and set it up as a check-in point and supply dump for time agents."

The breath's knocked out of me, but it's good for once. We won't have to rely on our cracked time tubes, after all. For the first time, I believe we have a real chance of making it home. Still, there's a flare of anger in there too. "Why didn't you tell us sooner?"

"Well, when someone killed my boss and fed her to a bunch of scavengers, it didn't leave me in a real trusting mood. Especially once the shooting started. And other things." Nakamura snorts and casts a dry look at Trifoso.

I wince. Fair.

The rain increases. Fat droplets fall through the screen of branches overhead. A stream of water gushes into our pit from above, and Trifoso jumps to his feet to get away. Coughing, he cries out in sudden pain from the movement, holding his side. I cross, ducking under his shoulder to steady him.

His eyes are pinched tight. "Poacher broke my ribs."

More water courses down the sides of the hole. The water level rises to waist-height.

"We should get out of here," I murmur.

Nakamura wades his way over to me, circling his arms wide as he walks to get momentum. "Okay, Doc. You first."

"Age before beauty?" I quip. "Oh, all right."

Nakamura cups his palms, and I brace my hands on his shoulders to jump. *One... two...* he boosts me up like a cheerleader. I dig my fingers deep into the wet wall, trying to find a hold. A clump of mud and roots falls apart in my hand, but my other fingers find purchase in a relatively dry patch. I inch higher.

Water slams into me from above, swatting me off the wall like an ant. My limbs sting as I hit the pool of water and bump the bottom of the pit. Nakamura must have tried to catch me because his limbs knock against me as we both thrash to stand up.

I break the surface and spit muddy water out. "*Shit.*"

Nakamura stares upward. "We could wait the storm out. The water might rise high enough we can climb out. Like a pool."

I shake my head. "Or the water might rise high enough we *can't* get out and we drown."

Trifoso presses against the wall, his voice is whistling, shallow. "And then there are the dinosaurs."

Nakamura blinks then pushes away from the wall, moving toward me. "Okay, Doc, let's get you up that wall."

The water pummeling my head gets worse, and I look up to see the branches above us move aside. Water falls straight on my face. The poacher girl, the young Asian one, stands there with her gun pointed at my head. The girl smirks down at us. "Thanks for this. I don't even have to dig your grav—"

A tremor shakes the ground. Thunder again or—

Lady C.'s head appears above the girl. Before I can even scream, the dinosaur snaps her jaws on the woman's shoulder. The poacher shrieks, and I hear one gunshot as she's snatched out of sight.

Nakamura and I instinctively rush toward the walls of the pit as the girl screams. But we're still stuck in the hole. My stomach is roiling, sourness in my throat as the screaming continues.

Trifoso puts his face in his hands.

A fleshy *crunch* sounds above us, and the screams abruptly stop.

Even over the rain I can hear Lady C. moving, the sounds of her breath, her heavy feet sinking and sucking in the mud as she walks. A fleshy piece of... something rolls over the edge and drops into the pit. The bit disappears beneath the shoulder-high water, and the water turns a vibrant red in its wake.

"Nobody look," I mutter. "I don't want to know."

A pat of mud splats against my shoulder from above, and huge clumps of it continue to plop into the pit's water.

Lady C. stands on the trap's edge, watching us. Her snout is bloody from the kill, but the rain is washing it clean.

"*No, no, no.*" Voice frantic, Trifoso darts toward Nakamura and snatches the gun out of his hands.

Nakamura reaches for him. "*Don't—*"

Trifoso fires. The bullet hits Lady C.'s tough, armor-plated hide but it doesn't go deep. It's more like a bee sting to the massive dino. Lady C. roars her fury.

"*Shit.*"

Bellowing loud enough to make my ribs vibrate, Lady C. lunges. Her teeth snap in front of me, a few feet from my face, and the fetid stench of her breath hits me.

I stumble, the men following me, all of us retreating as fast as we can. Nakamura trips, splashing under the water then coming up spitting. Our screams are so loud, so constant, I can't tell which one of us is loudest. My throat is raw.

The muddy walls crumble from the wet and Lady C.'s weight, but we're too low for her to reach. For now. Chunks of the ground fall and drop into the water. A rock slips free and smashes against Nakamura's head. He staggers, falls, and slides beneath the water.

"Nakamura!"

I haul him out and hold him up as he sags.

"I can't see straight. Oh, hell." His forehead bleeds freely, and his words are slurry.

More water gushes into the pit, raising the water level. It's up to my chin. Trifoso, desperate, fires the gun at Lady C. again. The dinosaur eases away, studying us quietly, tilting her head, like a bird trying to spear worms out of their hole.

Throat dry, I lift my own gun to take a shot.

A miniature flash flood roars into the pit. Water pounds against all of us, knocking us over and into each other. Lady C. lifts her feet, shifting and trying to stay balanced on the slippery ground. Trifoso's gun splashes into the water, and I barely keep hold of mine. Nakamura goes under.

A chunk of debris—sticks and branches washed from the trap's canopy—falls on top of me, pinning my arms, spearing my sides. I thrash against the wall, trying to get out from under it, but it's too heavy.

Faintly, I hear Nakamura scream, "Doc!"

I gulp in a last breath of air as the muddy water rises over my head.

Chapter Twenty-Seven

GRACE

The water's icy cold around me, and my lungs ache for air. I push against the debris pinning me under the water. No good. Nakamura wraps his fingers around mine. One small spot of warmth as everything in me coils tight with pain and fear.

I kick and claw at the twigs, trying to untangle myself. I grip Nakamura's hand hard. *Don't let me go. Don't stop.* The bones in my hand grind against his.

Something shifts. The branches pinning me move. I viciously brace my spine against the mud wall and kick. The pile shifts, and I push upright. Twigs catch at my hair, cut my face, but my head breaks the surface of the water. I gasp in a breath then another.

"Doc!" Nakamura yells it, over and over. More branches crack then he yanks me toward him, towing me through the water to wrap me in his arms. I cough, my throat burning, and I spit out water and bile.

Trifoso moves toward us, grinning, holding up the large knife he used to free me in triumph.

Lady C. lunges. I scream. She sinks her teeth deep into Trifoso's shoulder. Paul only grunts, his skin going ghastly pale, his eyes wide with fear. Lady C. rears, her prize dangling, clamped in her teeth. Trifoso screams at last as she lifts him up, and his knife falls. Water clouds my eyes. I stagger toward him, tripping and going under again. Nakamura swings his own knife, cutting deep into Lady C.'s neck. She growls but doesn't let Trifoso go.

Nakamura grabs Trifoso's hand, trying to yank him free.

"*Help.*" Trifoso's voice is hoarse, faint.

I tear into the debris pile and grab the stoutest, sharpest stick I can find. Lady C. lifts her head, trying to carry Trifoso off, but Nakamura's still holding on. Lady C. nearly lifts both men out of the water, but the weight's too much.

She adjusts her hold, biting down on Trifoso. He wails, a pitiful sound that stabs at my core.

"Drop him, you bitch!" I stab upward with my stick into Lady C.'s eye. There's some resistance, then the dinosaur recoils. Shrieking in pain, she drops Trifoso. Trying to claw the stick from her eye, she staggers from the pit edge, slipping and sliding in the mud. She disappears from sight, but the water of our pit trembles as she runs away.

"Paul!" I have to swim toward him because the water is too deep to walk.

Nakamura has one hand dug into the wall to brace himself. He holds Trifoso with the other, keeping my friend afloat. The water around Trifoso is deep red.

My nose and throat sting with tears. "Paul." I look around for supplies, anything. But all our supplies are washed away, lost, drowned.

All I can do is hold Trifoso's hand as his breath stops in a painful rattle.

A sob escapes me but I bite it back.

Gently, Nakamura moves Trifoso to the debris platform. My death trap is Trifoso's bier.

I'm shaking so hard my teeth clack together. Nakamura swims over and floats beside me. "I'm sorry, Doc, but I need to trigger his nanos."

"What?"

"To start his body decomposing. We don't want any scavengers to follow the smell and find us."

My whole body's numb. I can only nod.

Nakamura squeezes my hand then swims over to Trifoso. He does something to Paul's body, gently tapping pressure points it looks like. Trifoso's body begins to fold in on itself, decaying before my eyes.

Nakamura and I are both exhausted trying to stay afloat, so I grimly cling to the debris pile and watch, fascinated and horrified, as the last of Paul Trifoso crumbles away into the water. Efficient little nanos.

"No anomalies in the fossil record." A bleak laugh leaks out, and my eyes are stinging. I press my face into one hand and gasp in a ragged breath.

"It's all right, Doc." Nakamura wraps his arm around me, and I turn toward him, burying my face in his shoulder as the rain falls on me hard enough to hurt.

Chapter Twenty-Eight

JULIA

The rain gets to be too much for us, and Xia calls everyone home to camp after a near flash flood. One of our people, Yao, doesn't show, and we can't get her over the com. Her boyfriend, Quint, comes dragging in with a bloodied-up Daw. Quint takes the news of Yao's disappearance hard. His eyes shine, his face going red, before he storms to the far edge of the camp with a machete and chops away at one of the trees.

"She could just be missing," Xia murmurs, watching him but making no move to stop Quint's outburst.

"Hmm." We'll probably never even find Yao's body.

Everyone else in camp looks beaten, tired, and there are only a handful of us left. We can't last much longer, and I don't know how we'll ever catch up to the scientists. Or fight them for the time tubes. We can't even maintain this camp much longer. The sonic fence we've been using to keep the dinosaurs out shorted in the rain last night. We need to move, but we don't want to change locations until we're absolutely sure no one else is coming. We don't want to lose more people to this bloody, cursed forest needlessly.

I change clothes in my tent and throw on a heavy rain slicker, then I make my rounds through the lines of our "cargo." The animals huddle in their cages, wet, miserable. We have tarps for some but not enough.

I cross through the middle aisle of camp and make my way to the largest cage like I'm being pulled on a rope. Our Big Score. My son's golden ticket out of jail.

The young carnotaurus is drier than most of the animals because his cage is set beneath several trees, and I made sure his tarp was lined up all right again. He still looks cold and miserable, huddled in one corner. He chirrups and raises his head when I come forward. He looks cute, but I'm not at all tempted to reach through the bars this time.

I feel disconnected, unmoored. I'm not Dr. Julia Carson, head of the Campanian time displacement research team anymore. But my career as Bad Ass Julia, vital member of an elite poacher crew seems equally as dead.

I'm so mad at my son. And I miss him. And I'm furious at Grace.

And I miss her too.

"What are you doing?"

It's Xia. I half turn to watch her approach. She's got her rain coat on, too, and a big floppy hat, although her hair is still damp and scraggly beneath it. Her skin is blotchy and her eyes are red. I open my arms, and she bands hers around my waist, her head tucked neatly under my chin. "*It's my fault Yao was here,*" she whispers in Mandarin. "*She just wanted to earn some extra money, pay for school. I shouldn't have let her come.*"

I tuck a strand of hair behind her ear. "I wish we'd gotten out after last time. We could have taken our money and run. Retire and buy a nice island somewhere."

"I wanted to, but I thought you'd say no."

I might've. Then. "I've changed my mind."

She shoots me a wry, watery smile. "Too late. Anyway, what about your son?"

I flinch as I realize sometime in the last day I've lost all hope of helping my son. We can't even get our people out safe. No way we're getting that carnotaurus back to the future.

I make a noncommittal noise and pat her shoulders. Before I can offer any more awkward platitudes, she sniffs and steps away. Her features settle into a resolute mask.

Before I can ask what's wrong, I hear Daw behind us. "What a bloody fucking mess, Xia. I *told* you we should have killed the scientists when we had the chance." Daw advances on her. He's got a cut on his forehead, a trickle of blood dried along the side of his face that's dark and crusted enough the rain hasn't washed it all away yet. He's flushed, his eyes bulging with anger. "We lost a lot of good people in that forest because *you* decided to grow a conscience."

Xia cocks one eyebrow. "Killing everyone at the research station wouldn't have solved anything."

"We'd have the time tubes. We'd be *home*."

"You don't know that."

"What's the plan?" Daw surges forward, getting right up in Xia's face with his chest puffed out. "Run around in the forest until the dinosaurs pick all of us off? No. I'm done listening to *you*." He taps her chest hard with one finger. "And I bet everyone else is too."

I look around, doing a quick calculation of who's left, who would be on our side versus Daw's. I don't love the odds. Slowly, I sidle toward a pile of tools and stoop to pick up a pry bar. No one's watching me. Everyone's got eyes for the confrontation between Daw and Xia.

Xia doesn't flinch from him even though he dwarfs her by more than a head. "If you're done taking my orders, then you're off the payroll too. Grab your things and go. Good luck in the forest."

He lets out a low laugh and shakes his head. There's an unpleasant smirk twisting his mouth. Xia's hands are fisted at her sides although her expression doesn't betray any fear. "And miss out on the big payday after nearly having my head bit off? No way, Xia."

He goes for her, locking his hands around her throat. But Xia's too fast. She twists and breaks his hold then reaches across to punch the shit out of him. He takes the hit like a brick wall then catches her lower wrist and twists brutally. She bites a cry off but stomps on his foot even as he grabs her.

My heart's hammering, trying to keep up with the brutal fight, trying to figure out who's winning.

Daw bands his arms around her torso from behind, lifting her off her feet then slamming her down and punching her in the gut with his doubled fists. Xia drops, rasping to catch her breath. Daw kicks her in the ribs. "You and your girlfriend will take a walk into the forest. Right now. Or maybe we'll just save you the trouble and feed you both to Baby back there."

Heart trip-hammering, vision blurry, I rush him and swing with my pry bar, my old softball muscle memory kicking in. The metal bar connects with his head with a sickening melon *thump*, and Daw falls.

My knees give out, and I follow him to the ground. *I can't believe I did that. I can't...* The blood pouring out of the crack in his skull has a horrible fascination for me.

Xia pushes to her feet and scrapes the pry bar off the ground. She holds it loosely at her side as she looks around at the rest of the group. "Anyone else care to stage a mutiny?" She spits a gob of blood out and raises one eyebrow.

Slowly, the rest of them peel away and retire to their tents or idly return to what few duties we have left around the camp.

Xia stoops next to me and takes my chin, turning me so I can't look at Daw—at Daw's body—anymore. "Are you all right, Jules?"

In answer, I wheel away from her and vomit. After I wipe my mouth, I collapse in the mud and swipe the tear tracks off my face. "We have to get out of here, Xia. We need to leave."

"I know, Jules." She scrapes the hair off my damp forehead and kisses my skin. "I know."

Chapter Twenty-Nine

GRACE

The rain stops, but it's still a long, cold night at the bottom of our hole. Eventually, we get so cold, so desperate to dry off, we climb on top of the pile of twigs where Trifoso's body disintegrated. The nanobots are efficient. There isn't even a scrap of his clothing left. *Oh, Paul.*

I bite my lip and watch as the sun begins to rise, yellowing the gray sky with light. Small chirping and chewing noises sound above me. A tiny feathered dinosaur sits at the edge of our hole. It ignores us to gnaw happily on a fluffy mammal carcass that looks like a cross between a rat and an opossum.

The dinosaur weighs about five pounds, but he has an impressive tail with black rings like a raccoon's. The tail stands upright behind the dinosaur like an exclamation point to his every movement. He continues chewing but spares me a quick, vaguely confused *Why are you in my forest?* look.

I grin, watching him, happy for the distraction.

Nakamura stirs beside me and stretches one arm without taking the other from around my shoulders. "What is that?"

"It's a Hesperonychus."

"Gesundheit."

The hespy whips his tail at the sound of our voices, very much like an indignant squirrel. "Magnificent," I murmur. "Do you know this guy is one of the smallest carnivorous dinosaurs we've identified in North America?"

"Are we in North America?"

"Yeah. Welcome to L.A."

Nakamura shakes his head, frowning. "He looks like a roadrunner made babies with a squirrel or something. Not a proper dinosaur."

As if reacting to this remark, the dinosaur huffs, then spreads tiny arm-like wings and glides away over our pit, his kill clamped in his jaws.

I jab Nakamura in the ribs. "You just *had* to hurt his feelings."

"A thousand apologies." Nakamura looks at me, his gaze soft and kind. "Are you okay?"

I let out a ragged laugh. "No. Are you?"

His dimples flash. "No." He rests his cheek against the top of my hair, the one part of me that's managed to dry off. "I'm sorry about Dr. Trifoso."

Wincing, I blow my breath out on a sigh. "He didn't deserve to die like that."

"None of this is your fault."

"He wouldn't have come without me."

"Stubborn." But he gives me a squeeze as he says it.

I snuggle into his shoulder, telling myself I'm only seeking warmth. But his skin is soft, the muscles of his shoulders firm.

He twitches his shoulder beneath my cheek. "Don't get used to this, Doc. I'm still tripping you if I ever need to get away from a rampaging dinosaur."

"Likewise." The sunlight's pouring over the edge of the pit, gilding his face in gold.

His eyes are still shadowed, though, dark. "Well, Doc, what do you—"

"Grace," I murmur. "My name is Grace." A long pause follows, and I look away.

"Nice to meet you, Grace. I'm Ben." And I can hear the smile in his voice, the warm shyness when he says his own name.

My heart's pounding, so I push to my feet. I climb carefully off the makeshift platform of twigs. I steel myself and hold my breath as I sink my legs into the chill, muddy water of the pit.

Sunshine pours into our hole now, making the dirty water glint with flashes of silver, but the water itself is still freezing. "Rain's stopped," I say. "Walls have had a chance to dry. Maybe we can climb out." I go to the wall, running my palms over the dirt and dig in, creating my own handholds.

Behind me I hear a splash as Nakamura—as Ben jumps in after me. "So, you and Julia Carson. What's the story?" he asks.

I slip and land in the water with a splash. Ben helps me, but I shrug him off and go straight to the wall again without looking at his face. "You wanna talk about Dr. Carson and me?"

"Satisfy a dying man's curiosity."

"We're not dying."

"We're not getting out of this hole either."

I wince and huff out a sigh. "Adam."

"Adam?"

Hell. Might as well tell him myself. Get the story right at least. "Julia was my mentor." As I tell my tale, I keep scooping gobs of mud out of the wall, making my own footholds. That's the idea anyway. "Julia convinced me to travel here with her to study. 'There's only so much you can learn from bones, Gracie.'"

Ben copies me, scraping handholds out higher than my arms can reach.

I start climbing. "Julia secured the funding, set the lab up back here. Adam was her son." I snort, shaking my head at my twentysomething self. "He was the cutest damn thing I'd ever seen."

"Oh, yes?"

I look down, and Ben's grinning up at me, his eyes laughing. Cutest until you. I shake that thought away and return to my work. "I fell for Adam like the idiot girl I was. We got married too fast, and he came here to live with me. Julia hated that." I slip but Ben catches me about the waist. His hands are warm against the damp fabric of my shirt. I shiver. "Thanks."

"Why did she hate her prodigy and her son being together?"

I catch my breath then swallow, and my voice is wobbly. "She wanted him in the future, *safe*. When he first came here, he was trying to be a wildlife photographer. His photos sold, but it was because he was the only regular game in town. He bounced from gig to gig a lot. He'd been a bartender. Before that, he wanted to be an actor. When I *first* met him he was a med student. He dropped out the year we were married and followed me here. I thought he wanted to be with me. Now I question that. Here, hold on, I'm going to try." I ease away from Ben and climb again, digging my feet and fingers into the mud, fighting my way up the wall.

"When did your husband start his side business?"

"Is this an interrogation, Agent Nakamura?"

"Curiosity, Dr. Carson."

"From what I've learned, he started practically the first day he was here. Grabbing feathers off the carcasses we find sometimes, teeth. Small stuff, easy to hide. The big stuff, the live animals, that came later. It took about a year of him steadily selling on the black market before he drew the attention of some powerful people on the wrong side of the law. He knew how to operate our time tubes so he'd wait until we were all in the field then send his 'shipments' out. Right there, from my own lab."

"Holy shit."

"Yeah," I murmur. "The Time Guard always kept that bit classified."

"Well, yeah, generally we don't want anyone to know how bad the unregulated time travel can get. So your ex had time tubes and investors, and he decided to grow his business?"

"Oh, yes. He started bringing people through to be his crew. And they started pulling bigger jobs. Taking carcasses, taking eggs, then babies. Finally, they trapped and transported a full grown oviraptor. That's..." I trail off, bad memories rising like the taste of bile in my mouth.

But Ben's not letting this go. "That's when he got greedy?"

"That's when he got stupid," I snap. "He tried to trap a carnotaurus. The animal attacked them, a few of Adam's people died, and he radioed *me* from the forest.

Hurt. Scared. I went to get him." And it had taken everything I'd had not to strangle him on the way home. Selfish prick. My arms are shaking, and I can't tell if it's anger or the strain of the climb.

"And then you turned him in." I must have glared or something because Ben shakes his head. "What? I read the magazines: 'A Fall from Grace: the Dinosaur Lady and her Scandalous Criminal Husband.'"

"Yeah, I turned him in." I'm making good progress up the wall, remembered fury fueling me. "Do you know how hard his mother and I worked to get this program set up? To get the Time Guard to allow a research station in the Cretaceous? And Adam pisses all over that. Destroys his mother's career, tarnishes mine. They nearly shut the whole program down because Adam wanted some extra cash, wanted to feel like a big man with his criminal empire. It took me two years to convince the authorities I wasn't involved, and I had to do that by letting everyone know over and over how stupid I was. How little I actually knew about my husband. So, yeah, I turned the asshole in. You bet your ass I did."

"But Julia never forgave you."

I lean my cheek against my arm. "She never forgave me for bringing him along. He mostly hated it here. And she hated him being here. And I just wanted to please them both." I swallow. "She loved us both, but that doesn't mean we were good together." I dig my hand in, lift myself up. Something twists, and the rock I'm using as a foothold slides free from the wall under me. I slip, slide, mud collecting between my fingers, under my nails. And then I'm falling.

I hit the water then come up sputtering and spitting. "*Goddammit.*"

Ben lifts me up and wipes the mud off my face. "You okay?"

No. "Yeah." Resignation weighs me down. A despair so pervasive it might as well be numbness.

"Maybe it's time for teamwork, Dr. Carson?" Ben murmurs.

I hate asking for help. I hate needing it. But we're never getting out of this hole if we don't work together. "Boost me up."

Ben hoists me high with his hands on my waist. I sit on his shoulder and dig more handholds out of the muddy wall, higher than I was able to reach before. "I'm ready to try again."

I dig my hands and feet into the handholds we've made near the top, bracing myself. Ben gets his hands under my feet and basically hurls me toward the edge of the hole. I scrabble to hold onto the edge, but the mud's sliding away under my arms.

A hand reaches out and catches my forearm, locking like an iron band to keep me in place.

I look up, heart jackhammering, expecting to see a poacher.

But it's *Ben* staring back at me.

And then Ben calls out to me from the pit. "You okay up there, Doc?"

The Ben Nakamura holding my arm raises one eyebrow as I gape at him. He helps me to my feet and, now I've got a better look at him, I notice differences. There's a thin white scar through one eyebrow and curling down the bridge of his nose, and the Ben Nakamura in front of me looks slightly older than the one I left in the pit. More weathered. Tired.

He's also holding my arms just a shade too tight, and a muscle ticks in his jaw. His gaze is restless, as if he's as baffled to see me standing here as I am to see him.

I swallow, trying to take it all in. Maybe this is some kind of adrenaline-induced hallucination? "Um. Hi."

A weird, wry smile crimps his mouth. "Hiya, Doc."

I shake my head and retreat, rubbing the spots on my arms that are still warm from his hands. "Nakamura," I call down to the pit. "Do you have a brother?"

"No." Ben yells back at me from inside the pit. "Why?"

I wet my lips and turn to the other Ben Nakamura facing me. "Then we need to have a long talk. Right now."

Chapter Thirty

GRACE

Fortunately, Older Nakamura brought a rope along. Which makes getting Nakamura the Younger out of the pit much easier.

Shit. What do I call them to keep it straight? Older and Younger? Thing One, Thing Two? Make up totally new names for them? Lucy and Ethel? Calling the older one "Scar" feels a bit ableist.

I shake my head. "What do I call you?" I ask Older Nakamura.

Older Nakamura wets his lips, his gaze roving all over my face for a minute before he looks away. "Agent Nakamura is fine for me. Call him Ben." And he jerks his chin at his younger self.

"Why do *you* get to decide?" Younger Nakamura—*Ben* folds his arms over his chest.

Nakamura the Elder folds his own arms, eerily matching his other self's posture. "Because I'm older, and I outrank you."

"Motherfu..." Ben trails off and whirls around, scrubbing both hands over his face.

Nakamura grunts. "I know, kid, I know."

"Spare me that 'kid' bullshit," Ben snarls. "You're only a year or two older than I am, right?"

"Classified."

"Fuck. You."

"So." I step between the two of them and wave my arms in the air, taking a slow, deep breath to compose myself, then: "What the *fuck* is going on? He's a-a you from the future?"

"Correct."

"Yeah."

Older Nakamura looks much better prepared for the forest than we are. He's wearing a long-sleeved uniform and pants made out of a dark camo fabric. The uniform shifts even as I look at it, blending in perfectly to our forest surroundings. He's also got a heavy pack he flings off his shoulder to the ground.

"You two must be hungry." He gets out two ready meals then hands me a wrapped candy bar with a wink. "Little morale booster for you, Doc."

My mouth starts watering as soon as I recognize the label. "These are my favorite."

"I know."

I'm so hungry my stomach is cramping with it, but I stack my candy bar and meal together on a nearby log and instead watch the two of them. Ben's already sitting on the ground and digging into his meal, obeying the mantra of service personnel everywhere to eat and rest when you get the chance to. Older Nakamura, after a bland look my way, walks to the other end of my log and eases himself to sit. He doesn't quite have a limp, but there's a stiffness to his movements that speaks of some kind of mobility issue.

Ben watches his future self walk, a notch appearing between his brows. Probably worried what'll happen to his body in the future to cause that stiffness. Ben catches me watching him then looks away, shaking his head.

Nakamura starts eating and it is *so* strange watching the two of them. You know how siblings will sometimes have similar mannerisms, similar ways of talking or laughing? Watching the two Nakamuras is like that but worse, because it's not just similarity of movement. They are exactly the same from the way they hold their fork, to the way they chew, how they pick at their MRE tray...

I shiver, wrapping my arms around myself. "The Time Guard really does *this*? Lets you both be here at the same time?" I gesture at the two of them, and my head starts to pound.

Ben chews and swallows, looking at me levelly. "In certain special circumstances."

"But if he knows what happens in the past can't he, can't *you* change whatever you like?" I flap my hand at Agent Nakamura. "How long have you been here? Couldn't you have stopped the initial attack from ever happening?"

Agent Nakamura shakes his head. "They sent me *here*. To this exact second when I got you out of the pit."

"*Why?*"

Agent Nakamura jabs a finger at Ben. "Because that's what *you* told them happened."

Ben frowns and presses a hand over his mouth. "'It did happen, so it has to happen,'" he murmurs.

I restrain an urge to collapse into the mud and throw a tantrum, but I settle for a barely calm, "*What?*"

"The thing with time travel is—"

"The thing with time travel is—"

Yeah, they both started saying the exact same thing at the exact same time. This isn't freaky or unsettling. Nope. Not at all.

They toss annoyed looks at each other and both open their mouths to start talking again at the same time.

"Nope, nope." I jerk my chin toward Ben. "*You* explain. You can take the next one, Nakamura the Elder."

Agent Nakamura snorts and a makes a gracious 'go ahead' gesture to his younger self.

Ben rolls his eyes. "All right, so time travel is a big horrible, twisty mess, right? Or it can be? There's the grandmother paradox where you go back and kill your grandmother, but then how were you ever born to kill your grandmother, et cetera?"

"Right?" I finally break open my own MRE and dig in. The food is watery and tasteless, but my stomach is so empty I've eaten half my meal while Ben was drawing breath to talk.

"So the Time Guard had to adopt some kind of code," Ben continues, "some kind of guiding principle about the things they *could* change and the things they had to leave alone. That's what 'It did happen, so it has to happen' is about. Once a time agent's reported something occurred in the past, then the Time Guard has to make sure nothing intervenes to keep that event from happening. If I report my future self yanked me out of a pit, then at some point in the future they'll send me to this moment to make sure the loop doesn't break."

"The exceptions would be if someone were to successfully kill Hitler or save Kennedy or the like," Agent Nakamura puts in. "Giant world-shattering events are exempt from being fixed. Those are the kinds of things the Time Guard was created to defend."

"Because the Nixon administration was so much fun," I scoff.

Nakamura tilts his head to the side, and gives me a lopsided grin. "Come on, Doc. You know why we can't fix the past." He's older, scarred, a bit of a jackass so far, and he's not *my* Ben Nakamura—whatever that means—but his smirk still sets a hook in my gut and pulls.

"You're quizzing me?" I take a chomp out of my candy bar. "Because fixing the past could erase the future, erase the Time Guard, erase the moon landing, and so on and so forth?"

"Exactly."

"And the Time Guard won't want to undo the poachers' attack because they're worried it will change the future?"

"Well—"

"Well—"

Both of them did that talking at the same time in the same tone of voice thing again. Ben glares at his older self while Agent Nakamura gives him a bland smile in return.

"Nakamura the Elder," I say, "your turn."

Agent Nakamura leans forward. "The problem with fixing something like that is how far do you go?"

"What do you mean?"

"Do you undo this attack? Do you undo the whole return of the research team to this area? Do you undo the whole research program, period? If you decide to pick one thread loose the whole tapestry could unravel. That's why the Time Guard has such strict rules about how and when they can intervene."

My stomach drops, and a hollow ache starts in my chest. "So I can't save Trifoso? Or Meg? Even with a bloody time machine they're both just gone. And the others? What if they're dead too? The Time Guard would just let all those innocent people stay dead to preserve the timeline?"

Both of them make a move to comfort me, but Agent Nakamura cuts himself off, staggering to a jerky halt. Ben frowns at his double then reaches out to cradle my cheek. "I'm sorry, Grace. But this is why it's so important we get to a working set of time tubes as fast as we can. As soon as we send a report to the future, they can jump to the literal second after we report in and come mop everything up. The sooner we get home, the better chance we can save something from all this mess."

Right. I draw myself up. The mission hasn't changed just because there are two Nakamuras. We need to get to the old research station, find the spare time tubes, and pray they're working. And we need to avoid getting caught by the poachers while we do it.

Agent Nakamura gestures to me with his open palm. "You're the expert here, Doc. You know the terrain. Which way do we go?"

I recoil, startled. "You don't want to tell us what we did last time you were here? Save us the debate?"

He laughs. "That would be cheating. It might be useful for you to consider me mostly an observer."

I grit my teeth. "I'm so glad the Time Guard spent all that taxpayer money sending you to get us out of that hole."

Ben gets my attention before Nakamura can make a retort. "What are the options, Doc?"

"I've got a map." Agent Nakamura redeems himself somewhat when he produces a map and lays it down on the log. "We're here."

"All right. And the old research station is here. Maybe a day, day-and-a-half walk depending on which route we take." I tap the map, tracing my finger along one route then another. "There are two possibilities. But there are big predators no matter which way we go. If we go along the beach, we're sitting ducks for the giant pterosaurs and any of the sea predators that lurch out of the ocean. *This* path over the land shouldn't be bad until we hit Carson's Crossing here."

"What's Carson's Crossing?"

"River crossing. A shortcut to get to the old lab." I scrub my hands over my face. "If the river is low, then we should be all right."

Ben's eyebrows climb to his hairline. "And if all the rain has made the river rise?"

"Well, then we'll probably have to deal with the local float of *Deinosuchus*."

"Deinosuchus?" Ben asks.

"Big saltwater crocs," Nakamura explains, "Thirty-five feet long. Big enough to eat a T. rex." When Ben and I both give Agent Nakamura startled looks, he shrugs and looks away. "I, ah, did some studying when I found out they were sending me back here."

"So, that's the lay of the land." I send each of them a wide shit-eating grin. "Pick your poison, boys, by land or by sea? Death by air or death by water?"

Ben and Nakamura exchange a look. Agent Nakamura purses his lips but says nothing. Ben lets out a heavy sigh. "You choose, Doc. Maybe pick the path you believe we're least likely to get killed on?"

Great. No pressure. Hell, I'm the idiot who wanted to study dinosaurs in their natural habitat. I'm not sure how I thought this would end. Eaten by dinosaurs is pretty much the only way this *can* end, right?

I won't even get my name in the history books as the *first* human eaten by dinosaurs. One of the poachers already claimed that honor.

Ben reaches over and shakes my shoulder, rattling me out of my anxiety spiral. "It's okay, Grace. We're a good team. We can do this." He holds my gaze, and I can feel my shoulders bracing, feel some of the fear receding.

"We've made it this far," I murmur.

"Right."

I look at the map again and point. "This way then."

"Carson's Crossing?"

"Carson's Crossing."

Once we get on the rough trail through the trees, following a game trail, we're making good time, and the solid bulk of not one, but two highly competent and *armed* Time Guard agents can't help but be a comfort to me.

Agent Nakamura doesn't talk, which I find a bit unsettling, but Ben seems to take it as a relief. Nakamura walks in the rear and I take the lead on our column, mostly because I know where we're going.

My nerves are okay for most of the hike. Still, as the day wears on and we get closer and closer to the crossing, my stomach begins to churn with unease.

"Is 'Carson's Crossing' named after you?" Ben asks.

"No. My mother-in-law. She forded the river on her first trip. The one she made by herself." I huff out a breathless laugh. "She always said that trip was pure bravado. One woman alone in a dinosaur-infested forest for forty days and nights. But she knew if she made it then they'd *have* to give her the full research program. After all, if one woman alone could survive, then how dangerous could this place be?" I shake my head, laughing at the memory. It was another decade before she could get all the funding for the research stations, but getting clearance from the

Time Guard at all was the first big hurdle. "The study, the research station, they were her whole life's work." My cheek is still sore today, but whether the pain is from Julia's slap or the knocks that big meathead poacher gave me, who's to say? I bite my lip and shoot a look at Ben. "Do you think she was working with the poachers all along? Was the time displacement study *always* just a front for the poaching?" How stupid have I been? And for how long?

Ben strokes my cheek with his palm. His eyes are kind. "You can't let this eat you up. You trusted people, and they turned out not to be worthy. That's on them, not you."

"Right." I scoff. "I'm just the idiot who fell for it."

"The whole fucking Time Guard missed that this was going on. *Twice*, apparently. And this last time you reported what you saw. At least we had *some* warning when the attack came."

"It wasn't enough."

He sighs deeply and traces his thumb over my cheekbone. My cheeks heat, and I look away—right at Agent Nakamura, who's been watching this whole exchange with a pained expression.

I flinch, seeing that.

As soon as he notices me looking his way, Agent Nakamura smooths his expression to careful neutrality, but it's too late. Why does Agent Nakamura look so unhappy that Ben and I are getting closer?

A roar of rushing water reaches my awareness, and I freeze. "We're getting close." A few more strides, turn past the big pine tree, and there we are: Carson's Crossing.

Trees line the riverbank on both sides, some of their branches skimming the water as if to drink. The river's quiet here, a cool green, mostly still. Although you can see how fast the water's moving when it hits the edges of the crossing. It boils against the sides of the trail before flowing over the top of the rocks to reach the river on the other side. The crossing itself is a natural rise, a jagged line of stones where animals ford the river and hope for the best. Julia watched them do it then swam and waded her own way across. The deinosuchus left her alone although she did watch them grab a juvenile T. rex off the riverbank. But maybe humans are too small to be worth the effort to a thirty-five-foot croc?

"Croc." Ben points, his voice shaking only a little.

The deinosuchus is farther down the other side of the river, sunning itself with its eyes slitted closed and its mouth partially open. Since it's across the river from us, I can almost feel my brain trying to deny its size. It does look basically like a croc from our own time, after all: gray-green skin with black spots dotting the massive tail. But this one is as tall as a man at the shoulder, and from nose to tail tip it's half the size of an Olympic swimming pool. Also, despite the croc's I'm-no-threat-posture, I'm pretty sure if we dropped him into an Olympic pool, he would snap up all the swimmers.

"Well, there's only one. We can probably manage to avoid one, right?" Ben's voice is overly hearty, a sort of rallying cry.

I hate to burst his bubble. Fortunately, Agent Nakamura decides to do it for me. "For every croc you can see, there are ten more in the water you can't."

I shiver, staring at that cool green river, contemplating the danger hiding under the surface. Most of us have a primal fear about being grabbed and yanked under by something while we're swimming. The sudden pull, the shock, the release of air. Darkness. Pressure. Or, in this case, horrible pain as the croc shreds your limbs and rolls you over and over until you stop fighting—until you drown or bleed out. But that's a regular-sized croc. The deinosuchus could probably eat any one of us humans in one quick snap. No need for a death roll.

The water sounds so loud in my ears, a rush like a waterfall, but it's a quiet bit of the river. It shouldn't be that loud.

Ben brushes my arm, and I jump. "Sorry," he murmurs. "Should we backtrack, Doc? Take the other road?"

I glance over his shoulder, retracing our steps in my head. For some reason, my gut is telling me no. *Go now.* And a spike of fear fires in my blood before my brain can even catch up with what I'm seeing—movement deeper in the trees, an animal rushing toward us. Massive. Familiar. "*Run!*" I slap Nakamura's arm and haul on Ben's sleeve to get them both moving.

Lady C. has returned, mad as hell, and we've got nowhere to go *but* the river crossing.

Ben takes the lead, scrambling over the rugged line of stones. I follow, my heart hammering, and spare a look behind as Lady C. emerges from the trees. She snaps at the air above our heads, and the rush of hot, stinking breath hits my face like a slap.

I fall in the water, scraping my hands and knees. Nakamura yanks on my elbow to get me up and shoves me ahead of him.

She stops on the shore and roars, snapping her jaws open and closed. But she doesn't follow us onto the crossing. Instead, she scans the water, shifting from foot to foot in obvious agitation.

I accept that miracle and scramble over the nearest stones, breaking fingernails as I claw my way along, trying not to slip on the slick, mossy rocks.

A large splash from behind draws my eye to the other shore as the tip of the deinosuchus's tail slips beneath the water. The question is: Did the deinosuchus abandon its sunbathing for us or to make an attempt on Lady C.?

Doesn't matter. I force myself to focus on the crossing, on making sure I don't slip and fall again into that boil of green water against the bottom of the rocks.

Ben scrambles with strength and agility, clearly trying not to get too far ahead of me, but he's able to move much faster than I can. Agent Nakamura is lagging behind me, but, when I slow down to give him a hand, he waves me away and hisses, "Keep moving. *Don't wait for me.*"

We're about halfway across when there's a crash of water behind us, a roar and a hiss. I whirl. Lady C. managed to dodge the big croc's lunge, but now she's retreating, her long tail whipping behind as she runs into the forest. As fearsome as our carnotaurus is, she won't go head-to-head with the giant croc.

The deinosuchus stays on the shore, slowly closing its jaws, then it moves its lumbering body around until it can slide into the water and begin swimming again.

Toward us.

Chapter Thirty-One

GRACE

"Make a stand or keeping running, Doc?" It's Agent Nakamura who's asking, and he's already got his sidearm drawn. His weapon is like the one Nakamura, the *younger* Nakamura, used to kill that poor dinosaur the first night we were here. I hated the weapon then but, oh God, am I happy to see it now.

Heart hammering, I calculate how much more of the river we have to cross and how fast that ginormous croc is swimming toward us.

Only the tip of its nose is above the water, a small but relentless V swimming along the line of stones. It's hypnotic watching the sway of its tail, deceptively graceful and quiet.

Agent Nakamura and I are on a raised rock with some jagged points, so we could maybe scramble higher to avoid a lunge if we had to. Ben is on a lower rock a few yards ahead, ankle-deep in the river water, waiting to see what we decide.

"Keep going!" I yell, waving him on.

A fountain of water washes over Ben. Something's leapt out of the water at him. I scream as powerful jaws clamp onto Ben's leg and pull. He smashes his head against a rock as he falls. A spray of blood, and he's being dragged under by a smaller croc we never even noticed swimming up.

"*No!*" I draw my belt knife and throw myself at the croc trying to drag Ben away. This animal's maybe twenty to twenty-five feet, but I land on its hard scaly body and stab it in the soft spot where the leg joins to the hips. It hisses and releases Ben. He's floating facedown near the crossing, blood turning the water red by his head and his leg.

I stab the croc again and use my knife as a handhold when the croc underneath me rears. Its body contorts as it tries to throw me off or snap me up. I wrap my legs around its hard, pebbled body, my heart pounding loud enough in my ears I can't hear anything else. Sprays of water crash over my body like cold slaps, and I sputter.

"Grace! Be ready!" Agent Nakamura is brandishing that big boom boom stick of his. Face grim, he crosses to the head of the fearsome animal.

It hisses at him, and the powerful body beneath me braces for a lunge just as Agent Nakamura shoots it in the face, point-blank.

A terrible convulsion shudders through the whole thing's body, and it stiffens then goes limp beneath me. Blood leaks out of its mouth as it slides into the river.

Sobbing and shaking, I scramble off the carcass as it sinks. The body gets stuck in the gap between two stones, half in, half out of the water, eyes glassy, the terrifying mouth bloodied and gaping.

Agent Nakamura holsters his weapon and rushes to grab me the rest of the way out of the water, gripping my wrists tight enough to leave marks. I don't care. I so don't care. He can hold me tight enough to break a bone and I won't care at this point. As he hauls me onto solid footing, I cling to his arm, dry heaving so hard my stomach cramps.

"You're okay, Doc. You're okay." He gives me one last pat then lets me go.

I finally catch my breath and look desperately around. "Where's Ben?"

"I've got him." Agent Nakamura calls as he lifts Ben's body—his younger self's body—up off the rocks and carries him in a fireman's hold over his shoulders.

"Oh God. Is he breathing?" There's so much blood, and Ben is deathly pale and so still my heart clenches.

"We have to check later, Doc. Come on."

"Start moving. I'll catch up."

He doesn't argue, just takes off at the fastest pace he can manage on the slippery ground while holding a full-grown man's body over his shoulders.

It takes every bit of bravery I've got to turn toward the horrible corpse of the croc that attacked us, but I force myself to walk back. I force myself to touch the thing even as the rank stench leaking out of its mouth threatens to turn my stomach entirely inside out. My whole body is trembling, but I still manage to get my foot into its shoulder and kick, dislodging it from the stones where it was stuck. It starts to sink again but stops, still hung up, so I move to shove it again.

But then the dead thing moves, lurching sideways. I recoil so hard my muscles hurt afterward. But the damn thing is still dead. The movement was another deinosuchus gnawing on the tail, ready to make a meal of its dead fellow. Other crocs are swimming toward the area, scenting the blood in the water, no doubt. Good. "Enjoy the meal, fuckers." I shove to my feet, my body going numb from the cold, and I fumble over the rest of the crossing to the other side.

Agent Nakamura's waiting for me just far enough from the riverbank that the crocs would have to run to catch us before we hit the trees. He's got a first aid kit out, working on Ben's leg while Ben lies flat on the ground.

Ben's head wound has been left to bleed freely, and half of Ben's face is a pale red as the blood and the river water mix. The smell of bleach hits me as I get closer. Agent Nakamura isn't taking any chances with an infection—he's dosing poor Ben's wounds with a bleach solution strong enough to make me gag. Ben bites down a yell of pain as Agent Nakamura works. It's necessary, though. Croc mouths are notoriously filthy, and we can't take *any* chances with these prehistoric bacteria.

Ben's trembling so hard it's close to a convulsion, and he slaps his hand on the ground trying to fumble and find mine. I catch his myself and squeeze it. "You're all right, Ben." One-handed, I dig in Nakamura's kit until I can find a small foil packet. I tear it open with my teeth and toss the emergency thermal blanket over Ben's torso. It's probably not strictly necessary—the heat today is murderous, humid after all the rain, but I don't want him dying of shock on my watch.

I paw in the kit and get some gauze to start working on the head wound. Still one-handed because Ben still has a death grip—still has a hold of me.

I have to fold myself in half to work because I don't want to make him sit up with all his blood loss. Once I've got his face cleaned off, I can see the wound isn't too bad, a deep cut through his eyebrow and forehead that fortunately doesn't quite cut through his eye.

I frown over at Nakamura the Elder, and something about his face looks wrong to me. *His* scar is in almost but not quite the same place as the fresh wound on Ben's face. Nakamura the Elder's is closer to the bridge of his nose and only slightly cuts through his eyebrow.

But, even as I watch, his skin shifts, the scar moving to exactly match the fresh wound on Ben's face. What the actual hell?

Nakamura jabs Ben with a shot of something. At my questioning look, Nakamura murmurs. "Antibiotics. The strongest cocktail I've got in this field kit. We're lucky he's got the nanos, or he'd be dead already from blood loss."

"Doc." Ben holds onto my hand like he's being swept out to sea, and tears leak out of the corners of his eyes. Whether from pain or shock or something else, I don't know. "You saved my life. Thank you."

"You can return the favor sometime."

Agent Nakamura drops something with a clatter and swears under his breath.

I ignore him to turn to his other self and smile as I finish cleaning the wound and apply butterfly bandages. "Oh no. *Ben*, I just realized since you've got the scar too: How can I tell you guys apart?" I trace Ben's cheekbone as I say it, trying to radiate a light and calm I am so-very-far from feeling.

Ben gives a weak laugh. "Just remember I'm the cute one."

"Is that true?" I ask, turning to Nakamura, fighting for a carefree tone.

Agent Nakamura snorts. "Does that make me the smart one?"

We all laugh as the first aid continues and, for one fleeting moment, I can lie to myself that everything will be okay. If I can just ignore how ghastly pale and clammy Ben is. If I can forget the lie literally carved into Nakamura's face.

—⁓ello⁓—

As soon as he's bandaged satisfactorily, we haul Ben to his feet and get deeper into the forest, away from the damned water. We go as long as we can. Nakamura and I take turns supporting Ben. I notice Nakamura's slight limp is gone, but I don't say anything. Just file that away for later with all the other observations I'm compiling.

Eventually, we find a hollow under a large tree and set up camp. The three of us huddle as close to the massive trunk as we can. Agent Nakamura deals out more MREs, and we all choke it down. Ben falls asleep partway through his meal, the fork dropping from his fingers as his head lolls.

My heart's hammering as I check him, but he's still breathing. Somehow my voice stays calm even as my nerves jangle like alarm bells. "Did you drug his food?" I ask Agent Nakamura.

"After all the shit he's been through today? No, Doc, I didn't need to drug him." Agent Nakamura clears his throat. "He's out good, though. I'm guessing you want to talk to me. And I'm not sure he should hear it."

I grit my teeth and take very special care rolling the foil over the top of Ben's mostly eaten meal. I position his fork just so, setting everything carefully to the side in case he wants to finish it later. "I guess we should get the big one out of the way. Are you really Ben Nakamura from the future?" I finally force myself to look at him.

"I am." His voice is quiet in the moonlight. He sounds tender, but that's probably a reflection of the setting. The soft familiarity darkness can create.

The moon's up, and it illuminates the forest around us with a soft, silvery light. Under the branches of the tree, Agent Nakamura's face is mostly shadowed, the branches above throwing lines across his body like some kind of protective camouflage. I can't help but think if I'd been better at hiding my suspicion, we wouldn't be having this conversation at all. His face is carefully neutral, but his shoulders are braced with tension, and his hands are fisted against his knees.

I draw a deep breath in, trying to compose my thoughts and line my questions up. "You asked me what to do on the river, before the croc attacked. You should have *known* what happened, what we did, because you've already lived it." I take a breath. "But you didn't know. And your mobility magically improved. And your scar was in the wrong place. Now the scar's moved—which was *freaky*. Just by the way."

Nakamura tilts his head to the side, a lopsided grin on his face. "Very observant, Dr. Carson."

I shoot him a sour look. "I want a straight answer, Nakamura. You lied."

He eases back, leaning on his hands and stretching his legs out. "The first time we went through all this, when I was making my report, I told my superiors Future Me had appeared and helped us out of the pit then disappeared into the forest. I knew if I told them *that*, they'd have to send me here."

"But that's not what happened?"

"No. You got yourself out of the pit and helped me up."

"So, you're from the future, but this isn't the way the past originally played out for you. Is that it?"

"Correct." He looks away and rubs his hand over his calf, massaging the muscle as if he's unfamiliar with it. "The first time we went through this, we took the beach route. A croc got me then, too, but we didn't have bleach and antibiotics. We didn't have a first aid kit at all. Nasty infection started immediately. I lost part of my leg and nearly died."

"If you knew we'd be attacked, why didn't you come with full body armor for all of us? Or a jeep so we could drive around the crocs or—"

He waves his hands to stop my flurry of questions. "Well, first of all, if I gave you all body armor, you'd probably have a sense of invincibility that would make you more reckless. I *know* my past self probably would've done something stupid. The same thing applies if I try to warn you two what might happen. You'll believe you know where to run, what to do, but I could be wrong. Or you could second-guess yourself and make things worse. *Also*," his voice goes sharp and hard, like he wants to make sure I'm paying attention, "at this point events are proceeding closely enough to the way they happened originally, so my advance knowledge is likely still useful. If I introduce too many new variables—like armor or more weapons or better transport—the timeline could change too much, and my knowledge becomes obsolete. I might as well not have come here at all." He rubs his temple, his eyes fluttering closed as if weariness has overtaken him.

"Is that why you lied to get here to the past? To save your leg?"

"More or less." He bites the words out, but it's not anger coloring his tone, it's desperation.

A storm of emotions surges through me, leaving my stomach knotted. "People have died. Why were they less important than saving your leg?"

His shoulders slump and he half turns from me. "I couldn't save everyone," he whispers. "I couldn't make a big change, or the Time Guard would notice and try to stop me. But I thought one small change might go unnoticed."

"What about the butterfly effect? Small changes causing big effects other places."

"Eh, in my experience it's more like knitting: you can drop back some columns and reknit them without redoing the entire fabric. I've already seen that." He points toward Ben's sleeping form. "Even though we went a different route, he still got bit by the croc. The fabric of events is still pretty much the same as what I know."

I pick up a stick to fidget with it, drawing nonsense shapes in the dirt just to have something to do. "What if the Time Guard figures out you did this?"

He shrugs. "I don't know. Either no one has ever successfully done what I did or no one has ever been caught. *Or* it happens all the time, and they just look the other way when it does." He chews his cheek, a nervous tic I haven't noticed in him before, and he meets my eyes with his own. There are dark circles there, and a shimmering pain that makes me want to reach for him.

I shake the urge off and hug my arms around myself. "You don't like it when Ben and I touch or—or flirt. Do things end badly between us?"

"Doc."

"Should I give him up?" I whisper. "Is it better if I walk away?"

I can't make myself look at him, but I can hear Nakamura fiddling with the detritus of his MRE, rolling the wrapper closed, stacking our trash all together to dispose of it. Finally, he lets out a long, drawn-out sigh. "*Can* you walk away from him now?" There's a gentleness to his voice, a kindness underneath that nearly undoes me.

As much as I can pretend to myself he's not "my" Ben Nakamura, this *is* the same man. And the thought of walking away, of never being close to him, never exploring what we could have, makes everything in me turn to lead. It's like I'm anchored to this spot and there's no point in moving ever again. Which is a pretty clear answer how I feel about Ben Nakamura. If I'm in the mood for being honest with myself.

"You're tired, Grace." Nakamura meets my gaze and gives a pained swallow. "Interrogation over, Dr. Carson."

Shame burns through my chest, and I curl my knees against myself. "We should try to sleep. Do you want me to take first watch?"

He gives a small laugh. "That won't be necessary." And he points upward.

That's when I hear an engine purring above us, and one of our familiar beat-up hover-jeeps appears in the air fifty feet up. "I'll be damned." I shoot to my feet and wave, yelling I don't even know what to try to get their attention.

They flash the high beams at me in acknowledgment, and someone hollers out the window, "Wait there!" then the jeep circles off. Looking for someplace to land probably.

My heart races with elation, and my knees actually wobble, but I have to stay standing for a few more minutes at least. The jeep circles and lands, and I turn to Nakamura, grinning wide.

He's been watching me, and although he returns my smile, his eyes are still shadowed, his posture still watchful and tense. It finally—belatedly—occurs to me if all he came for was to save his leg, shouldn't he be relaxed? Mission accomplished, right? The antibiotics and cleaning the wound thoroughly seem to have mostly done the trick.

So, if Nakamura is *still* on high alert, then what else might go wrong? What else might he have come back in time to fix?

Chapter Thirty-Two

JULIA

After the confrontation with Daw, Quint takes care of the body for us, dragging Daw's lifeless corpse with the smashed head out of sight. Probably to dump in the forest somewhere away from camp. Funny, I would've pinned Quint as a Daw supporter, but maybe he's just out for himself now with Yao gone.

Xia and I clean ourselves up as best we can although we're both running low on clothes. Not exactly easy to do laundry in 73 million BC. My stomach is still inclined to revolt, but Xia takes me to her tent, and we curl around each other, just seeking and giving warmth. I bury my nose in the silk of her hair and try to remember there's a world waiting for us beyond this camp, beyond this wretched forest. If only we can get those time tubes.

I'm close to drifting off, my heart finally calm and beating steady, when Xia shakes my shoulder.

"Do you hear that?" she asks.

"Hear what?" I burrow into the fall of her hair.

She sits up, putting me away from her. "Screaming." Xia shoves her boots on and ties her hair out of her face, so fast I can barely follow her with my eyes. She's out of the tent while I'm still looking for my first shoe. I hear it now too. Screaming from the edge of the camp. Not just human. The animals are freaking out too, shrieks and trills. Loudest of all, the baby carnotaurus hoots and chirps with a joy that might be beautiful to hear if I didn't have this sinking dread in my gut. I get my shoes on and throw myself out of the tent in Xia's wake.

We collide with each other and nearly fall to the ground before we manage to stabilize.

I can't see her yet, the mama carnotaurus, but I know she's coming. The camp is chaos, humans running, animals screaming.

"Move, move!" Xia shoves me toward the nearest vehicle ten feet away. The ground shakes, and I fall, my hands and knees sinking into the mud. Xia hoists me up by my collar, even though she's a foot shorter than me, and throws me into one of the nearby cars. I fall against the seat edge, my breath punching out of me. I gasp, *"Xia—"*

She slams the car door in my face and rushes to the baby's cage. I start to open the car door to head out. Then I hear the roar. I think I was still holding out some hope I was wrong, that she wasn't coming for us, that Xia was overreacting.

But no, Mama Carnotaurus has found our camp. Probably while we were chasing the scientists, she was tracking us. And our sonic fence failed, so there's nothing to deter her.

Screams rip through the tents, and I scramble into the front seat of the car, looking for the keys.

I'm half-distracted. My heart is in my throat as I watch the carnotaurus bull-doze her way through our crew. She stomps on one person, snaps another in half. She doesn't even stop to feed. This attack isn't about that.

Meanwhile, Xia is still out there, fighting with the lock on the baby carnotau-rus' cage, trying to avoid his snapping jaws while all the time his mama sneaks up on her.

"Forget this." I chivvy my ass into the driver's seat and paw through the glove box. The keys are in there, trapped in the folds of someone's Michael Crichton paperback. I start the engine and swing the wheel around—just as Mama makes a charge for Xia.

I slam my foot on the gas and shove the car in between Xia and the charging dinosaur, hovering close to the ground. Mama Dino kicks at me, making my hover-jeep sway in the air, and cracking one of the rear windows. I nose the vehicle over, bumping her knees, and the dinosaur jumps in surprise. Xia, meanwhile, hefts a rock high and bashes the lock on the baby's cage.

I fling the passenger-side door open. Xia throws herself inside just as the baby butts his cage door wide. She's not fast enough. He catches her by the ankle and bites down. Xia screams and kicks with her other foot. I throw the car in park and climb over the center console, looking for a weapon. My heart's sick with its own pounding fear as Mama Dino stomps on our car, smashing it into the mud and roaring. Above me, the metal of the car ceiling groans in protest.

"RAWWW!" Not a dinosaur. It's that meathead Quint. He *literally* punches the baby dinosaur in the head then pries its jaws open with his bare hands. Xia slides her foot free and claws her way into my car. I slam her door shut myself and flop into the driver side. Quint fumbles with the rear door, and I belatedly remember to unlock it. He tumbles in. "Go, go!"

I'm shaking and crying and laughing. Xia groans, but she's laughing under her breath too. Mass hysteria. I yank on the controls for a steep ascent, and Mama makes one last snap but misses our bumper. When I look down, the baby has snuggled beneath her while she begins butting him with her head, herding him into the tree line and far away from us.

"Ho-ly shee-it." Quint puffs his breath out. "Bitch tore the whole camp apart."

Most of the cages have been knocked over, the locks breaking on impact. A flutter of wings passes the side windows, and I can't help but beam as the pterosaurs flee into the sky where they belong.

I never was a very good poacher.

"Are there more survivors?" Xia asks.

I wince. She wasn't watching the carnotaurus' rampage.

Quint's face falls. "No. She got everyone that was left except us." I watch him in the rearview as he folds his arms and stares out the side window. A muscle tics in his jaw. "I want to go home."

Ever practical, Xia's already dug up the medkit and passes it to Quint. "Make yourself useful, kid." With some grunts and hisses of pain, she manages to get herself positioned with her leg draped over the dash so he can bandage it.

Quint rubs his cheeks, wiping a betraying wetness from his eyes until it blends with the sweat beading his face. "Okay." Fortunately, everyone in camp knows some basics of field medicine, so he does a good enough job wrapping her ankle to slow the bleeding. Xia winces as he patches her up, biting her lower lip until the skin goes white. I wish I could reach over, hold her hand, stroke her hair. But I need two hands to fly this thing.

"Where are the scientists going?" Xia asks, her voice taut with pain.

"What do you mean?"

She takes a labored breath. "We were tracking them for a couple days. It seems to me they had a pretty clear path in mind. They weren't just running from us. They were running toward something. So where were they heading? What else is back here?"

"Oh, shit." I punch the steering wheel, pissed at myself for not remembering sooner. "The old research station. They shut the place up after Adam, but I don't think they ever tore it down. I bet that's where they're heading."

Xia purses her lips. "There might be spare time tubes there. After all, what are the odds the Time Guard would send people through with only one pair?"

"What else is left to try?" I flip a U-turn in the sky and take us toward the rising sun and the old research station.

Chapter Thirty-Three

GRACE

Once the jeep finally lands, I'm worried the flutter of hope in my heart might strangle me as I wait to see who it is. Who else survived the attack on the research station.

Srinivasan gets out first and waves as she walks toward us, backlit by the head-lights of the jeep. "I can't believe you two made it," she says.

"Who else is with you?" I ask, cutting off the end of her sentence.

She sends me a kind look. "Both your grad students, Dr. Carson. Sona and I got out together during the attack, and we found Jax about a day later. Jax is injured, but they're all right."

My knees give out in a release of tension and fear and guilt so immense I just fold over once it's gone. Srinivasan half catches me, gripping both my elbows.

"You're all right, Dr. Carson." She eases me to the ground where I let my head fall between my knees, my breath jittering in and out of my chest.

I can tell the instant Srinivasan notices there are two Nakamuras because she goes absolutely still, and the breath puffs out of her like she's been punched. "Oh."

I scoff. "Yeah. *He* can explain." Either one. I don't specify. Ben has been roused by his older self, but Agent Nakamura prevents him from rising. There's a sheen of sweat beading Ben's face, and he's still paler than I'd like. Infection setting in, after all?

Srinivasan crosses to the two Nakamuras and hunkers down, most of her attention focused on Nakamura the Elder.

Ben grins at me, and I see my own joy shining out of his handsome face. We aren't alone, the others aren't all dead. After a beat, his attention is drawn to the conversation between Srinivasan and Agent Nakamura.

Srinivasan asks them both something in a sharp, low voice, too quiet for me to hear. Agent Nakamura makes a negating gesture with his hand and actually steps away from her.

She frowns and folds her arms, then storms away.

Curiosity pulls me forward, and I fold my legs under me to sit next to Ben.

He makes a small "Hmm" noise as he watches Srinivasan stalk over to the jeep.

"What was that all about?" I murmur.

"We told her about Dr. Trifoso. Then she asked if he knows who killed Agent Zaran. And why. And my... counterpart told her he doesn't know anything."

Agent Nakamura flops onto the ground apart from us. "I told her I don't know who it was," he keeps his voice very quiet. "We never solved the case." A muscle bunches in his jaw. "She doesn't seem to realize my life won't be worth spit if I say I know who the traitor is. Or maybe she doesn't care."

"*Do* you know who it is?" Ben keeps his voice very bland.

Agent Nakamura clicks his tongue. "I just said we never solved the case."

This whole conversation is like having ice water poured through my veins. Somehow I managed to block out the murder, managed to forget there's probably a traitor among us. It could have been Trifoso, of course. He had the sleeping pills, after all. And Trifoso is safely dead and easy to accuse. But no, the poachers didn't give any sign of having known Paul. And why would he have let them beat him, why would he have run off with us when they attacked if he could've gone to them for safety?

No, as tidy as that would be, I don't believe Trifoso lured Meg Zaran into the dark and stabbed her to death, fed her body to scavengers to try to cover up the killing.

After everything we've been through—and maybe this is naïve, especially after Adam—but I can't believe Ben would've done that either.

So, it has to be one of the other three survivors: Jax. Sona. Or Agent Srinivasan.

The rear door opens, and Jax hops out with Sona's help. Jax is favoring their right leg where a heavy field dressing covers their thigh.

"Sona. Jax." I force myself to smile even as my stomach squirms. I find I'm too tired to rush over for a proper greeting.

Sona gives me a wan wave, looking far too young and bruised to be dangerous. "Hello, Dr. Carson." She settles in our circle, blinks at the sight of two Naka-muras, then snaps her mouth shut with a click. Only her widening eyes betray her curiosity.

Jax's skin is badly sunburned, and their lips are chapped. We all look pretty bad, but Jax looks the worst. Jax settles on the ground with some help from Sona then reaches out to grip my hand. My grad student's face is alight with the joy I myself was feeling only an instant before. "Dr. Carson, I'm so glad you made it."

"Me too, Jax. It's good to see you. All of you." And I grin at our band of survivors, meaning it, but also trying to hide the black spot on my heart, the suspicion darkening what should be this joyful interlude.

Srinivasan rejoins us once Nakamura produces more of the MREs. We're quite the merry band, perched and sprawled and leaning on the tree's massive roots. But, like the darkness looming outside our circle of light, I can feel the heaviness of what we've been through almost like a physical weight. Meg dead. Paul dead. A traitor. We can put on a show, but it's brittle, and could fall apart at any moment.

Ben finishes the meal he fell asleep halfway through and quietly thanks me for setting it aside. I pat his hand then wrap myself up in one of the blankets Srinivasan brought over from the jeep. The jeep had blankets and radios, water jugs, notebooks, some weapons, and tools for hiking. But only enough food for *one* person for six days, so our three fellow survivors have been forced to ration.

They give us blankets, and we swap back MREs. Dry socks for a rat bar. Water for ammo. It's quite a trading outpost we've got going. Srinivasan and the rest dig into their meals with gusto and, for a long minute, the sound of their chewing is the only thing to hear.

I notice Sona and Jax both have guns at their hips, and I don't know quite what to think. Loans from Srinivasan, I suppose?

Srinivasan notices me looking and sets her tray down with a sharp clatter. "They needed to be able to defend themselves. I couldn't do everything myself."

I'm not sure why she's so defensive about this, so I just give a small nod and bundle up in my blanket. It only takes me a few minutes to become comfortable in my wrap, and my eyes drift closed. I'm leaning against something solid, a thick arm around my shoulders. I blink up at Ben, sleepy. "Sorry." I try to sit up, my cheeks hot.

He gives me a small half-hug. "Don't worry about it, Doc."

I want to sink into his warmth, let myself fall away and sleep, but the others are finally finishing their meal, and I need to hear what they have to say.

Srinivasan starts the narrative. "I got Sona and myself out the first day, stole the extra jeep and took off. The poachers shot at the bumper and tried to chase us in one of their vehicles. Took forever to lose them. The solar cell on the jeep was gone by the time we landed. So we had to hole up for a day, hope they passed us by while the battery charged. Once I was pretty sure the coast was clear, I went to the research station, but the time tubes were gone. And all of you were missing."

"We had the tubes," I murmur, "but they got destroyed." There was nothing to salvage after the carnotaurus attack in the pit trap.

Srinivasan gives a slow nod. "I figured that must be the case when help didn't immediately arrive. Then I figured you all might be heading for the old research station and the hope of a backup pair."

"We are."

"When we circled around to the research station again, I ran a search pattern to see if we could find anyone else. That's when we picked up Jax."

Jax eases forward, their eyes heavy, their shoulders slumped. "Dr. Trifoso was gone when I heard the shots, and I ran outside as fast as I could. I made it out the fence and into the forest. I was panicking, not looking where I was going. I made it all the way to the coast of the inland sea and startled a bunch of pterosaurs off the rocks. Some pterosaurs started swooping at me. One of them picked me up by the leg and flew off with me. I... it was..." Jax buries their face in their hands, shaking all over.

I rub their shoulder, offering silent reassurance.

Jax pats my hand and draws in a long, shaky breath before continuing, "I had my pocket knife on me, and I cut the ptero's leg, bad, and he dropped me into the ocean. I kind of flailed to shore. It's hard for me to walk, so I was doing the best I could, trying to make it on the beach. Hoping someone would come along. And Srinivasan found me." Jax spares a beatific look for Srinivasan.

Srinivasan ducks her head and takes the thread up. "Once it was clear we weren't finding any more survivors near home base, I figured we needed to head toward the old research station. But I didn't think it was a great idea to drive straight, so we've been taking a circuitous route, trying to fly through the tree line where we can, flying at night in a straighter shot."

"How'd you find us?" I ask.

"That foil emergency blanket you've got Nakamura wrapped up in. Not much in this forest produces a shine like that, so I thought it was worth checking. I'm glad we did."

"Us too." Ben laughs. "Less walking now."

We're all beat-up, filthy, exhausted. Maybe it makes sense to wait until morning to push on for the research station. But, if we take the jeep, we're so close I can taste it.

Srinivasan catches my eye and raises one eyebrow. "What are you thinking, Dr. Carson?"

I clasp my hands together in my lap. "We should push for the research station tonight. Like you said, we can go faster in the darkness. And if we can get to the time tubes, then we can collapse and all be done and let your Time Guard reinforcements mop everything up."

Ben makes a small "hmm" noise beside me, shaking his head. "There's something to be said, though, for resting and tackling the final push to the base when we're all fresh. We don't know what we'll find there, after all. And we don't know what we'll encounter on the way."

I grunt. "Why do you have to be so reasonable?"

Srinivasan looks over to Agent Nakamura. "Anything from the peanut gallery?"

Agent Nakamura works his jaw, and his gaze flicks over Sona and Ben and me, for some reason. "Leave the wounded behind with someone armed. We don't know what we'll find. They might be in greater danger if they go with us."

Ben lurches forward to lean on his arm and glower around me at his other self. "We should all stay together."

Agent Nakamura shakes his head, his brows crimped together. "We won't all fit in that jeep. It's got, what, four seats? Besides"—he crosses his arms over his chest—"you need to rest. Don't forget I *know* how badly you're injured. How much pain you're in. You should stay here and rest, wait for reinforcements."

Ben *hmphs* at that and flops back.

Srinivasan scoops a gob of gray mush into the bowl of her spoon and sits contemplating it as she addresses Nakamura. "Who are you proposing stays behind, Agent Nakamura?" Her gaze flicks between the two of them. "The senior."

Agent Nakamura clears his throat. "Jax and Ben here for sure. And I was thinking, you, Agent Srinivasan."

"*Me?*"

I wish I had popcorn. Srinivasan's face screws up in a frown of total distaste. Perhaps she believes she's been babysitting too long, taking care of Jax and Sona all these days?

"It shouldn't take us long to get there," Agent Nakamura continues, his tone even and infinitely reasonable. "It'll be no time at all for the reinforcements to come fetch you once we've called them. We could leave Sona here, too, as extra hands, if you like."

"No way." Sona clips the words out, not yelling, but very firm.

"Excuse me?"

Sona folds her arms and glares at Agent Nakamura. "No. I'm not staying out here in the open while you run off in the jeep. No offense to Agent Srinivasan. She did a great job keeping us all alive, but I am *not* staying behind while you drive off in the jeep. I'm coming with you." Perhaps she can read disapproval in my face or Nakamura's or both because she tips her chin up and licks her lips. "I'm sure Agent Srinivasan can handle everything just fine. Besides, she'll have one of the Agent Nakamuras with her too. That's plenty of help."

Short of tying Sona to the tree or some other equally ugly scene, there doesn't seem to be a way to stop her. And there *are* enough seats in the jeep, after all. Maybe I'm just too tired to fight about anything anymore.

Srinivasan claps her hands to temporarily end the discussion. "Look, no one should go anywhere without getting some rest first." She huffs her breath out, glaring at Agent Nakamura. "I *will* stay here with the wounded. But I want everyone to get an hour or so of rest first before you set out. Otherwise, you'll be bumbling off in the dark and doom us all."

Agent Nakamura tilts his head sideways then nods. "Fair enough."

As antsy as I am to be moving, I still manage to fall asleep instantly once I curl up in the blanket. All of us sleep close to each other, a pile of lumps under the base of the tree with Ben and Sona standing watch.

But for his guard duty, Ben might have offered his shoulder to me as a pillow. I might have taken him up on it and fallen asleep with the sound of his heartbeat in my ear.

Waking up is hard, and I know I'm not the only one cursing Agent Nakamura as he moves among us and hustles us out of our warm blanket cocoons. I'm dying of thirst, and I can't seem to keep my hands still. I want to get to the research station and, at the same time, I don't ever want to leave this small measure of safety we've found.

While Srinivasan and Agent Nakamura are trading supplies in and out of the jeep, I help Ben stand and lead him apart from the others, out of sight.

He holds my hand and raises his eyebrows at me. "What's up, Do—"

"Don't." But I'm chuckling as I say it.

He bites the inside of his cheek to keep his own grin in check, then he sobers and ducks his head to meet my eyes. "What's going on?"

I wet my lips and swallow, then I step into his bubble of personal space and put my palm over his heart. His eyes go warm and soft in a way that makes my toes curl. I haven't been with anyone since Adam, haven't even wanted anyone since Adam. And Ben and I are filthy, exhausted, injured, on our last legs. And I still want to kiss him so bad my teeth ache. "Ben."

"Grace?" He cradles my jaw and leans closer, as if he can tell how hard this is for me. Maybe both. But he doesn't make it easy for me. He doesn't steal the kiss I'm offering.

He's so close his breath stirs against my cheek.

"I'm sorry I have such horrible timing," I whisper.

"It's all right, Doc—"

I pop onto my tiptoes and press my lips against his. He makes a small noise of surprise, then a happy growl against my mouth. He draws me to him, wrapping those strong arms around me, and he kisses me, *finally*, his mouth soft against mine. Without hesitation, I loop my arms around his neck.

It's a long kiss. A sweet kiss. A perfect, desperate drowning of a kiss.

When we break apart, it's only far enough to breathe, and I keep my forehead pressed against his. My heart's hammering like I've run a mile, and all my limbs are warm and loose.

Ben brushes a tender kiss over my nose. "What was that for, Grace?"

I close my eyes and band my arms around his waist. "I'm not sure we'll get the chance to later."

"Grace—"

"Dr. Carson, time to go." Agent Nakamura—our own personal bloody chaperone—pokes his head around the side of the tree. His mouth turns down when he sees Ben and I embracing, but he doesn't excuse himself. Just stands there, staring at me expectantly.

I ease myself out of Ben's arms, and it's like I've left something of myself behind in the shade of that tree.

"Good luck, Grace," Ben calls softly after me.

"Stay safe, Ben," I reply as I fall in step with Agent Nakamura. Please, please stay safe. Which thought makes me glance over at the grumpy man stomping next to me toward the jeep. We're far enough away from Ben and the others they probably can't hear us.

Agent Nakamura catches me looking and turns to me with raised eyebrows. "Yes, Dr. Carson?"

"*You* stay safe too."

"I didn't know you cared, Doc." He's teasing me, sounding like his cocky younger self.

It makes something twist in my heart, and I stop next to the jeep and boldly meet his gaze. "I *do* care. Even if you won't tell me why I shouldn't anymore."

That startles him. "Grace, I can't—"

"Spare me," I murmur. "I just couldn't leave without telling Ben. Showing him how I feel. Even if I *do* have you looming like the Ghost of Christmas Future projecting doom and gloom. You understand?"

Agent Nakamura's jaw tightens, and his eyes burn as he meets my gaze. "I understand. Believe me, I do." He raises his hand, almost touching my face.

I catch my breath. It's a bit like seeing some rare animal in the wild. I'm scared if I breathe wrong, he'll fly away.

Instead, his hand trembles as he places one knuckle, as gentle as a whisper, against my cheekbone.

Every beat of my heart is too slow, like it's coming from the bottom of my toes. This reminds me of that first moment when he lifted me out of the pit trap and just looked at me, as if he hadn't seen me in years. As if he was trying to memorize my face.

My stomach drops, remembering that haunted look. "Nakamura—*Ben*, how worried should I be? What are we walking into?"

"I honestly don't know." He keeps his voice low. "I was delirious with fever at this point before. I never made it to the other research station. And, if an agent isn't there, the Time Guard doesn't brief you on events in detail. Just the broad strokes. Sometimes not even that."

I puff my breath out, my stomach hollow, bitterness coating my mouth. "Fantastic."

He gives me a lopsided grin. "Sorry I'm not the get-out-of-jail-free card you were hoping for, Doc. I guess I'm not as full of juicy secrets as I led you to believe."

"Admit it. You've just been trying to cultivate that dashing Man of Mystery air about you."

He places a hand over his heart. "My greatest ambition in life."

I chew my lip to keep from laughing. Oh, this is dangerous. So dangerous. He's acting more like himself. His sweetly familiar face finally syncing up to the fun personality of his younger self. Handling one charming bastard is hard enough, but two? Very dangerous for my health.

Sona clears her throat behind us. "Are we going?"

Ah yes, it's finally time to pile into the jeep. Nakamura surprises me when he asks me to drive to the research station. "You know the way best, I figure." His eyes are shadowed, and he can't quite stifle a yawn as he asks me. The man is more than due for a break, so I hop into the driver's seat.

Nakamura slides into the front next to me. Sona climbs into the rear.

I don't know if the other two sense my tension about returning to the lab or maybe they're just as tired as me. Whatever the reason, we don't talk as I drive the hover-jeep through the air. I keep close to the tree line but just above it. The jeep is pretty exposed, but driving through the trees at ground level just doesn't seem safe to me. Maybe Srinivasan is a better driver than I am if she's actually been driving *through* the forest for days.

Dawn is coming, but the sky is still dark enough that our visibility isn't great.

As I drive, trees and other landmarks start to look familiar, limned by the golden light of dawn breaking—an outcrop of boulders, the outline of the hills. Finally, I can see the building ahead, a long spire still in shadow, like the dark tower out of some fantasy novel. There's a catch in my throat. We're so close to the first lab. The one Julia and I set up together.

I swing the jeep up toward the roof. A shadow passes over the windshield, darkening the car. My skin pebbles with goose bumps. The shadow passes again, and my hands tense on the wheel. In the side seat, Nakamura rolls the window down and cranks his head out the side.

"You see something, Nakamura?"

"A pterosaur. Above us. S'huge." It's probably a testament to how much we've all been through that his voice is perfectly calm as he relates this fact.

I crane my head around and look up. I can make out the pterosaur's silhouette against the rising sun, like a black paper cutout or a shadow puppet. "I think it's a quetzalcoatlus."

Quetzalcoatlus have always seemed to me like one of the more ridiculous animals to exist, like something out of a child's imaginings. As tall as a giraffe and with a wingspan to match, they're sharp-beaked dragons brought to life. Very big, very territorial, and very violent when they get angry.

Sweat pops out on my forehead, and I slam my foot on the gas, hoping I can get us to the lab faster than the quetzy can catch us.

The top of the old lab comes into sight. If only I can land and get us all inside—

Giant wings unfurl, and bodies as tall as a giraffe's push themselves upright on top of the old lab's roof. The heads of the creatures are long and narrow, with the sharply pointed beaks of pterosaurs. More quetzys then. A goddamn colony of them, fluttering and lounging together. The top of the lab building is covered in their chalky-white guano.

"I'm guessing those weren't here when the advance team stashed the tubes." Agent Nakamura's voice is sheepish.

As the hover-jeep draws closer to the lab, two of the quetzys cock their heads then spread their massive wings and launch themselves off the lab building.

"Shit!" I spin the wheel, rolling the car over sideways and flipping us around to head toward the sheltering forest.

"What are you *doing*?" Sona screams.

"I'm taking us down and heading for the trees."

"Do we have any ammo left? Or anything to... throw at them?" Nakamura asks.

"Do you really think that will do any good?" Sona snarls. But she rolls her window down and pops a few shots off with her borrowed handgun. Nakamura fumbles his sidearm out—

The first quetzy hits us. His body thumps hard against the roof, pushing us down out of the air. I toggle the wheel, tipping him off the top as he loses his balance, but another comes up behind us and pecks the rear windshield out. Sona cries out behind me, but I can't turn to check on her.

Twenty yards to the tree line. I stamp my foot down, wishing I could get more speed out of this thing. The second quetzy flaps beside us and snaps the side mirror off.

Sona tosses something out the side window. A tarp. It covers the quetzy's head, and the pterosaur peels away from us, squawking and thrashing, trying to get the tarp off.

"Good job!" Ten yards to the tree line—

The jeep jolts as two of the quetzys land on top of it at once. The metal of the roof and hood shrieks as their talons puncture it. I smell burnt wiring, and smoke is starting to fill the car.

"Everybody buckle up!" I jerk my own seat belt tight then drop the controls in a nosedive straight for the ground. Wind from the broken window rips at my hair, flicking it like a whip against my face. Sona screams in the back seat, a long, drawn out wail the whole way down. Nakamura is grimly holding on to the roll bar, mouth pursed into a thin, white line.

The ground's coming up fast, and the quetzys squawk and throw their huge wings open, trying to slow their own fall. The jeep jumps as the two quetzys release us, not willing to splat against the ground just for a meal.

I yank on the controls, battling to pull us up. The wheel fights me, and my arms shake hard enough to hurt as I hold on. Nakamura throws himself over, adding his strength to mine. We get the nose up in time and zip forward just a few feet above the ground.

The tree line comes up too quick. I stomp the brake, but it doesn't do any good. Swearing, screaming, I jerk the wheel over. We clip one of the trees, bounce off a boulder, and my stomach swoops as the car spirals through the air.

Still upside down, we slam against the ground, the roof of our car crunching as we finally crash to a stop.

Chapter Thirty-Four

GRACE

Our hover-car is still upside down, and damned if I can figure out how to get out. My blood pounds inside me, and I have to breathe through my mouth to hold back a wave of nausea.

"Nice parking job, Doc." There's a laugh in Nakamura's voice, and I let out a small puff of relief he's okay enough to tease me.

"Well, you know, I just couldn't find the valet station."

Nakamura snorts.

"Everybody all right?" I ask, ignoring the fact that *I* am clearly not.

"You're *insane!*" Sona grinds out.

Nakamura carefully unbelts himself with his weight braced to keep from falling on his head. He kicks out the side window then crawls through.

I'm way too tired to do anything like that, but by then he's circled around and popped my door open from the outside. With a sigh, and a *lot* less coordination, I unbuckle then fall and fumble my way out of the jeep.

Nakamura moves to the rear to help Sona crawl out. His face and arms are cut up from the glass, and he's still filthy with mud. But, when he smiles reassurance at me, the breath catches in my chest.

He brushes his knuckles over my forehead, and it stings, so I must have a cut there. I lean into his caress anyway.

"Well," Sona says, her voice calmer, "what do we do?"

I frown. "Get into the lab. What else?"

"How do you plan to get past the quetzys?" she demands, her skin blanched from the shock of the crash.

"We can figure something out," Nakamura says, his voice mild. "Maybe when the sun sets." He has an odd twitchiness to him, a braced watchfulness that makes me edgy.

I tap his shoulder to get his attention. "How long will you need to install the tubes in the time room and get the time field up and running?"

"These tubes are a new prototype, experimental. They have a keypad on the tubes themselves. We don't need a time room or a console, just the tubes."

Sona's mouth actually falls open in shock. My own mind kind of blanks out at the enormity of what he just said. Of course everyone's been hoping for more portable time machines for forever, but the Time Guard has always pushed back on that. Part of the way they keep criminal activity down is by keeping time machines large and unwieldy. Small and portable tubes are a game changer. "We can't let Julia and her poacher friends get their hands on those prototypes. We should go *now*."

"You're right." Nakamura shakes himself and starts weaving through the trees toward the clearing where the lab sits.

The brush rustles, and we all freeze. Nakamura shoves Sona behind himself. *My* first worry is it's the quetzys returning. But then an Asian woman steps into the clearing, her gun pointed at my head. "Good morning, agent. You're right. I'm very interested in those prototypes you mentioned. Why don't you show us where you've hidden them?"

I'm braced for another fight or beating or just to be gunned down, but when the rest of the poacher crew steps forward, it's only Julia and the big guy, Quint. They're all just as dirty and beat-up as us. Julia's gaze crosses with mine before she hurriedly looks away.

"Where's the rest of your crew, Julia?" I call out.

She flicks me an irritated glance. "Hiding. With their guns pointed right at your head."

"Somehow I doubt it. It's a tough forest out there."

"Try me."

"Like this, you mean?" Nakamura draws his gun with a clear shot at Julia's head.

She gives an impatient *tsk*. She has a gun of her own, but she's not even holding it up at him. "This doesn't have to be messy. You can go through the time tubes too. We just want to go through *first*."

"Not her." It's the big poacher speaking, Quint. The one who broke poor Trifoso's ribs and punched me. Quint looks much the worse for wear with a black eye—courtesy of Nakamura, I think—and bloody cuts on his arms. The poacher's eyes are wet, his face splotchy with tears. "Not her," he says again, angrier.

I believe he's talking about me, but then he staggers right past me and starts screaming, "She died because of you! This is your fault!" He gets his hands around Sona's throat. "If you hadn't murdered that agent, if we'd just gone home when we were supposed to! She'd be here! Yao would be alive!"

Nakamura hesitates then takes his gun off Julia to rush toward Sona. Me, I'm just tired.

A gunshot rings out, and another. We all jump, then Quint falls to the ground, two neat bullet holes through his chest. His breath rattles out of him as he stares blankly at the sky.

I guess Trifoso wasn't the turncoat.

"You little bitch!" The Asian woman, the leader I guess, starts forward, limping, but Sona trains her gun on the poacher. Sona's hand is steady, her eyes cold. It's like the flaky grad student I know never existed.

"Julia, is it? Drop your gun," Sona says.

"Why the hell would I do that?"

"Because I'll shoot Xia in the head if you don't."

Julia hesitates, and I can see her pulse jumping.

I hold my hand out. "Julia, don't—"

Too late. Julia sets the gun aside and kicks it away.

"You too, Agent Nakamura." Sona's gun swerves over to point at me. Sweat pops out at the base of my spine, and my heart punches against my ribs.

Nakamura snorts. "Drop my gun so you can shoot us all at your leisure?"

"Look." Sona wets her lips, her gaze flicking around to take us all in. "The poachers made me do it. They threatened me."

"Bullshit." Xia spits at her feet. "She came to me. Last year, two runs ago. She figured out where we were based on the camera trap data and offered to keep quiet if we paid. Offered to sell us intel and warn us if the Time Guard started to get close. But this time you got spooked and killed that time agent. That's when everything went south."

"They're *lying*." Sona's gaze flicks to me, and for a minute she looks young again and fragile and scared. "I had to help them. They would've killed me."

I'd like to believe her, but... "Who killed Meg?" I ask.

"They did!"

"With a knife?" Nakamura takes the thread up. "And then they just slipped away in the dark to attack again in the morning?" He moves a step closer to her.

"Srinivasan got you out too fast when they attacked." I frown as I start trying to put it all together, and my mind feels like a computer with the fan whirring. "Otherwise, you would've run to the poachers for rescue. But you were too far away, paired up with a time agent, and you didn't dare try to navigate the forest by yourself. You're not brave enough for that, are you?"

"Sona, it's over." Nakamura inches forward, keeping his voice soft, his hands up. "You can go into that building for the time tubes, but you won't make it out."

Her nostrils flare, and a muscle clenches in her jaw. "Then you'll have to get the time tubes for me. And I know the perfect motivation so you don't dawdle." She smirks, her eyes bright as she trains her gun on me.

My world slows, narrowing only to the image of her finger squeezing the trigger. The muzzle flashes. Something slams into me, knocking me to the ground. Warmth soaks into my chest, but it's not my own blood.

I roll Nakamura off me, just in time to see the red stain spurt and spread across his chest.

Chapter Thirty-Five

GRACE

"No!" The sound tears out of my throat as I kneel over Nakamura's body. My hands tremble as I try to staunch the blood. It's horrifyingly warm against my palms. "The kit! Where's the first aid kit?"

"Here." The poacher, Xia, kneels beside me, and she has a kit, but it's their own. She starts working on Nakamura, cuts his shirt open and applies some kind of gauze tape over the open bullet wound in his chest.

"Shit. Well, guess you're on the hook to get me the tubes then, Dr. Carson." Behind me, Sona huffs with impatience. "What are you waiting for?"

I wheel around, pluck a rock from the ground, and throw it at her head. *"Fuck you!"*

The rock misses, but I still lunge forward, kicking up dust. Someone catches me with an arm around my stomach, holding me off Sona. *"Don't."* It's Julia. "She'll just shoot you too."

I shove Julia away, roughly enough that she stumbles.

Sona's hand shakes as she levels the gun at me, but she tries to brazen her way through, tossing her hair out of her face. "You're just going to let him bleed then?" Her voice goes low, throbbing with the melodrama of it all. "When you might be able to save him? If only you could get to those time tubes." Clearly, Sona's warming right up to her role as the villain of the piece.

I take a quick breath then let it out slow, trying to tamp down the murderous rage barreling through me like a freight train. It doesn't quite work, but my voice is steady at least when I say, "If I get those tubes then you let Nakamura go through *first*."

Sona narrows her eyes, debating, then she nods. "Fair enough."

Julia steps forward. "I want to make the same deal."

"For yourself?"

"For Xia. She's injured. Besides, a two-person team will have a better chance of success. And nobody knows this old lab better than Grace and I." She very carefully avoids looking at me through her speech.

What the hell is she playing at?

"Fine." Sona starts to point with the gun then thinks better of it. "The wounded go first, then me. Then the rest of you can do what you like."

Julia turns to me, her face blank and still as a frozen pond. "That okay with you?"

No, but there's no time to fight this out. "Yeah." I'm already moving toward Nakamura. The woman Xia's done a pretty good field dressing, but he's covered in blood and ghastly pale. *Not again.* The thought's so silly, but it resonates through my whole body with a shocky kind of impact. *Not again.* I just watched him nearly bleed to death. This isn't fair. I grit my teeth and fight the urge to throw another rock at Sona's head.

His palm is clammy, his warm brown skin going pale as I knit my fingers through his. "It was me, wasn't it?" I whisper. "You came to save me. Not your leg."

He squeezes my hand. "The brass told me you died. They didn't say how. I was hoping it was a dinosaur. Getting shot *hurts*."

My core is aching cold and shivery, like frozen moths are banging around my insides. "Ben, thank you. *Thank you*. But you didn't have to do this."

"You'd do it for me. You did do it for me. Yesterday. I watched you jump on a croc's back to save my life."

"Yeah, but I'm an idiot." This hurts. Oh God, this hurts. I have to go. Now. Before I turn into an even bigger wreck. I rub my cheek against his knuckles. "If you die, I will never forgive you." I let his hand go.

When I turn, ready to go at last, Julia is still standing with Xia, their heads bent together, bickering.

⁓ℓℓ⁓

JULIA

"It should be me, Jules."

"You're injured, Xia."

Xia's lips compress, and her gaze flickers over to something behind me. "She'll double-cross you. What incentive do any of them have to help us?"

"You watch out for that bitch grad student. I've got Grace."

A muscle tics in Xia's jaw, and her eyes go shiny. "Take care of yourself then."

"You too."

I'm unprepared when she throws herself at me, her arms banding around my waist. She practically knocks me off my feet, but it's still wonderful. I hug her and rest my cheek against the silk of her dark hair. "I wish we'd had more time," I murmur. "And fewer dinosaurs."

"Stop talking, Jules." Her mouth finds mine in a quick kiss, brief, hard, and I think my heart must have stopped for a second.

But I can't look at her once I've stepped away. If I do, I won't go. "See you." I release her and jog to the edge of the tree line before I can change my mind. We need those time tubes, and this is the only way to get them.

Feet crunch through the brush behind me, and I turn toward Grace. I wait for the familiar flare of anger, but all I have is wan resignation. I'm too tired to be angry anymore.

"We can't outrun them." I nod toward the quetzys, who are all still stirred up from Grace's grand bloody entrance. The big pterosaurs flap their wings and snap at each other like small buildings colliding.

Grace wipes some sweat off her brow with the hem of her bloodied shirt, and her gaze fastens on the wreck of their jeep. She raises an eyebrow. "Do *you* still have a vehicle?"

I'm already shaking my head. "Not happening. Nope. If we total my vehicle, too, then everyone will be stuck here with no ride."

"We're already stuck here without the time tubes."

Xia can't walk. If I can't finish this, if I get killed, then she'll be all alone with Sona and a dying or dead time agent. Without our hover-car, Xia will most likely be the first one picked off by predators in the forest.

But if we don't get these tubes, then there's no guarantee any of us will survive long enough to see a rescue. Grace is right, unfortunately. If we two puny humans try to run across that open plain, we'll just get eaten.

Well, dismembered then eaten.

"Where'd you park?" she asks.

GRACE

"This is nuts." Julia has herself braced against the doorframe and the dashboard in her car as we zoom over the ground. "I've changed my mind, Grace."

"Too late!" Me, I've got my foot flat on the gas, taking us like an arrow straight for the front of the old lab. "You're supposed to be my lookout, Julia. Remember?"

"Bite me." But she rolls her window down and leans out to look, gripping the car frame. "Balls. One just took off from the roof. He's diving!" She scoots inside and flops into her seat, snapping her seat buckle in place. Twisting around to see up through the front windshield, she rests the back of her head against the dash. "Go to the right... now!"

I jerk the wheel over as one of the quetzys just misses us in a deadly dive-bomb. The car tilts sideways, listing on the displaced air of the animal's wing stroke. I can see in the rearview as he flaps awkwardly to the ground then, balancing on his hind feet and the small toes on his wings, he takes off in a run after us.

"Shit."

"What?"

"Just watch the sky." I tense my jaw, wishing this cursed machine could go about ten times faster. The walls of the lab loom above us. We're so close—

"Another one's diving."

I start to zig left when the one on the ground catches up, closing in on the left side. Julia screams, and I turn us the other way just as a shadow darkens the car.

I squeeze a little more speed out, and the second quetzy misses us as she stops her dive with an ungainly flail of wings. She tumbles into the one already on the ground. He hisses and snaps his neck to peck at her. I brake, watching their struggle, and flex my hands on the steering wheel.

Julia bounces in her seat, checking the skies, turning to watch the dueling quetzys on the ground. "They're between us and the building."

"I *know*, Julia."

The quetzys have forgotten us as they snap at each other, flapping their wings in a display of force. Any other time, and I'd be digging for my field notes. The hover-jeep's motor hums like a kitten purr, but as soon as we start moving again they'll be on us.

"We can outrun them," Julia murmurs.

"What?"

"They aren't as fast on the ground. Floor it. We can make it."

Hell. Just hell.

I stomp my foot on the gas again, and we jump forward. The quetzys, still caught up in their fight, scatter like bowling pins as we zoom between their tangled wings. They hiss and start after us, and I'm not sure how accurate Julia's assertion is because they're moving pretty damn fast on the ground. But there's the old lab right ahead. Beautiful. Perfect.

But if I stop—if we hop out and try to run for the lab entrance—they'll snap us up like a pelican scooping fish out of the water. We need the hard shell of the car between us and them. We need protection. I brace my arms against the steering wheel, stiffen my knee until I'm sure my foot is pressing against the gas as hard as it can.

Julia jerks around to stare at me. "Are you going to stop?"

"No." I close my eyes, bracing myself as we slam through the side of the building.

Chapter Thirty-Six

JULIA

I could kill Grace. See, I thought I wanted to before, but that anger has nothing on this. I'm not a young woman. She's just lucky I didn't keel over on her when she drove through the fucking wall. "You crazy bi—"

"I know, I know."

The windshield's spiderwebbed, and the car's covered in building dust. Bloody Grace. I jump as my car door pops, but it's only Grace opening it for me.

"We'd better move," she says. "The quetzys can't fit through the hole, but they're still digging around it trying to get in."

"Perfect." I grit my teeth and climb out. My chest is sore, bruised from the seat belt. Grace starts to put her hand under my elbow, stops herself, then goes ahead and does it anyway. I bite my lip and look away. "This is so ridiculous."

"Tell me about it."

"Did your time agent describe just where he hid the time tubes?"

"Up."

We start toward the staircase, but after the first step, my foot sinks into something squishy and slides out from under me.

Grace catches me, holds on until I'm steady. I nod my thanks then kneel to see what I stepped in. "Shit."

"What's wrong?"

"No, it's literally shit."

"Oh. Okay." She crouches beside me, and we both examine the spoor together. "This is too small to be from the quetzys. Those look like partially digested egg pieces, maybe some vertebrate here from another meal."

"Small predator?"

"Most definitely. Maybe a troodon or one of the raptor species."

"It looks fresh." And something in my tone must have given me away because Grace shoots me a very sour look indeed.

"I'm not the grad student anymore, Julia. *You* check it."

With a long-suffering sigh, I stick my finger in. "It's warm."

Grace grimaces and hands me a pack of muddy tissues from her pocket. I nod my thanks and wipe my hand off.

"There's more over there." Her voice is quieter.

I spot several more dung piles—old and new. "We seem to have stumbled into a predator's turf."

"But are they home?"

"This is why I hate fieldwork." I start up the stairs. But, even as my rational self is scared out of my mind, the idiotic, irrational scientist deep inside me is just *fascinated* by all of this.

We find the animals on the second floor: an entire colony of troodons, complete with nests and at least six adults.

I retreat slowly out of the doorway on the second floor landing. Grace and I rush up to the next floor. Thankfully, the third floor looks clear of dinosaurs.

"The quetzys probably took the roof because of the heaters up there. Nakamura said the Time Guard isn't actively using this place, but they keep the power on because it's useful as a staging area for operations."

I keep my gaze down, picking my careful way past the bones and other bits of carcasses on the stairs. "And the troodons probably like the shelter from predators and egg stealers, but how do they get in and out with the quetzys on the roof?"

"They're probably nocturnal. The quetzys settle down for the night, the troodons come out and hunt. They're scavengers too. They probably pick up some of the quetzys' leftovers on occasion."

"It's a good theory, Dr. Carson."

Grace gives a good-natured snort. "Thank you, Dr. Carson."

That used to be our in-joke after she married my son. The two Dr. Carsons. Dammit, I'd thought she'd be so good for him, but it all went so wrong.

Grace must be thinking along the same lines because her brow furrows, and she looks away. "Nakamura said it's on the fourth floor."

"Okay."

We walk in silence up the next staircase, our steps echoing loudly through the empty chamber.

"And just what *did* turn you into a poacher, Julia?" Grace bites the words out, her shoulders stiff.

"Take a look out the window, Grace. There isn't a shortage of dinosaurs around here. It's not exactly condors we're hunting."

Grace just shakes her head, her jaw set. She's so annoyingly energetic as she climbs the stairs. Young, healthy. Meanwhile, I'm puffing behind her and my calves are burning, sweat pouring down my temples.

"It was after you got my son arrested," I tell her.

She flicks a startled glance at me. "What?"

I pass her on the stairs. "The legal fees were piling up and that civil suit with the injured girl. I went out for a walk in the forest here one night. I was so sure the university would rescind my funding, and I'd be stuck in the future forever. So I kept walking, hoping something would eat me and end it all—"

"Julia—"

"But Xia and her people found me first. I knew who she was, how good she was—Adam had told me. So we decided to work together, and she helped me get money to Adam." I'm ahead of Grace on the stairs. "I didn't do enough for him before, Grace. I'd do anything—I *have* to do anything for him now."

Grace just shakes her head.

"I—I'm sorry it came to this, Grace." Foolish old woman that I am, I've got tears stinging my eyes.

"Me too." Her voice is hoarse. "Through here."

The fourth floor is the dormitory space, and it's eerie to see the place empty, all the rooms bare with the floors covered in a fine coating of dust.

Grace counts off rooms then finally turns into one of them and goes to the closet. She steps inside and pats along the wall, then she smiles at me. "We're good." She yanks hard on something and returns with a long black crate in her arms. "We just have to figure out how to get back."

I open my mouth to reply but then I hear it—a skittering behind me, feet on the stairs.

I shoot Grace a wry glance. "Nocturnal, huh?"

"Well, unless something tasty stumbles into their lair."

"Troodons don't attack larger prey usually," I murmur.

"Yes, but do we count as larger? Especially when it's three to one in their favor."

"Hell."

Chapter Thirty-Seven

GRACE

I run into the hallway with Julia on my heels. I'm hoping we can beat the dinosaurs, make it out before they see us.

Nope.

Three adult troodons are already ahead of us, coming off the stair landing. They're maybe chest high on me and a little over waist height on Julia. Their huge eyes are wide, dark pools in the poor light. They were made to hunt in the low light, and we were not. One of them still has his claws through the door handle on the stairwell. Too smart. The animals freeze when they see us, but almost immediately they start toward us again. Are these the same tool users from the other day in the forest? I hope not. I hope these are their much stupider cousins.

I back down the hallway, Julia at my side. She draws a large knife from her belt, and I take the time tube case in one hand to tug out my borrowed knife from Nakamura.

"If we run they'll chase us." Julia's voice breaks.

"We can't make it past them down the stairs."

She slides her foot behind herself, slowly moving away. "Medbay was on this level, wasn't it?"

"You think there'll be anything there?"

"Let's go look."

We turn tail and run. Behind me, the troodons' claws clack as the dinosaurs pick up speed to chase us. Something knocks into me, and the time tube case slides out of my hands and down the hall to bang against Julia's foot. She hops backward and sees me. Her eyes go wide. She bends to pick the case off the ground. *I just hope she lets Nakamura go through.*

The dinosaur pinning me to the ground latches onto my shoulder, his teeth sinking in. Hurts like a bitch. I twist and thrash, screaming, trying to get him off. I stab behind me with my knife. No good.

"Get off her!" Julia runs up and kicks the dinosaur off me. She yanks me to my feet with one hand and hauls me forward when I stumble. She's holding the time tube case in a white-knuckled grip with her other hand. Julia shoves me ahead of her into the medbay, knocking over a broom that was in the corner. She slides the time tube case into the room then wheels to slam the door closed.

But the two troodons fly through the air toward her, banging the door open. Their disemboweling claws flick out. I swing the broom, knocking one away. The other slams into Julia's side, digging its claws into her thigh and biting hard at her stomach as the two of them crash against the doorframe. Julia screams and thrashes. She manages to plunge her big knife into the animal's side. I whack the troodon all the way off her with the broken broom handle and kick it into the hallway.

Using my good arm, I grab her by the shoulders and drag her inside the room. I shove the door closed behind me then collapse against it. Pain flares along my back, and I recoil, remembering my own wounds too late. "Shit. Ow."

"Oww." Julia's moaning rouses me, and I push to my feet, leaving a bloody handprint on the wall.

"Lock it." Julia grinds out.

Right. Tool-users. Goddamn troodons.

My body is on fire, stinging and cringing every time I move, and I might have a broken rib or two from the troodon landing on me. Still, Julia looks worse. Her entire right side is slick and shiny with blood, and the breath rattles in and out of her in an alarming way.

I look around the medbay and let out a gasp of relief. The room's been sealed against the elements, and it's still stocked with supplies. "I guess the Time Guard really wanted their time agents to have a fallback position."

Julia grunts, her eyes closed.

I swallow. *Nakamura*. He needs this medbay worse than either of us, but he needs the time tubes more. A field hospital wouldn't be enough.

The tubes. I flick the case open. The tubes look the same as the ones I know from the bigger machines, but the keypad is a mess of confusing buttons. I could just start hitting things, but I might send us off to medieval England and the Black Death or Pompeii right before the volcano erupts. Time travel isn't something you want to screw up.

"Do you have any idea how to use those?" Julia asks.

My shoulders slump. "No. You?"

"If only."

Crap, well, that method of escape is temporarily closed. Time to see what else we have to work with.

Julia manages to get herself onto one of the bunks. There's still a med scanner in one corner, but when I try to power it up the machine just grinds gears and fills the room with an unpleasant burning smell. I switch it off again.

Julia shakes her head. "Cheapskates at the university. Never buy equipment that's worth anything."

"That's okay." I keep my voice chipper. "We'll manage just fine without it."

Julia snorts and lifts both her hands away from her bloody gut. "Spare me, kiddo. Just find me some morphine then figure out how *you'll* get out."

"I'm not leaving you here." I jog over to the medical cabinets only to find them sadly disorganized. Still, I start sorting through the detritus.

"You just want to make sure I'm in jail where I belong."

"I want to save your life."

"I'll only slow you down." She turns her head away as a tear trails out the corner of her eye.

When I open the next cabinet, a box of gloves and other supplies spill out, hitting me on the face and head.

Julia growls. "Grace, you're wasting time—"

I grip the counter edge, my pulse thudding. "You damned stubborn old woman, just... let me save you."

A silence falls, and I can hear the troodons scratching at the door. The force of their efforts makes the door rattle against its frame.

"I'm not old," Julia mutters.

I laugh and start digging through the supplies again. My heart lifts as I unearth a small bottle out of a top cabinet. "Ah-ha."

"What's that?"

I brandish the bottle and a wrapped syringe. "I found your morphine. We'll give it to you right before we go, though, so you're not too groggy."

Julia widens her eyes then nods. "Okay. Find me some Advil in the meantime."

I toss her the syringe and morphine vial then rifle through the cabinets again for bandages and some antibiotic ointment.

Julia and I manage to peel her ripped and bloody shirt off. I start to sponge the blood, but she waves me away. "I can do this. You keep looking for something we can use to get out of here."

"All right." I tear through more of the cabinets while the pounding of the troodons continues against the door. Claws flash occasionally under the frame, making my nerves jump.

I bend to check one of the lower cabinets and freeze as I open it. "Well, thank goodness for the infamous Time Guard paranoia."

"What?"

"They didn't just leave the time agents some medical supplies." I trace my hands over the sleek metal case I've found and hold my breath as I pop the clasps. When I flip the top open, I can't help but giggle with happiness.

Julia sits up on the bed. "A tranq gun."

"Dr. Carson, I think we're in business."

"We should wait until the night to go. The quetzys will be asleep."

I look out at the sky. It's just past noon. "Nakamura can't wait that long. *You* can't wait that long."

She folds her arms, grumpy. "Well, what are we going to do then?"

The door rattles against its hinges as one of the troodons throws itself against the wood. Probably as frustrated as we are.

"Well, I've got a really bad idea we can try."

Chapter Thirty-Eight

JULIA

Sitting on my musty cot, waiting for death to come through the door, I wish I had a cigarette. If I'm about to die, I'd at least like to get one last smoke in first. "This is a bloody stupid idea," I mutter.

"You agreed." Grace's voice floats to me from somewhere in the dark room.

"Doesn't mean it's not a stupid idea."

"Duly noted, Dr. Carson."

I snort and settle against the pillows of my medbay bed. I've got my knife in my lap, gripping it tight enough to turn my knuckles white. It's slick in my hand, though, gummy with a mix of sweat and sticky blood.

"Ready?" Grace asks.

"No."

She waits, and I can taste her impatience on the air.

I try to wet my lips, but all my spit has dried up. "Okay. Go."

A minute passes, then I hear the flick of the door lock. The first troodon pushes through, his large eyes shining with cunning and an almost uncanny intelligence.

My stomach turns when he looks up and sees me on the bed. I can hear him sniffing, hear his claws clicking as he walks forward across the tiled floor. Another one comes through, pushing the door open wider with his snout.

The two dinosaurs circle me, edging closer. They can smell the blood of my wound. They want me, I know it. A nice fat carcass to drag to their young on the second floor.

I watch them, trying to track their movements. The first one's legs tense for a spring. "Now, Grace!"

The room's door bangs closed and Grace steps out from behind the wood, the tranq gun at her shoulder. She fires as the first one launches himself. The dart hits him in the side, and he flops over midleap, missing the foot of my bed by mere inches. The second one starts toward Grace while she loads her next dart. She swings at the dinosaur with the butt of the rifle, knocking him away, then she flips the gun right way round and fires the dart into his neck at point blank range.

"Two down," she says, breathing hard.

"Four to go." I slide off the bed and grab the crutch we've already prepared for me.

Grace hands me the gun, and I reload it while she wrenches the mattress off the bed frame. She and I both rolled around on it to make sure the whole mattress reeked of blood.

I cross to the window, stepping over one of the troodons' collapsed forms, and flip the glass open.

Grace wrestles the mattress across the room then shoves it out the window with her shoulder. The mattress sails to the ground, flipping blood-side down to land in the dirt.

"Crap."

We wait, holding our breaths. Two quetzys swoop out of the sky, landing on the mattress and proceeding immediately to tear the thing apart.

"Okay." Grace grins and shoves our second blood-prepped mattress out another window.

I wanted to use the troodon bodies but Grace vetoed that idea. She's still a softie when it comes to dinosaurs.

She takes the lead down the hallway, and I put a hand to her shoulder to make sure she doesn't outpace me. We hit the stairs. I try two of them with the crutch then give up and chuck it ahead of me to clatter down the stairs. I grit my teeth and stagger on with my bad leg. *When the* hell *are my painkillers kicking in?*

On the third floor landing, the troodons leap out at us from the foot of the stairs. I kneel behind Grace. She fires the first shot then hands me the gun to reload. I go as fast as I can, but one troodon charges up the staircase. Grace slashes it with a knife, and it retreats, hissing. I hand her the gun, and when the dinosaur charges again, she hits it in the gut with the dart.

The troodon's limp body slides down the stairs, knocking into its relatives. They chirp and scatter, running away.

Grace grins. "I guess they finally figured out *we* are the big animals."

"Guess so."

We clear the stairs and hit the lobby. Grace pauses next to our hover-jeep, but the thing's a wreck.

"Looks like we're walking it, Dr. Carson," I say.

Grace yanks one of the doors open for me. "Shall we, Dr. Carson?"

What a day. What a fucking *day.* I laugh. "Yes. Let's."

The two of us take off sprinting—well, me hobbling—out the door.

GRACE

As soon as we're out the door, I let Julia pass me. I look over and the four quetzys are still heavily occupied tearing up the mattresses. Bits of downy white fluff dances on the air. It looks like the pterosaurs are playing.

I pick up speed, the gun and the time tube case both banging against my thighs.

I don't want to discard the gun, not yet, but I might have to—

A familiar shadow looms over me. I drop and roll into a ball. A large beak stabs into the ground by my side. I roll away, groping for the gun.

When I turn over, the quetzy towers above, its massive wings tented around me. I fire a dart into its neck. The animal flinches but this thing is five times the size of the troodons, and it just keeps coming. I fumble another dart out anyway and reload. When I shoot the quetzy again, it hisses and snaps. I dodge to the side and lurch to my feet, pressing against the leathery skin of its wing. The quetzy snaps at me again but misses, unable to crane his neck around all the way.

I thumb another dart out of the string on my belt, but I drop it. The quetzy shifts and knocks me sideways. As I stumble, I hear the glass dart crunch under my foot. *So much for that.*

The quetzy studies me with sharp yellow eyes, and I'm oddly peaceful studying him. It feels almost like being caught in the time field: displaced, floating, a held breath.

But the moment passes, and his head shoots forward, striking toward me. At the last second, he reels away, his head missing my body as he shrieks in pain. I see Julia's silhouette behind his wing. She's cut a large tear through his thin membrane there. Blood spurts from the vertical line.

"Run!" Julia screams.

I drop the gun and scoop the time tubes up. The tree line looms ahead of us, tantalizingly close. I can see Sona beckoning me forward. *Come on, come on—*

I turn. Julia's way behind me, fumbling forward in lurching strides, limping badly. She's yelling and waving me onward. "Go! Go!" Behind her, the quetzy staggers toward her, hissing but stumbling like a drunk on a Saturday night with its injured wing.

I wheel toward Sona and lift the time tube case high. "Catch."

Her eyes go wide, but she darts forward as I throw, and the case falls neatly into her arms.

I whirl and run to Julia, sliding to a stop beside her. I can hear the quetzy running after us, but I don't turn.

Sweat pours down Julia's face, and her breath rasps loud in my ear. "I always liked you, kiddo."

"You too."

A tall shadow stretches over the ground ahead of us—the quetzy running up from behind. I shove Julia forward into the trees and throw myself after her, a clumsy, full-bodied dive for home base. I scrape my chin and chest up good and get a mouthful of dirt for my trouble.

The quetzy tries to follow us through the trees, but the trunks are too close together for him to get to us. Julia's partner, Xia, finally scares the thing away when she starts throwing rocks at its head with painful accuracy. With one last hiss, the quetzy staggers away.

"Nicely done. Dr. Carson. Dr. Carson." Sona saunters up to the two of us.

"Wonder if Xia has any stones left," I mutter. Julia grunts a laugh out.

Everything hurts. Everything. But I haul myself to my feet somehow to face Sona.

Xia swears as she wrestles with the time tubes a few feet away. These new prototypes of Nakamura's are the same long rods like the ones I'm used to, but these are clearly built to take a bit more of a beating. They're encased in a layer of protective metal, with a panel at the top of one to enter time coordinates. Any other time, I'd be hovering over the tubes, trying to get a closer look at these new toys. Instead, I shuffle my aching self toward the corner where Nakamura lies stretched out on the ground, his torso red with blood. Okay, *now* everything hurts. *Don't you die on me, you bastard.* "How are the time tubes coming?"

"Booting up... I think," Xia says. "Your time agent told me what to do."

My time agent.

With a hum and a crackle of electricity, the time tubes go live, and a wave of energy springs up between the two poles like a heat mirage in the desert. A ripple of muted excitement passes through our small group.

Sona starts shuffling toward the time field. I yank her arm. "Nakamura first. Remember?" I hold Sona's gaze, my other hand clenched into a fist. I'll tear her to pieces if she tries to welch on this deal.

She waves her hands, irritated. "Yes, yes."

I jog to Nakamura and take his shoulders while Xia helps with his feet.

Nakamura stirs to life, and his eyes flutter open as he looks at me. "You made it."

"Yes, and you owe me a drink later."

"Of course."

"A big one."

We set him on the ground beside the time field. Tubes this small, only one person can go through at a time, so we can't carry him over. And he's so beat-up we can't just push him.

"Roll him in," Xia says. "The field will catch and draw him the rest of the way through."

"How undignified," he mutters.

"You'll live."

"Yes." He catches my hand and presses a fluttering kiss to the palm. His eyes are bright, probably with fever—maybe with something else too. "I *will* be seeing you again, Doc. I didn't take this bullet just to lose you."

My throat's scratchy, eyes burning. "It's a date."

His hand falls away from mine, into the time field, and, just like Xia said, the field yanks him the rest of the way through. In a blink, he's gone.

I'll probably never see him again.

There's a crackle in the air, and all the hair on my body stands up with static electricity. Julia and Xia run—well, stagger—toward the time tubes. Sona, startled maybe, lets off a shot that knocks Julia into the ground.

"*No.*" I start forward.

A burst of light crackles in the air then explodes outward. The shock wave knocks me and the others off our feet. Julia is the first one to get up, and she keeps running straight for our time tubes as they sizzle with energy.

"This is the Time Guard! Nobody move!"

"*No, no, no!*" It's Sona, screaming like a toddler in a toy store as two officers grab her arms and subdue her.

Julia has one hand at the panel of the time tubes while Xia rattles off a string of coordinates in Mandarin, too fast for me to catch. Julia's fingers dance over the keys as she inputs the new coordinates. Blood stains the shoulder of the scrub shirt we took from the medbay for her.

"You first, Julia," Xia yells.

"Forget about me." Julia puts her foot behind Xia's knee, knocking her off-balance. While Xia is pinwheeling, trying not to fall over, Julia shoves the other woman, and she falls into the time field and disappears.

I roll over, trying to blink the rest of the afterimage of light out of my eyes.

"*Hey*." Two Time Guard officers descend from the trees and press Julia to the ground, twisting her arms behind her.

"She's injured," I call out and start elbow crawling toward her.

Julia's still got her cheek pressed into the dirt and the knee of one of the officers digging into her spine. She beams at me anyway.

I stagger toward her and shove the officer off of Julia. "Get a medic," I bark at him.

I ease her onto her back and put her head in my lap. "Why didn't you save yourself?"

"Xia has a family. They need her." Tears trail out of the corners of her eyes.

I wipe the tears away with my thumbs, retracing the trails on her cheek to erase all the evidence. "You have a family too."

She closes her eyes and gropes for my hand. "I know."

"Julia—"

She's trembling all over. "You'll visit me in jail, won't you? If you can?"

"Of course."

"Good." She closes her eyes. "Good."

"Excuse me, ma'am." It's the medic, and I press Julia's hand one last time then step to the side so they can work on her.

"Fuck. I'm tired." I recognize the voice and turn to see Agent Srinivasan.

I walk over to join her. "How did the Time Guard get here so fast? Doesn't it take hours to assemble a strike team?"

Srinivasan gives a deep, satisfied laugh. "Sure it does. On the other end. And there are rules about interfering with the timeline, of course, so even once they knew what happened they couldn't come any sooner than the instant after Nakamura went forward. But the second Nakamura made it home, they could come in right behind him and clean this mess up."

I shake my head. "That's cheating."

"That's time travel."

We watch together as three agents drag Sona to the time portal, fiddle with the coordinates again, then shove her through—no doubt into the arms of three more agents waiting in the future to receive her.

"Agent Nakamura?" I ask Srinivasan.

She tilts her head, her face soft with sympathy. "Which one?"

I rub my forehead. "Either. Both."

"They're both in treatment. I'm sorry, but it'll probably be awhile before you'll see him again."

If he lives, she doesn't bother to say.

I nod and swallow, my throat thick with emotion.

"He'll need to be debriefed," she continues, "and the whole *two* of them thing means extra time sorting everything out. Where he can be, when. How much you can talk to each other."

Right. I'm *sure* the Time Guard won't let me see Nakamura the Younger. They can't risk me telling him what happens, that he lied to return here, that he gets shot to save me. And Nakamura the Elder... there was so much blood. He was so pale.

No, I'm not sure I'll ever see him again at all.

Srinivasan shakes my shoulder. "You're next, Dr. Carson." She nods toward the time portal.

Oh. Of course.

Of course I don't get to stay, go home to my research station, and pretend everything's fine. I don't even have a research team anymore, after all. Still, there's a sort of silvery grief attached to the realization. Even after everything my prehistoric world has put me through, I still love it here. I still want it and all the mysteries it holds. I look around at my lush green world, fill my lungs with the clean, crisp air one last time, then I turn to Srinivasan. "Okay. I'm ready."

Chapter Thirty-Nine

GRACE

Here we go again. Somehow getting scanned in and going through security weren't enough to trigger my nostalgia, but finally stepping into the terminal hits me like a punch to the solar plexus. It's the same bustle as always, the same mix of historical dress and Time Guard uniforms.

It's been six months since I returned from my last ill-fated mission to the past, and in that time, I've been pretty busy. It was touch-and-go whether the university would let me keep the research station going. But then, a week or so after I made it to the future, my university received a large anonymous donation with the stipulation that half the money could go to whatever they wanted, but the other half *had* to go to me. They didn't like it, but they took the money and shut up about closing my lab. I figure Julia had her friend Xia take care of the money somehow. We've got a proper foundation now, and we named it after Paul Trifoso.

The Time Guard was a bit thornier about the whole thing, but once I casually let it drop I knew about their portable time tubes, and might conveniently forget they were top secret, the Time Guard suddenly became a lot more willing to give me what I want. That might bite me in the ass later—not a great idea to piss the Time Guard off—but that's a risk I decided to take with my eyes open.

I don't know what happened to Julia. Once she got out of the hospital, the Time Guard effectively disappeared her. I'm sad I won't get the chance to honor my promise. I would have liked to visit her.

Her associate Xia is still location unknown on the Time Guard Most Wanted list, last I heard. The Time Guard tried to track the coordinates Julia sent her to, but the location had already been cleared. They found traces of time residue and Xia's blood. Xia's still at large, and somehow I suspect she'll see Julia before I do, one way or another.

No one's given me word on Ben Nakamura, except that he's alive. I sent him several notes through Srinivasan but haven't heard anything. My messages were probably too brusque, too short, but it's hard to pour your heart out when you know the Time Guard is reading over your shoulder.

I don't know if he's not talking to me because he's in some top secret safe house or because he doesn't want to see me. I wouldn't blame him if he decided I was more trouble than I was worth. Especially because as soon as I could, I started pushing to get back to the prehistoric world that almost killed him. Twice.

"Dr. Carson!" I turn at the familiar voice and grin as Jax approaches me. Apparently, some people are as devoted to dinosaurs as I am, because Jax signed up for another tour of duty in the past before I could even finish making the offer.

We hug, and when I step away I shake my head. "You can call me Grace."

Jax gives a sheepish grin. "I'll try to remember. Is our gate ready yet?"

I shake my head. "No, some kind of delay. Our lead time agent is probably late. It's some new person. The original lead agent had to take a leave of absence unexpectedly. So we're getting a last minute addition. They weren't even sure who it would be as of yesterday."

"Great." Jax rolls their eyes. "I'm so glad they made *us* go through all that psychological testing to qualify for this post. Meanwhile, the time agent gets to breeze in with a free pass."

"I know." I point toward a small cluster of folks surrounding a pallet of supplies. "That's our team." A mess of scientists and a whole pack of time agents. The Time Guard isn't taking any chances this time. Of course, that's what I thought *last* time but, well, we'll see what happens. "You go say hi. I'll scare up some coffee before we leave."

Jax shivers. "Good luck." Clearly, Jax has tried the time terminal's coffee before.

Still, needs must drive, so I leave my stuff with Jax and wander toward the small coffee shop. I don't need coffee. Truth be told, I'm anxious, heavy in the gut and quivery in my nerves. Am I really going back *again*? Am I really ready for this?

And am I throwing away something precious by not trying harder to reach Ben Nakamura? One last, *last* try and all that? Of course, I waited around six months for the man to find me. And, apparently, the Time Guard has dropped him in some deep, dark hole never to return. I've tried to talk to him over and over, to find him. Maybe I need to accept he doesn't want to be found.

The thought makes my shoulders slump, but I try to shake it off as my turn in line comes. But, just before I can step up to order, someone taps my shoulder. "Can I buy you that coffee? Shitty as it is. I do owe you a drink."

His voice sends shivers down my spine, making my skin prickle with heat and awareness. I wheel around. "It's you."

"Hiya, Doc. Sorry I'm late." He taps my cheek with one knuckle.

I throw my arms around him, my eyes stinging. "*Ben.*"

He catches me close and traces a hand over my hair.

We stand like that for several heartbeats, until I can convince myself this is real and my heart slows down a bit, then I ease back to look at him.

"Grace." He grins. That old familiar grin.

That old familiar kick starts in my gut at the sight of it.

"Wait." I hold a hand up. "Which one are you? Elder or Younger?"

He squints his eyes, thinking. "Me. Just me. I am the one who got shot, though, if that's what you're asking. So I'm, ah, fully up-to-date on our timeline together."

I blow my breath out on a huff. Time travel. Yeesh. I shake my head and grip his hands. "*Thank you*. Did I say that enough before and in the notes? Thank you for what you did."

He slides his fingers into my hair and cups my jaw. "I know I told you before I couldn't save everyone. I couldn't make a big change like that, or they'd notice. But I thought—I hoped I could save you."

I catch his hand, my breath snagging somewhere under my rib cage, my heart hammering. "Ben, I—"

He swallows and raises a hand to stop me. "I wanted to tell you... I hope you know you don't owe me *anything*. I don't expect anything from you. And if you're uncomfortable having me on your team, I understand, and I'll apply for a transfer—"

"My team?"

He clears his throat. "I'm, ah, head time agent for the 73 million BC time-displacement study. There was a last minute opening, I put in an application and, well, since I had so much experience with the era, my bosses thought I'd be the best person for the job." He takes a breath and winds down as if he's just figured out he's rambling.

I bite back a laugh at his nerves and keep my face composed.

Ben's shoulders roll down, and he smiles. "I'm going with you. If you're okay with that. If you want me there—"

"Yes, Ben. *Yes*." My professional restraint deserts me, and I throw myself at him again. He catches me in both arms and swings me around so my feet leave the ground. I dig my fingers through the black softness of his hair, feeling light, feeling happy.

He sets me down and stares into my eyes, his gaze bringing warmth to my cheeks. "What horrible prehistoric beasts will be trying to eat us this time?"

I rock back on my heels and give him an innocent look. "How do you feel about giant marine reptiles? Mosasaurs? Elasmosaurs? Thalattosuchians—"

He groans. "Please stop talking now."

I laugh. I missed him. Oh, I missed him.

"Well, here we go again." He grins. "Ready for another adventure, Doc?"

"Absolutely." Bad coffee entirely forgotten, we link hands and head toward our team and our departure terminal. We've both got one-way tickets out of this geological era, after all, and for once I am right on time.

Thank you so much for reading *Time Traitors*. If you enjoyed it, please consider leaving a review on the retailer's site to help other readers discover it.

Would you like to join my Reader Group and stay up to date on all my news & new releases? Anyone who joins my Reader Group will receive a free short story.

You can sign up on my website: www.elidonovan.wordpress.com

Acknowledgments

It's been a loooong time getting this story out into the world. Almost every character's name has changed from draft to draft to draft (although Grace's never has). But it feels so good that a story I've been working on since 2013 is finally going to see more than the light of my critique groups. After such a long journey I, unsurprisingly, have a bunch of folks to thank...

Thank you to the field researchers who answered so many questions for me and recommended some fantastic resources: Anne Hilborn, Arjun Dheer, and Asia Murphy. Asia, in particular, went above and beyond answering ALL my nosy questions about camera traps. Anything I got right or authentic, you can thank them. Any mistakes or inaccuracies about the field work are entirely my own fault.

For my beta readers of this story in all its various and many forms, thank you: Veronica Scott, Nadya Duke, M.E. Garber, Karen Anderson, Leigh Wallace, Laurence Brothers, Michael R. Johnson, Sam Midwood, Megan Hannay, Andrea Zevallos, and my former teacher Larry Wilson.

Thank you to the wonderful community on Codex; you've helped me grow and learn so much.

Thank you to my Futurescapes 2018 writer faculty Mary Robinette Kowal and the rest of MRK's group who helped me get my beginning into much better shape.

Thank you #2 to MRK for acting as my Nebulas mentor in 2021 and giving me a much needed kick in the pants.

Thank you so much to Maria Christian for everything. She knows why.

Thank you to my kids, you are my miracles. Thank you to my husband who always tells me "do what you need to do" and his unwavering support of my writing. Thank you to my mom for acting as my PA while I tried to get this darn book out the door.

And, lastly, much love and thanks and gratitude to all my 7P folks. You're the best group of writer buddies anyone could ask for, and I'm grateful every day to be among a group of such excellent people.

Also By Eli Donovan

Science Fiction with Romantic Elements (and time travel!)
Time Traitors
Time Traitor Files: Agent Nakamura

*

Standalone SF Romance with some heat
Jacen
Zandro

*

Sweet Feminist Fairy Tale Retellings
The Fairy Tales of Lyond Series:
The Beauty's Beast
Enchanting the King
The Apprentice Sorceress
The Changeling Child

About the Author

Eli Donovan is an author who thinks dinosaurs are just neat and grew up reading too many Jane Goodall biographies. Eli lives in Southern California with a husband, kids, and one grumpy elderly cat.